IZZY
AT THE END
OF THE
WORLD

IZZY
AT THE END
OF THE
WORLD

K. A. REYNOLDS

CLARION BOOKS

An Imprint of HarperCollins *Publishers*

ISBN 978-0-35-846777-9

Typography by Carla Weise
23 24 25 26 27 LBC 5 4 3 2 1

First Edition

For my husband, Bob. The man who saw my light when the world went dark. Who always told me I was the prettiest lady in the world. Who taught our kids to laugh hard and loud, played them guitar, and took them on countless adventures. Who held my hand as our babies were born and again as you died. Thank you for sharing my journey for twenty-seven unbelievable years. For loving me like a force through our impossible, beautiful life. For teaching me the true meaning of unconditional love, and for the chance to teach you the same. So many miles, Honey. Cheers. This one's for you.

———

(And to the one reading this now who's been through the darkest dark. The one who's hurt so badly, you didn't know if you'd survive. If nobody's ever told you, I see the light in you. That a new dawn will rise just for you, born by the power of you. Thank you for coming on this journey with me. It sure is nice having a friend at the end of the world.)

FOREWORD

HELLO. My name is Isadora Wilder, but most people call me Izzy. I am fourteen years old, and everything I'm about to tell you is true.

The first thing you should know about me is that I'm autistic. For those who don't have experience with autism, how I speak and act, and the ways I process things, might seem unrealistic, frustrating, or just plain wrong. But this is just me being me, the only way I know how, and I won't apologize for that. I also have anxiety and depression. So, opening all the way up to people can be hard for me. Especially because some adults don't like the personal things I have to say. It makes them uncomfortable to hear the pain kids like us go through. But I say those folks are wrong. Us kids are stronger, smarter, and braver than adults could ever understand.

That's why I'm opening my story to you. Because maybe you've gone through hard stuff, too. Maybe you've felt the way-deep-down hurt like me and need a friend who knows what it's like to be scared and misunderstood. Someone who knows what it's like to feel alone in this great big world. And if the adults don't like it, tough.

Us kids need to stick together.

A FEW WORDS OF WARNING, THOUGH: this book contains triggers.

Those with anxiety, panic attacks, depression, abuse, death, cancer, and/or suicide triggers might not want to read on. But if you do decide to come with me through my story, I sure hope you find something inside it that helps you through your own story, too.

Either way, know I'm sending you love to wherever you are, and I wish you a life of love, healing, and joy. Thanks for being here.

Much love,

Izzy Wilder

In the end, there is no turning back.

CHAPTER 1

THEY'RE HERE

THIRTY-SIX MINUTES BEFORE EVERYONE VANISHED,
I was playing video games with my little sister, Maple.
We were tucked up cozy and warm in a house on top of
a mountain, high enough to touch the night sky. It was
late summer in Vermont. September 19, to be exact.
A cool breeze slipped through the evening air, per-
fumed with woodsmoke and pine. My grandparents
were awake, talking real quiet on the couch, almost
asleep. Me and Maple were creating new avatars in
our favorite game—if you call rolling on the floor and
laughing while making up hilarious character names
actually playing the game. Everything was normal.
Nice. Quiet. At least it was, until my sister made me
yell at her—again.

"Maple, no! You can*not* name your night elf Fart-Master19!" We were howling so loud, Grams startled awake on the couch and hollered at us to hush.

"What?" Maple, twelve going on eighteen, answered while shaping FartMaster19's nose.

"It's not like your cat lady's name is any better?"

I whipped around fast, laughter gone. "How dare you talk about OMG-I-Love-Corn that way! She's a serious and smart cat lady who just *happens* to enjoy corn. Everyone thinks she's amazing, see?" I pointed my controller at the townsfolk and dragon on-screen, reflected in Maple's big hazel eyes. "Here comes the dragon-slayer lady to worship OMG-I-Love-Corn." Maple gave me a look from behind a wave of brown hair that said, *Ew, I'm embarrassed to know you and I couldn't love you more.*

I knew how Maple felt. Because that's how I felt about her, too.

"Okay, *fiiine*," Maple groaned, and deleted the name FartMaster19. "If I can't use the name I want, what about something we agree on—like your cat lady stinks and so do you." She ducked before I threw my pillow at her head like she knew I would.

I gasped. "How dare you. I do not stink, and my cat lady can't help smelling like corn—it's literally all she eats!"

"Oh, I dare." Maple tried not to laugh. "And I'd dare all the way over again, too."

I gasped and collapsed dramatically on the floor. "Fine. Change it back to FartMaster19 if you want. But if the villagers make fun of her, that's on you."

Pleased with herself, Maple grinned and changed her avatar's name back to FartMaster19 like she'd planned to do all along.

"Elves," I mumbled, grabbing my controller with a ghost of a smile. Then we joked and fought and played until Maple got sleepy and went to bed—bragging about FartMaster19 the whole way.

While Grams scrolled her phone on the couch, and Pops heated the oil for popcorn, I snuck outside to peer up at the glitter-bright stars. Out on the deck by myself, it was just me and my thoughts and all the peace in the world.

As always, I gravitated to my mom's amethyst necklace, strung by a silver chain at my neck. Amethyst was my birthstone, and my mom's necklace was special. Twirling the raw oversize stone comforted and grounded me. Just touching it made me feel closer to her.

The deck lights flickered.

"Izzy!" Grams hollered at me on the deck, and I jumped. "How long are you gonna be out there? It's cold!" Grams had a mess of curly brown hair like mine topping her head. A set of dimples like mine poked her cheeks. All the love and fire in the universe flickered inside her fierce brown eyes. But goodness, was she always worrying about me being cold. I'd only been outside a few minutes, but according to her, I might as well have been lost in the arctic for years.

I stared at her through the sliding glass doors and knew exactly what her next words would be: "You'll catch your death out there, Isadora! Now come on and get your sweater." I squeezed my mom's amethyst in my fist and sighed. I already *had* on a sweater. A *Star Wars* one Grams had made me with Yoda on the back, *Strong, you are* knit-written underneath. Not to mention my fleece leggings and thick wool socks.

I *definitely* was not cold.

My grandfather, who I'd always called Pops, grinned at me from the kitchen with smiley blue eyes, like he knew all the secrets of the world. "Do what she wants, Izzy," he called through the glass doors. "You know she's always right." He gave Grams a side-eyed smirk. She looked back at him, nodded, and laughed.

And it was good. It was right. It felt like the dark days of our history, all the hard times that came before this, were light-years away.

We locked eyes then. First me and Grams, then me

and Pops—the two of them inside, safe and sound; me outside on my own, night winds stripping me to bones. I'll never forget that moment. As if all the words we never said to each other whispered between us. Who would have guessed that look we were sharing was goodbye?

When I turned back around to the stars, an odd light gleamed at the far edge of the sky. The light was twice the width of Venus and shone brighter than the whole blanket of stars. It was like the mysterious light had pinned itself to the heavens as if waiting for me to find it.

Most would have said, "That's just another star." And I thought that at first, too. Until my brain said, *Uh-uh, Izzy. You've been watching this same sky since you were born. Your brain knows that light wasn't there before. Trust your brain. That light is no star.*

Suddenly, I really *was* cold. Freezing-water-down-my-spine cold. "Do you see that?" I asked Grams and Pops without looking back. But the wind stole my voice and dropped it into the valley before they heard me.

So, I kept watch. Pushing the curls away from my face and digging deeper into the mystery. Grams's eyes were so hot on my back, I thought Yoda might catch fire.

But tonight, I couldn't look away from that strange light in the sky. And I had this nagging feeling that light was watching me, too.

"Isadora Bellamy Wilder!" I nearly leaped out of my socks. Pops looked on from the kitchen, about to pour in the kernels of corn. Grams stormed toward the glass deck doors, sweater in hand, angry face on, spicy words ready to fly. "I *said*, get your—" When she slid open the doors, our dog, a shepherd-mix disaster named Akka, galloped through the living room in a whoosh. He snaked past Grams's legs and out the door, almost knocking her down. "You naughty old thing!" Grams told Akka, trying not to grin through her show of mad. "What's gotten into you?"

Akka barked. He sat at my feet grinning like the devil, and I couldn't help laughing. That dog loved me more than anything, and I loved him the same. We'd found Akka at the shelter a month after Mom died. It was love at first sight. Akka understood me like no one else and had been my soul mate ever since.

"I can't help it if he loves me best," I told Grams, brows high, giving her the same exasperated love-you-no-matter-what-but-oh-are-you-trouble look she gave Akka.

"Of course he does," Pops added through the open door. "Who wouldn't love you?" Those were the last words I heard Pops say. Because right then, the not-a-star light—*moved*.

I did a double take. Like, did I really just see that thing move? The second I questioned it, the ball of light sprang forward, getting bigger the faster it came.

The deck lights flickered and zapped. The trees surrounding us shivered. The boughs bent, and tips swayed. Akka barked and barked as hundreds more of the same giant white lights filled the sky. A low hum vibrated through everything. The living room lit up in white.

Grams, halfway inside the deck doors, dropped my sweater, fixed on the lights coming fast. Our hair rose and danced in the wind. Grams and I shared the same look—one that whispered of terror and fear, a second before our eyes screamed, *RUN*.

But where was there to run to?

Grams shouted at Pops, "Get Maple!" her voice shaky and sharp. Pops sprang from the kitchen in a flash and sped off after my sister, no questions asked.

Popcorn was just starting to pop in the background when Grams reached out to grab me. She caught my arm as one of the lights lowered over our house. Everything glowed in pulsing white light. The object was huge, like a meteor from the center of space. Grams's eyes grew, gaping up at the brightly lit object hovering outside.

I squinted up into the glare, still clamped on to Akka's collar, as the wind really started to blow. The only place the giant light wasn't lit was a black circle in the center.

"*Bork-bork-bork!*" Akka lunged at the light over our house and busted me out of my trance. My arms almost ripped from my sockets and Akka escaped my grip.

"Akka!" I sprang after him, and barely caught him trying to jump off the deck.

The drop was fifteen feet to the ground.

He could have died.

Heart pounding, I pulled Akka toward the house, but he fought me the whole way.

Hurricane winds prickled with pine needles swirled around me and my boy. My hair lifted like an uprooted tree, gnarled roots whipping this way and that. I shoved my hair off my face and called to Grams, "Help me! Akka won't come inside." But Grams didn't move from the doorway. Her arm was still outstretched where she'd been holding my sweater, her wild eyes fixed on the lights.

Like she couldn't see anything else.

Pops and Maple ran downstairs and set their eyes on the lights. Maple had put on her sweater. I'd never seen my sister so scared. I'd just locked eyes with her when—

FLASH.

Megawatt spotlights of gold beamed to earth from the objects filling the sky. A shock of pain zapped through me. The amethyst on my mom's necklace seared against my skin. When I tried to touch it, when I tried to pull Akka inside, when I tried to move forward, I couldn't. I couldn't even shift my eyes. Suddenly, I was unable to move. The soft hum from the lights grew so loud, my eyes shook in their sockets. My body felt inside out.

Before I could even process what was happening, the countless illuminated objects parked over Vermont shut off their lights. And all at once, I could move.

The dark quiet of the mountaintop returned like nothing unusual had happened. I thought the worst was over.

But our nightmare had just begun.

CHAPTER 2

THEY'RE GONE

I'D BEEN SCARED PLENTY OF TIMES. SO SCARED, I wondered if I'd ever stop feeling afraid. But it wasn't until unidentified flying lights swarmed my mountain, I knew how deep fear could go. How fast my safe world could slip away. I guess that's the difference between reading a thing and living it: until you actually lived the story, it was just someone else's dream. But this time, the protagonist was me.

Night wrapped around me and Akka like we'd been folded into black paper. I couldn't see any more unidentified flying lights, but we were still frozen on the deck—a couple of Han Solos stuck in carbonite. All I could think was, *Is this the real world?*

Until the force field gluing us to the deck let go.

I threw my head back and gasped like I'd sprung up from the bottom of the sea. Wind rushed my ears. Akka lunged toward the house and slipped from my grip. The world sped up real quick after that.

I rushed inside and shut the deck door, a million questions swarming my mind. *What were those lights? Where did they come from? Were they military? Are we at war?*

Were they UFOs?

"Grams?" The stink of burned popcorn hit my nose. "Pops? Maple?"

The stove was still on, and the popcorn was starting to smoke.

Why wasn't Pops shutting it off?

"Pops! Grams! Maple!" Feet numb, I tripped over some stuff on the floor but kept moving. "Where are you?" My voice echoed through the house the way it might in space. Endlessly. Unheard. I slid across the wood floor to the kitchen, heart pounding in my ears, lights flickering on and off.

"Hello?" Popcorn spilled out the top of the pot and onto the floor. "Pops?" Smoke stung my eyes. I shut off the stove. *"Grams?"* Any more smoke and the alarms would go off, and alarms were too much for my ears, so I didn't want that.

I opened the kitchen windows and turned on the fan. *"Maple!"*

My scalp prickled like pins poking my brain.

Something was wrong.

About to check upstairs, I was stopped by Akka's high-pitched cries. He was sniffing the stuff by the deck doors I'd tripped over when I ran inside. My heart jumped when I realized what the stuff was. The extra sweater Grams wanted me to take. A pack of mint gum and cherry lip balm—Maple's. Pops's wallet, phone, and Allen wrench set. Grams's worry stone from Gimli, phone, and change purse. Everything they'd had in their pockets had dropped to the floor.

Heart wild as a wolf in a trap, I sprang toward the staircase, tripped, and slammed into a wall. Mom's amethyst dug into my chest, and I hollered in pain.

Akka sat at my feet, whining up at me. "It's okay," I lied. "I'm okay." He pawed my leg, unconvinced, as I pulled open the neck of my shirt. A big angry burn marked my chest. I'd been so frantic, I hadn't even noticed the pain.

A memory flashed. The lights. Mom's amethyst burned hot with the lights. A really terrible awful bad thought slithered in next. *What if Grams, Maple, and Pops were vaporized in the lights and only their stuff was left behind.*

"No. No, no, no."

I galloped up the stairs, choking on bile. *"Maple!*

Grams! Pops!" Sobs of fear cluttered my words. *"Answer me!"*

Akka click-click-clicked after me. I vomited on the stairway and didn't stop to clean it. I wondered what Grams would say if she knew I didn't clean it up, then started to frantic cry. Tears shuddered out of my chest and burst from my mouth like a million stirred crows. Nothing felt real. Bad thoughts pounded my mind:

They're gone.

You're alone.

Nobody's coming back.

The lights.

They're gone with the lights.

I checked the whole upstairs, but they weren't there either and panic took hold.

I sprinted into my bedroom so fast, the door slammed the wall with a bang. Everything looked normal. My bed, still a tumble of sheets. Clothes and homework scattered my floor. I blinked at the poster of Akka the Flame, a half-elf, half-fawn fire mage from the *Moonlight Society* trilogy, the namesake of my best boy. Akka the Flame aimed his athame at the caption above him: *Your power is waiting.*

But I felt more powerless than ever.

I covered my mouth in a silent scream and fell to my knees. "My family has to be here somewhere.

Lights don't just fly to earth and take people." I shook my head and covered my ears, rocking back and forth. "No. No. No. There's a reasonable explanation to all of this, I just have to figure out what it is." Akka whined at me, then sneak-licked my nose. I cradled his fluff-head with shaking hands and put my forehead to his. "They can't be gone. Because we're still here. If those lights took people, they'd have taken us, too."

Akka nudged my arm with his nose. His way of saying, *I completely agree as always, now get up, Izzy. It's okay. I am still here for you.*

I hugged my best boy till my tears stopped, then forced myself to my feet. My family had to be somewhere. And me and Akka would find them.

I raced downstairs, thinking maybe Grams got confused in the lights and left the house. Maybe Maple and Pops went after her? Grams *was* in the early stages of dementia. It wouldn't be the first time she got confused and wandered off alone.

Last month, Grams took me shopping for a new bra. Oh, my goodness, was that embarrassing. She kept holding different ones to my chest as people walked by, asking me questions like, "How's this? You think this'll fit?" while eyeballing my chest. I wanted to shrivel up and turn to dust on the floor.

"Hush it, Grams!" I hissed, cheeks on fire. "I'm not twelve. I can do this myself."

Skin crawling with horror, I was about to hide under the nearest clothes rack or run away and become a bog hag when she told me she needed the bathroom and would be right back. I checked out the clothes while I waited and discovered she'd left the store without me.

If it happened once, it could happen again. And if Grams left the house, Pops and Maple would've definitely gone looking for her.

I had to check for them outside.

"Akka, come on. Let's—"

Akka cried somewhere in the burned-stink kitchen. Windows open, the house was cold. The air seemed thicker, too. The scent of ozone, like in spring after the first rain, drifted inside. I shut the kitchen windows and found Akka wedged in the corner, ears down, eyes sad, tail between his legs.

"Akka?" My throat had a lump so big, my words barely squeezed out. "It's okay." But I felt like a liar. Nothing was okay. I smiled into his scared eyes. "We'll find them, good boy," I promised, needing to believe it, too. "They have to be here somewhere."

That's when I saw the puddle running across the floor. Shame dragged Akka's face—he never peed in the house. Ever. I sniffed back the tears burning behind my eyes and put a smile on just for him. "When I was little, I peed on this floor, too, so you're in good company." I cuddled him tight enough to feel his rabbit heartbeat, close enough for him to feel my truth. "Don't worry, Akka. You're still the best boy in the world."

A sudden shriek echoed outside, and I jumped. Akka growled, low and deep, hair raised.

Was it an animal?

Mechanical?

Human?

Something else?

What if it was Pops, Grams, or Maple?

We needed to hurry.

"Akka. Wanna go outside?" Akka didn't mess around. Even now, the mention of going out had him doing the "outside is the best side" full-body-butt-wag dance of joy, scream forgotten. But all I could think was how much I didn't want to go. How screams, even in movies, were a trigger for me. How they made me jump with worry and fear. How whatever screamed might not be from this world. Worse. It might have come from someone I loved.

I grabbed Akka's leash, snapped it on, and opened

the front door. On the way out, I spotted the flashlight by the microwave—one of those crank ones for emergencies—and grabbed it. Akka yipped, ready to go.

I took a deep breath in the silence and chased the scream into the dark.

CHAPTER 3
THE CRASH

I SCREAMED WHEN I FOUND OUT MY MOM DIED. I couldn't believe my mom, Annie Elizabeth Wilder, one of the kindest people on earth, was gone, and there was nothing anyone could do about it.

"A brain tumor?" Me and Maple stared at Grams. "How could she have died of a brain tumor? I didn't even know she was sick." Grams said Mom hid her cancer from everyone. And when I asked why Mom kept her sickness a secret, I'll never forget what Grams said.

"Your mom liked to carry secrets the way dark stars carry light. They keep that light to themselves, tucked up real tight, light-years away from the wishers below."

"But why wouldn't she tell us she was dying?" Maple asked through tears. "Why wouldn't she let us help her?"

Grams rocked us in the La-Z-Boy like we were five, sniffing back her own dark-star tears. "I don't know." Rock, rock, rock. "I guess she kept that secret from us, too."

As I ran outside now with Akka, I thought maybe when someone's world shook to the roots, the only thing left to do was scream. A survivor's cry to let the world know, I'm still here. I'm hurting.

But I am still alive.

On the front porch, the wind blew cold. I gazed into the trees, looking for unidentified flying lights, but found only questions. Where was my family? What were those lights? And why were me and Akka left behind?

Akka pressed his body against me, scanning the woods for sound. I cranked on the emergency flashlight and followed its shine up the gravel drive. We were the only house at the end of our road. No neighbors for a sixteenth of a mile.

I didn't hear any more screams.

"Grams?" I called quietly toward the valley to my left. "Pops?" I said louder up the hill to my right. "Maple?" Nothing. The woods were dead silent. The earth felt so *empty*. Like it lightened its load—laid its burden down after billions of years of carrying humankind.

Usually, this time of night, coyotes howled, crickets chirped, trains rolled, and owls sang songs to the stars. But now, nothing moved, and no living thing sang.

It was too quiet. Akka stopped at Grams's car and growled, ears swiveling like satellites, nose aimed at the sky. I followed his stare, but only the black pitch of night stared back.

When I opened Grams's Subaru door, it creaked loud as a siren. The inside light didn't turn on. I wondered if Grams had left the lights on again and the battery died. Maple's anime backpack sat in the front seat. The three-legged plush fox she always carried stuck out and sent a wave of panic through me. Maple was terrified of the dark. The thought of her in the woods, maybe alone, made me want to cut down the whole forest searching for her. Grams had Pops, but Maple was mine to protect. And I failed.

Where was my Maple bug now? I didn't understand where my family went, or how to find them, or what I was supposed to do.

I checked Pops's truck. His Toyota was still broken, and the inside was a mess. Cupholders full of change. Spilled coffee. Tools lining the back seat. I moved away from Pops's truck, filled with guilt for telling Pops his truck was nasty. Because now, everything inside felt like a precious treasure, rather than the biggest disaster on earth.

Wait.

The biggest disaster . . .

The Wilder Disaster Plan. I'd forgotten about it!

After Hurricane Irene, my grandparents insisted we have an emergency plan in case of another disaster. Grams said, "If disaster hits and we're not home, go to our bedroom closet and wait out the storm. If we're not back by morning, try the neighbors' or Joe and Maryanne at the River Bend Market. Ask for help. Be smart. Be safe. And of course, keep trying 911."

I gaped at Akka. "Their phones." I'd left them on the floor. Grams and Pops hushed their ringers for movie night. What if they'd been trying to call? "Akka. Come on."

Racing up the drive, I thought about Nora. The last time I saw her long pink hair, brown eyes, and big smile was yesterday at school in study hall—working hard at not working. Since we'd already finished our work, we were watching the trailer for a new horror movie. And while Ms. Mehta and Ms. Fedorowich whispered in the corner, Nora asked me, "If you were in a horror movie and had to choose one person to help keep you alive, who would it be?" She batted those long lashes, wearing an innocent grin—though nothing about Nora Singh was innocent.

I gave her a look like, *Are you kidding?* "You. Obviously."

She slid her chair closer and rested her head on my shoulder. "Why?"

I leaned back into Nora, the scent of her body spray drifting over me. "Uhhh, because you're the scariest person I know? I faint at the sight of blood and freeze at the first sign of danger, so if you want me to survive, I need you."

Nora patted my hand. "You've made the right choice."

Nora was my best friend. I couldn't believe I hadn't thought of her till now. Was she home? Did she see the lights? Were the Singhs safe?

Am I the last person on earth?

Me and Akka had just gotten to our walkway when a deep hum vibrated the night air. Leaves stirred at our feet. Akka growled at the trees, and we stopped in our tracks. All at once, the darkness felt alive.

"Bork-bork-bork!" Akka jumped onto his hind legs. I held him back and followed his gaze to the sky. The hundreds of lights I thought had left, blazed to life.

The lights had been there all along.

A gold spotlight beamed over us. I shielded my eyes from the glare and screamed, "Akka, *run!*" Me and Akka sprang fast toward home. Gravel bit into my feet as we ran. I tripped up the front steps as the unidentified flying lights shut off.

Vermont went dark. The wind died. Akka borked his brains out while I fumbled the doorknob. "Akka, hush!" I shoved open the door.

I locked the door behind us and collapsed to the floor. Every bit of me shook with adrenaline. Akka ran toward the deck doors like a dog possessed. *"Bork-bork-bork!"*

I sprang to grab him and reeled my boy back. "Quiet, Akka, please." He hushed, panting at my side. "Maybe the lights are g—"

FLASH.

Ultraviolet beams lit Vermont in electric-purple shine. My mom's amethyst heated hot as flames. Akka pulled toward the deck, borking louder, pulling harder. I had to get out of this light. I pushed my mom's amethyst over my shirt, dragged him under the dining room table, and squinted outside at the UFLs (unidentified flying lights). I wanted a better look at what they were, but the lights were too bright. It was like staring into the sun. I dropped my gaze to the base of the beams, and what I saw blew my mind.

Real live monsters were lowering to earth through the violet beams. Humongous creatures with giant heads, red eyes, and long tentacle arms snapping in and out of the purple shine were suddenly swarming the mountains outside my back door. A fine black mist drifted down with them and dispersed on the wind. I shook my head, fingers curling Akka's fur as he borked, whispering, "How is this real?" After the last monster dropped, the UFLs went dark and shot back into space.

Akka squirmed out of my grip and galloped toward the deck doors, growling and snapping at the glass. I scrambled out from under the table, ran after him, and blinked out into the night. One of the UFLs was coming back. No—it was plunging toward earth.

I pressed my palms to the glass. The object was dark, oval, and shaped like a massive rock. I could see it fine as it fell. I watched, expecting a crash, my heart scrambling like a cat in a bag. But two seconds before the UFL hit the mountains, it blinked out of sight.

Then *boom*. The deck trembled. The hills echoed like thunder. Smoke rose in the place I was sure the object crashed. I peered outside in silence, fists clenching until my hands hurt, mind racing with fear.

What were those monsters and why are they here?

Why did the UFL vanish right before it crashed? Where is my family? What are me and Akka gonna do now?

Why were we left here alone?

Heart rapid-firing, I checked the doors to make sure they were locked, fighting to understand this new life. A life where monsters dropped to earth and no one came running. No grandparents asking, "Izzy, are you okay?" A life where no sirens wailed or emergency alarms signaled. Where no instructions came on for what to do.

It was just me and Akka, alone at the end of the world.

Inside the too-quiet house, my body went into revolt. My ears rang. My thoughts rapid-fired. And I was woozy like I might barf.

So, I lowered to the floor and rocked like I did when my mind was too slippery to calm. Whispering, "Izzy, keep breathing, just keep breathing," until my calm flew back like a night bird from the dark. Eventually, my calm always came back to me.

Akka had his head on my leg, eyebrows bobbing with concern, waiting for me to rise. I took one last deep breath and whispered, "It's just you and me for a bit, Akka. But don't worry. I'll never let anything bad happen to you." When Akka licked my nose, I knew he believed me.

I picked up my grandparents' phones off the floor, still wondering how they'd gotten there. Grams's phone shocked me when I touched it. Lights and electronics had a way of acting up around me. Their cells were the only phones in the house—on account of Maple dropped hers in the toilet an hour after she got her first phone, and I lost mine in the mall bathroom for the second time and Grams wasn't having any of that. "No more phones until you can afford to break your own," she said. "And don't even *think* about touching ours."

But I bet she wouldn't mind if I used them now.

I turned Grams's phone on, still shaky with nerves, and—it worked! I grinned at Akka and checked for messages as he drank from his bowl.

No messages.

"That's okay." I checked Pops's phone next. He had a message! But it was from the automated car warranty lady that always made Pops so mad.

The internet. Maybe there was something about what's going on. But as many links as I clicked, and as much as I scrolled, there was nothing about any lights or monsters or anything. I stared at his cell like a zombie. His wallpaper was a photo of me, Maple, Mom, and Grams. I squeezed his phone tight and pressed it over my heart. *Where are they? Why am I here alone?*

Wait. The TV.

I raced to every television in the house and flipped on each news channel I could find, but the only stories playing were old. Like before-the-lights-came old. And most of the other channels wouldn't even work.

Nervous energy jumping my hands, I focused on what came next in the Wilder Disaster Plan. Since it was nighttime, I wasn't supposed to go to the neighbors' because it was so far away. With those creatures out there, Grams would fire up hot if I did something so careless, so I decided to call the neighbors instead.

No answer.

Pacing faster, I called Nora. But nobody picked up. *Nora.*

Swiping hot tears from my cheeks, I called the firehouse. The police station. 911. The River Bend Farm Market. Grams's friends from the beauty salon. Pops's old buddies from work. But nobody picked up anywhere.

"Okay then, Akka." I shook my fear off like a coat and twisted my necklace. "I guess we keep trying numbers and wait until morning." I forced a smile for Akka. "Maybe Grams, Pops, and Maple will be here when we wake up." If we had to stay here tonight, I needed to lock down the house. Those ugly things from the lights were nothing I wanted in here. So, I locked every door. Closed the blinds. Then flopped onto the couch where Grams had just been and broke down sobbing. The blanket still smelled like her. The air smelled like burned popcorn from Pops. And when I closed my eyes, Maple's face smiled back.

"I lost Mom last year. I can't lose them, too." I wiped my face and shook off my tears. "If they're not back by morning, we'll pack a bag and go find them." Akka sneezed. He hated my plan—and could I blame him? The thought of walking down the mountain with those monsters in the woods terrified me, too. But even when things looked their darkest, I could usually find a flicker of hope. Rays of light I'd tucked away from my best days to save for my worst.

So, after I cleaned up Akka's accident in the kitchen and my vomit on the stairs, I led Akka to my grandparents' bedroom and locked the door. I tried not to cry about how their bed smelled like Grams's perfume and Pops's nag champa incense. Or wonder if Maple was alone and crying for me. I snuggled up close to my already snoring dog like this was all we knew how to do and imagined my family someplace safe. Then I let it all go.

"That's right, baby girl," Grams would say when me or Maple were sad. "Let the dark thoughts go until there's only light. That's where I'll always be, sitting right here, waiting for you. Always inside that light." And I fell asleep to the soft lilt of her words.

Drifting into the dark, hanging tight to that memory of hope.

CHAPTER 4
SOMETHING'S INSIDE

I WAS DREAMING.

It was the deep, dark heart of night. Fog seeped slowly through the trees. My breath frosted the cool air as I stood alongside my house, in the small side yard facing the woods. The sliver moon bobbed on a sea of mauve clouds. Akka was at my side, and everything shimmered like sweet, soft magic.

But something was terribly wrong.

Akka sprang into the forest without warning, glancing back like he wanted me to follow. I took off after him and trailed his glowing green eyes to the witch's hut in the forest. Me and Maple built the tumbledown shack from Pops's leftover scraps of roof metal and wood. We stuck two old chairs, a rug, and a fold-up table inside the hut so we could enjoy Grams's famous blackberry tea and cookies in style. But now, there was no Maple. No Grams, Pops, cookies, or blackberry tea. Only me and Akka outside the witch's hut door.

I was about to enter when a soft golden light burst through the hut's cracks. Music rose softly after. "Blackbird," by the Beatles.

My mom's favorite song.

"Mom?" I leaned in close to the door and peered straight into the light, hair standing on end.

"Hey, Izzy-girl," my mom replied.

I jumped. Glass shattered close by. And the borks of the best boy in the world crossed the barrier of dreams to wake me.

"Bork-bork-bork!" Akka jumped off the bed and banged the door with his paw. When I remembered all that had happened, my heart jump-started and pounded the same.

I sprang up in a sweat, skin cold as a Neanderthal thawing from ice. My grandparents' bedroom was the cool shade of morning twilight. "Blackbird" still played in the back of my mind.

Mom. That was the first time I'd dreamed of her since she died.

She sounded so alive.

"Bork-bork-bork!" Akka nosed me under the sheets, then ran back to the door like, *Izzy, we don't have much time, please hurry.* As always, Akka was right.

I threw off the covers and bolted from bed, hoping that while I was asleep, Grams, Pops, and Maple had returned. And with a shiny grin of hope on my face, I flung the door open. But the second I got into the hallway, Akka shot downstairs, snarling and borking in fear.

Dread flattened my grin.

Akka would never snarl at them.

Out the hall windows, Vermont was dipped in steel blue and lime. Black dust blew up the stairs on a soft breeze, grazing my wild mess of curls.

The black dust that dropped from the lights.

The house was void of sound. Movement. Family. When I reached the bottom of the stairs, my heart thundered, loud and wild.

One of the sliding glass doors was shattered.

I heard smashing glass in my dream.

Before I could stop him, Akka lunged for the hole in the door. *"Bork-bork-bork!"* I sprang after him and screamed.

One of the monsters from the lights was on my deck. Its big red eyes zeroed in on me as it shoved its long limbs through the door.

No time to think, I dragged Akka away from the creature straight out of a horror movie. The monster was charcoal gray and big as a truck. It had the elongated body of a prehistoric octopus but stood like an evil, long-legged spider on the tips of dagger-sharp arms. Dozens of barbed tentacles squirmed and snapped around its huge, gaping fanged mouth. The creature paused inside the deck doors, bulbous red eyes on me. Akka scrambled across the slippery floor, borking and pulling to attack. I held him as long as I could before I was forced to let go.

"Akka!" The monster thrust a few limbs through the broken deck door to grab my boy. Akka snarled and dodged one limb, then went after another as it swished across the floor. Adrenaline speeding through me, I dove like a superhero and grabbed Akka before another of the monster's limbs smacked him down.

Broken glass sprayed in the fray as I dragged my frantic boy toward the kitchen. The creature screamed two hundred decibels too loud, while pushing itself through the door. Akka twisted free from my grip and raced across the dining room to bite the monster and missed. I screamed at him, *"Stop!"* but Akka was hot with rage and went after it again.

The creature tried another time to squeeze through the hole in the glass but got stuck. It shrieked and pushed more limbs inside. The ugly thing kept trying to knock us down. For a while, me and Akka were too fast to catch. Until one of its limbs wrapped my ankle and pulled me toward the door.

"Akka!" Akka latched on and bit the ugly thing hard. The monster shrieked, locked me in its dead-eye stare, and let me go.

I scrambled toward Akka to get him out of there. But before I knew what was happening, one of the creature's limbs came at me from behind and knocked me to the ground.

Akka barked. Stars and black spots invaded my vision, but I felt no pain and kept on. I crawled over a layer of broken glass to get Akka before he attacked the monster coming for me. But I was too late. The ugly thing latched on to my good boy's leg and took him down.

"No, you do not!"

Akka yelped. I yanked Akka back, but the tip of the creature's sharp limb had burrowed into his thigh. Akka shrieked in a way that made me want to cry and run at the same time. Except when I saw

Pops's aluminum baseball bat—reserved especially for intruders—standing by the basement door, I let go of Akka and grabbed it, braver than I'd ever been.

I battle-cried like the devil had me and lunged. I fought it in a fog of adrenaline, of family and survival and nobody hurts my dog!

Alien goo and stink spilled from the monster and sprayed all over me, but that only fueled me on. I whacked the gray ugly thing until it let Akka go. The creature flailed and pushed to break down the doors, glaring at me with its enormous red eyes. All I could think was, *How is this real?*

"You get away, you hear me?" I told big and ugly, thrashing half in and out of the broken deck door. Akka growled beside me, ready to spring back into action. I aimed my bat at the beast. *"You get all the way away, and don't ever come back!"*

The creature tilted its head and made a clicking noise like a cicada. It stared at me like it was deciding what sauce to dip me in on the side. Before it could choose, someone whistled in the distance. An actual other person whistling.

Maybe I'm not the last person on earth.

The hideous goo-dripping monster turned toward the whistle and called a sharp cry in return. Like it was answering back.

Wait. Were the monsters being controlled by the one whistling? What if the whistler came from the UFLs with the monsters and wasn't human at all?

With a final siren cry, old ugly and its limbs slipped out of my house and gave me one last look. A bold-faced stare like it was saying, *I'll be back*. Still huffing and puffing from battle, dripping with monster juice and black dust, I met its stare with my own. It faced the sky, leaped off the deck, and flung itself into the trees, chasing the whistle into the woods. I had just enough strength to drag Akka away from the door and collapse with him in my arms.

My insides buzzed like a swarm of bees. Then came the fear, hitting hard with used-up adrenaline. I dry heaved. My hands shook. My thoughts were loud and getting louder. I dug my fingers into my thigh hard enough to hurt. To roust me from the moment— to remind myself I was still alive.

Bat still in hand, guts and goo slicking me and my dog, I felt that aliveness rush into my chest and throat and burst out at once . . . in a laugh.

I dropped the bat and turned to my panting, sticky, slobbering, beautiful Akka and laughed from way down deep. "You brave, stubborn, wonderful boy." I almost peed and for some reason could not stop laughing. "It thought you were lunch, but you showed it, didn't you!" Akka looked at me like I was three pancakes short of a stack, but I kept laughing because a real live monster didn't eat us, and we survived. "You know it's bad when all you have to laugh about is that a monster from a real live nightmare didn't slurp you up, but we're still here, so I call that a victory, don't you?"

Akka scrambled up and barked. I swear, my boy was smiling, too. I grabbed him and hugged him hard. My laughter turned to relieved tears. "Thank you," I whispered over the lump in my throat. "Thank you for not leaving me."

Akka licked my nose. And I knew he was thanking me, too.

My hand came away sticky. Blood. I lifted Akka's back leg to check his wound. It was bleeding from where the gray ugly—what I'd decided to call the monsters—latched on with its tentacle. The wound was a couple of inches wide—raw, but not too deep—on his left thigh.

But like it or not, daylight had come. And like Grams and Pops's emergency plan said, if they weren't back by daylight, it was time to go.

I grabbed the goo-crusted baseball bat and started for the stairs, thinking about all we had to do to leave. Pack supplies. Feed Akka. Disinfect his wound. I ran upstairs, thinking about the whistle that called the gray ugly away. If it was a regular someone like me, and they were surviving in the woods, there was hope for my family, and for me and Akka, too.

When we got to the bathroom to wash Akka's wound, I caught myself in the mirror and found a stranger staring back. Bigfoot-wild hair, haunted green eyes, blood streaked from a cut I didn't remember getting. I looked like Princess Mononoke—face smeared with gore, wolf at my side. Funny how one minute you can be playing video games with your sister and the next you're battling a ten-foot-tall monster, smeared in blood, fighting for your life.

I scrubbed the goo and blood off of us and the bat, too. I cleaned our wounds in a did-I-really-just-attack-a-monster-with-a-baseball-bat daze, then hurried to my bedroom to change. Akka followed, tripping over my feet. "Don't worry. I'm not going anywhere without you."

I grabbed clothes from my drawer, my favorite shirt of Akka the Flame and a pair of black jeans, and dressed in a trance. I even put my Yoda sweater back on (*Strong, you are*), blood splatter and all. I'd just scooped more clothes from my drawers when I remembered Pops's off-limits bowie knife hidden in my grandparents' closet. I didn't like deadly things: guns, knives, arrows, axes, anything threatening. But today, I'd treat that beautiful bowie like a close personal friend and slay anything in the way of me and my dog.

My grandparents' walk-in closet was huge and stuffed with every last thing. Akka sniffed Pops's suits and Grams's endless racks of shoes; Grams's perfume and Pops's cologne were all I could smell. Memories rose up inside me. I felt hollow with the absence of them. Like if they didn't return, I'd never be happy again.

Just yesterday, Grams was teasing me that "if you ever get married, you better believe I'll be fighting my way up to that podium to tell everyone that when you were a toddler, you named your butt Richie, and when you passed gas, you had the nerve to blame it on Richie." I gasped. "You wouldn't!" And all she said was, "Change your F to a C in math and we'll talk."

They were all here yesterday. How could they just be gone?

Fighting back tears, I set down my spare clothes and the bat and climbed the shoe rack to reach the top shelf. An old blanket draped the bowie. When I shook it loose, I found an unfamiliar box hidden behind the knife. On the box were three words that suddenly became the most important words ever: *Annie Elizabeth Wilder.*

I blew out a slow breath and remembered my dream.

Hey, Izzy-girl.

Mom.

CHAPTER 5

"DON'T YOU (FORGET ABOUT ME)"

TWO MONTHS BEFORE MY MOM DIED, WE DROVE to Brattleboro and walked the town at night. Each time we walked under a streetlight, I swear, the bulb would go out. She used to tell me I was magic. That I was powerful enough to do anything. Even survive the end of the world.

I forgot about that night until now.

An electric charge rolled through me as I placed Pops's bowie on the floor and took down the box. I'd never seen this box before, but it called to me. Like my mom was whispering, *Izzy, there's something you need to see.* I knew this wasn't the best time for a memory lane stroll. But one thing about me, when I was focused on a task, no matter what was happening around me, I didn't want to break focus for anything. So, I sat down on the grass-green carpet and opened Mom's box. If you were me, I bet you would, too.

The first thing I found was a pair of eyeglasses. I traced the bite marks on each arm. Made by the same teeth that gleamed when she smiled. I looked so much like her, when people who knew her saw me, they would say, "Izzy, you look just like your mom." When they walked away, my heart broke. I was a living reminder my mom was gone. I wanted to tell them, *I know I look like her. But I wish you could see me, too.*

Under her glasses was a square black electronic thing with buttons on the side, a door on the front, and headphones still attached. Wait. I'd seen pictures of Mom wearing this. Holy crow.

This was her old Sony Discman music player. It plays CD's and even has a radio inside.

I popped the Discman open and found a CD labeled, Playlist for the End of the World. A shiver slid up my belly. I didn't know why Grams and Pops hid this box from me and Maple, but finding it now sure felt like fate.

About to press play to check if the player worked, I spied a bright yellow journal stuffed with loose pages at the bottom of the box. When I opened the cover, the inside flap read, The Life and Times of Annie Elizabeth Wilder. Chills hit the second I touched it.

I didn't know my mom kept a journal. And I didn't know why, but this book, and her CD, felt important. Like something inside them was reaching out to me.

I flipped through my mom's journal. The beginning seemed normal—regular entries of regular days, starting about fifteen years back. Mom talking about being pregnant with me. How sad and angry she was that my father left us before I was born. How she moved in with my grandparents. How she loved rocking me to sleep. How exhausted but in love with me she was, and how she said I made her shine. Then came entries of little Maple. How she was the best surprise. How Maple was so fun and sweet and hilarious, she had all of us wrapped around her fat little finger, still true to this day. I had to laugh when she referred to Maple as *Shriek* though. When she was a toddler, Maple made a noise like a banshee whenever she wanted attention. And she always wanted attention.

Maple. I curled my body, knees to chest, and read on.

"Today, Maple got her first period! Poor thing was wearing white jeans. . . ." "Today on my way to work, a bear walked in front of my car. . . ." "Today, Izzy saw a therapist for depression. She reminds me so much of myself. . . ." Every entry, no matter how normal, felt like a punch to the heart. I missed her so much, it felt like when she died, half of me did, too.

Halfway into the journal, my mom's entries changed. They got sadder and more hopeless about a year before she died.

> I have to apologize for not writing sooner, but things got in the way. Right now I am very depressed. It's times like this that you wonder what you are here for. . . . Sometimes things are so good and sweet, and other times . . . I just don't know.

Some pages were crumpled and loose. I think some were even tearstained. I didn't know how, but I could sense her sad heart through the page.

> It hurts living here some days. I find myself reliving things that happened. Good, bad, everything. Sometimes I lie awake at night remembering every detail of our lives here, and mentally go back in time. It feels so good to be home again (mentally anyway!). I really miss the old days. It's funny all the memories that come back when I think of all of

us together, Pop, Mom, Izzy, Maple, and me. We had some terrific times, all right. And that's good that we can go back in our mind to find the fragments of days past. It helps keep one going, doesn't it? The house used to be my security blanket. But I don't even have that anymore. . . .

Some entries were just sketches, or song lyrics, or pages shaded gold. A few pages were colored in violet and labeled, *Darklights*. These pages hid shadowy shapes inside. She'd also drawn charcoal sketches of large black flowers. Under the weird blooms, she'd written: "What are these?" I flipped past doodles of red palm prints titled, THIS MEANS SOMETHING. Elaborate sketches of constellations and deserted roads. There were crude drawings of people choking labeled, THEY SHOWED ME THESE—WHY? Crumbled buildings. Deer, bears, foxes, and squirrels with Xs over their faces. The number 312 and 951 written over and over again. Art of a black and broken earth titled, *Our Fate?* And tiny pencil-tip dots scattered every page.

But the things she wrote near the end were the most disturbing of all.

They speak to me. Do things to me. Things I know they're going to do to more people soon. I've been studying ways others escaped them. I even bought an amethyst necklace for protection from the lights. I'm scared. Mostly because they warned me not to tell. I beg them to leave me alone. To stop doing what they're doing to me and others. But I have a feeling I'll never be free of the lights.

My hands trembled around my mom's necklace as I breathed through a terrible feeling I couldn't explain. Like this CD and journal were tied up with what's happening now. But what did her entries mean? What did "they speak to me" mean—*who* is speaking to her? What happened to my mom? I squeezed her amethyst crystal tight and wondered, Was this the stone she bought for protection from the lights? And what were the chances her lights were the same ones as mine?

I had to find out.

On the next two pages, she'd sketched a field alongside a moonlit dirt road in charcoal. Her car's headlights gleamed into the tall grass. Above her, three giant oval lights hung over the field. UFLs. Same as we saw last night. Except, without the glare of actual light, you could see the doors and windows on each ship. In my mom's drawings, the lights looked like real UFOs.

I flipped the page. Next, she'd drawn gold streaks of light beaming into her car and shining all over her. Above it she wrote: "The last thing I remember." Under this she scribbled, "Blackbird" and "radio" and how she woke eight hours later in her car by a field in a flash of purple light, but it felt like only a split second had passed. The field looked familiar, but I couldn't place it. The next page was just these words on repeat:

Nobody believes me. Nobody believes me. Nobody believes me.

I sat in my grandparents' closet, rocking back and forth with tears in my eyes. *Was Mom taken by the lights?*

No. Not the lights.

She was abducted by UFOs.

Is this real?

Suddenly, a loose page slipped from the journal, which made my chest ache.

It sure can get depressing when you feel so alone. When nobody understands . . . when you can't

tell what's real and you don't even believe yourself.
It makes me wonder. . . .

Do you believe?

"Ahh!" I dropped the journal on Akka's head.
"Sorry, bud." Akka yawned and gave up on sleep. I
stroked his soft head and thought I smelled my mom's
orange perfume.

No. I squeezed my eyes tight and shut the book.
I was so overwhelmed with information, revelations,
and sadness about my poor mom, I could barely keep
my thoughts and feelings straight.

How did I not see her depression?

Why did she hide everything she was going
through?

Were the lights that took my mom the same ones
that came here last night?

Were they really UFOs? Did they take Grams,
Pops, and Maple, too?

And if so, why hadn't they brought them back like
they did Mom?

It can't be a coincidence I found Mom's journal. I'd
been begging the universe for a sign she was still with
me. Maybe this was it. Maybe the information in her
journal could even help me find out what happened

to Grams, Maple, and Pops—maybe even how to get them back.

Akka gave me a "Woof!" Like, *Izzy, enough reading, not enough leaving*. I jumped at his bark. But as usual, Akka was right.

"Okay." I stuffed the loose papers into the journal and shoved the book down my pants. All the time, my mom's necklace banged my chest. I wondered how she thought it would protect her and wished so badly it had. "Let's go bring our people home." I grabbed my change of clothes and Pops's monster-bashing bat. Stashed his bowie knife and Mom's Discman, then left the closet behind.

Downstairs, I packed food and supplies for me and Akka, not knowing what would happen once we left home. Or if we'd find another human alive. All I knew was I had the best dog in the world at my side, and no matter how far I had to go, or how long it took, or how many monsters I had to fight, I'd do everything in my power to keep Akka safe and find my family. I'd do whatever it took to survive.

Pushing my worries aside, I readjusted my heavy pack and remembered Mom's Discman. I still hadn't checked if it worked.

When I pressed the button, my mom's voice

crackled through the headphones: "Song one of Annie's Alt. Mix, 'Don't You (Forget about Me),' by Simple Minds." I covered my grin with both hands, sobbing through tears.

"Akka—it's her!"

Everything else fell away. We were together, her and me inside the song, in a time far away, in a space between worlds.

As the song played, I wrote a note.

Sept. 19
Dear Grams, Pops, and Maple,

If you find this, you're home safe, and that's the best news ever. 😊 Me and Akka left for the River Bend like your emergency plan said. If you're not there, we'll keep walking till we find you. We'll stay on Route 30 and head toward Brattleboro in case you're looking for us, too. We love you more than anything and hope to see you soon.

Always, Izzy

P.S.: Sorry about the deck door. I'll tell you about it when I see you.

I shut the Discman off, left the note on the counter, clipped on Akka's harness, and tried to sound brave for him, like Pops and Grams did for me and Maple. "You ready for an adventure, Akka?"

"Bark!" He gave me happy tail wags and a tongue-out smile.

Yup, he was ready.

"Good." Akka at my side, a loose plan at the ready, I felt like maybe we could actually find them. I hefted Pops's bat, took a last look behind me, and opened the door. "Let's go, good boy."

Mom's music in my head, I left home singing.

CHAPTER 6

SIGNS

THE OUTDOORS LOOKED HAUNTED. THE SUN HAD been eaten by clouds, and darkness fell like a storm. I clomped down the front steps, black dust billowing from the sky. This must be the dust that fell from the lights. Black powder. Like in my dream. The fine black dust floated past us, coating everything in sight. My nostrils and lungs burned. The air stank like bleach. How would plants and trees breathe under all this dust? How would animals and insects survive? The sketch in the journal of animals with Xs over their faces jumped into my head. What if that meant the animals were gone, too? The world was dusty as a forgotten tomb.

The cemetery of the old world.

I shifted my backpack nervously as we passed Grams's and Pops's cars. I tried not to cry, but there was suddenly so much to cry about. I scanned the trees for the monsters I'd started calling gray uglies. I couldn't see them. I felt them watching us, though, in the raised hairs on my neck. But I kept going. I refused to let my fear stop me from finding the people I loved. I wouldn't stop until I figured out what was happening to my world.

Squinting against the dust, me and Akka walked the long road toward our neighbors, taking in the dark reality of our new earth. The trees, grass, and gravel slicked with oily black dust, choking out my world. Everywhere I looked, plant life was dying, and it broke my heart. I pulled my *Moonlight Society* scarf over my nose and mouth and hoped with whatever magic I possessed that my little family would be waiting for us someplace up the road.

When we arrived at Ben and Fee's ski shack, all their lights were still on, but they weren't home. Akka sniffed a clump of white fur on the welcome mat and glanced at me. *Where is Moss?* Moss, the neighbor's border collie, was a good boy, too. If they were home, Moss would be barking by now.

We knocked on every house on our street, but they were just as empty. I kept trying Grams's and Pops's phones—911, fire department, Nora and her family, my therapist. But nobody picked up. By the time we got to the street sign at the end of our mile-long road, I was already out of breath. My overstuffed back-pack dug into my shoulders. Pops's bat felt like it weighed a million pounds. My lungs burned. Akka sniffed the black grass and coughed. I wished I had a mask for him.

As we turned left onto the big road leading down our mountain, something out of place caught my atten-tion. Large, weird weeds hemmed the dirt road. No, not weeds. Pods. Like the pods on milkweed plants. Except these were the shade of sealskin, shaped like footballs, and floating on top of the ditchwater. They looked like flowers.

Akka pulled on the leash to sniff the weird plants, but I dragged him away. "Akka, no. Have a num-num instead." I passed him one of the dog cookies I'd stashed in my pocket, gripped my bat tighter, and hurried my boy down Taft Road.

Everything on the big road was just as eerily silent. Many houselights were on, but nobody was home. There were no birds singing. No chipmunks chittering or bugs buzzing. No truck drivers driving. No joggers jogging. No vehicle sounds in the distance. The world felt empty. Like nothing was breathing. It was just wind whistling through pines, our feet scraping road, and three questions spinning my mind.

Did I really hear whistling before, or did I imagine it? Was it another human or not?

Will I ever find my family alive?

With each step, I became more aware of the creatures from the lights in the woods. The Green Mountains were so thick, a bigfoot army could be living in there and no one would know. Me and Akka listened close. Scanned the trees on either side of the road. I saw no long limbs reaching from the shadows, but that didn't mean they weren't there.

To keep from panicking, I pressed play on Mom's Discman. Goose bumps prickled my arms at her voice. "Song two of Annie's Alt. Mix, 'I Believe,' by R.E.M." Tears rolled before I could stop them when she said, "I believe in you."

Do you believe?

The music burst through the headphones and immediately made me smile. It reminded me so much of her. But the harder I listened to the lyrics, the more they unnerved me. The guy sang about changes. How his throat hurt, finding the key, and what to do.

And how he believed.

Akka paused at the stop sign to do his business. A cold, black-dust breeze blew past. I put my back to the wind till it stopped, but I swear, again, I smelled my mom's orange perfume.

I whipped around searching for someone but found something else instead. The stop sign had a sticker on it I'd never noticed before: "Do You Believe?"

If this were a movie, I'd tell Nora, *That can't be a coincidence.*

I shut off my mom's Discman, heart trying to vault out my chest, and wondered if, when she was alive, she'd experienced synchronicities like this, too.

Three-quarters of the way down the mountain, the first drops of rain splashed my nose. Akka ran ahead, barking and snapping at the falling rain because he loved the rain. But ugh. I forgot to pack rain gear. Everything in my bag would get soaked.

I stopped to bury my mom's Discman and headphones in my backpack. Grams's and Pops's phones, too. Akka took this moment to sniff one of those weird pods in the ditch. I yelled at him to stop but pulled him away too late. He started sneezing. And when he raised his head, a drop of something fell from his nose.

Blood.

A second later, the rain really started to pour. I stared down the mountain road.

"Let's hurry, okay?" Akka licked my forehead, then barked. I forced myself to stop thinking the worst and jogged faster toward the bottom of the hill.

Around the next bend, a car had flipped over in the road. I hurried toward it, worried someone was injured but also scared of finding someone dead inside. I wiped the window of rain. All I saw was a pizza box and uneaten pizza and a six-pack of Coke on the over-turned roof.

"They're gone, too." My words were muffled through my wet scarf. "But you're right here, Akka." His nose had stopped bleeding. "At least I have you." We passed two more vehicles—one crashed into a house, another into a tree, both empty like every house on the road. We passed more of those creepy pods, too. This time, I kept Akka away.

Almost to Route 30, I was soaked and stinking like bleached rain, and my mom's necklace burned hot as flames. Then something in the woods screamed.

Gray uglies.

"Bork-bork-bork!" Akka lunged back the way we came. His leash was slippery with rain. I tightened my grip on the bat and growled at him to hush.

Akka stopped borking. His ears swiveled for sound. The shrieks grew louder. Closer. Branches snapped to our left. The monsters from the lights were coming. I had to do something. I blinked at Akka.

The only thing to do was run.

"Akka, come on!" We sprinted so hard toward Route 30, I thought my lungs would collapse and legs would snap. I tasted blood on my tongue. My nose was bleeding now, too. We had to get to the River Bend Farm Market on the other side of Route 30 and fast.

A gray ugly taller than the one on my deck burst out of the woods and blocked the road. Akka skidded to a halt ten feet from the monster. I tangled in his leash and almost fell in a puddle. Akka lunged at the giant, and my calm shut down for good.

"Bork-bork-bork!" Akka wanted revenge on the uglies for munching his leg. Too bad. I loved my best boy too much to let him die and yanked his butt back just in time.

"Akka, stay with me!"

The gray ugly came toward us real slow on the tips of its limbs, staring me down with its red bowling-ball gaze. Other uglies screamed from the trees, but Akka stayed at my side. I searched for a way out of becoming this dumb butt's lunch but found no safe escape. We had to get gone or we were toast.

Nerves on fire, rain pouring down, the River Bend Farm Market minutes away, I held Pops's bat high and screamed, "Run!"

"Bork!"

Me and Akka sprang for the woods and got exactly

two feet before—

Crack-rip-*pop*. Crack-rip-*pop*.

The pods in the ditches cracked open. And baby uglies pushed out.

Me and Akka skidded to a stop. He growled and snapped as baby uglies slithered from the pods, blocking our way to the woods on both sides of the road. Our only choice was to skirt the monster and head straight for Route 30.

Nose gushing blood, I pulled Akka forward and ran right by big mama ugly without her even stopping me. Not until I glanced over my shoulder did I see why.

The rainwater rivers at the sides of Taft Road had swept the babies away.

The giant ugly blocking our way pitched an end-of-the-world cry. Like a rally for war. Similar cries—like banshees baying into microphones—erupted from the woods. Akka writhed and screamed from their shrieks. My ears shredded inside the noise. I didn't know if the gray uglies were coming for me and Akka or for their babies, but I wouldn't wait to find out.

"*Akka*, keep running, go!" I shouted over the ugly's cries and rain, and pulled him toward Route 30. I thought we were in the clear until Akka dropped to the ground.

CHAPTER 7

PANIC

"AKKA!" I DROPPED THE BAT AND FELL IN THE DIRT beside my boy. Water surged down the trenches on either side of the dirt road, sweeping baby monsters away. "Akka, get up." I couldn't catch my breath. "Look at me!" His nose bled harder. He was cold, wet, and crying, and I was done playing nice with these monsters—nobody hurts my dog!

The giant gray ugly blocking the road hovered over me and shrieked, strings of black drool oozing from its teeth. I guarded Akka and screamed, *"Get away from him!"* I thought we were goners, but before eating us up, the gray ugly sprang after the pod babies, leaving me and Akka alone.

I hung my head and breathed fast with relief.

"Akka, I've got you, good boy." I put the bat in my pack, then lifted his soaking-wet body off the ground using every muscle I didn't know I had. "Please be okay." Then I cradled him like a baby and ran.

Route 30 was like the roads in the Stephen King book *The Stand*. Vehicles cluttered the pavement. Some crisscrossed the road; others were flipped upside down.

Cold water seeped into my soul.

The only one here is you.

The River Bend Farm Market was across the street and to the left. Runoff waters roared on either side of the two-lane highway. I pushed my body across Route 30, tears mixing with rain, and ran, not looking back. Akka's legs bumped against me until we got to the market door.

The automatic doors burst open. The inside was heated and warm but completely empty.

"Hello?" My boots squeaked on the tile as I set Akka on the floor. "Anyone here?" No Joe or Mary-anne like Grams and Pops told me to find for help.

Forget them. Focus on your boy.

"Akka," I whispered, trying not to panic. I brushed the wet fur from Akka's eyes. "Can you hear me?" He looked tired and weak but stopped shaking when his eyes opened on me. "You're okay!" My sadness flipped to grins. "Are you okay?" I hugged him close, never so relieved in my life. He lay still for a minute, then twisted to his feet, licked my nose, and shook off the black-dusted rain like nothing was wrong.

I sat with him for a while to make sure he was all right and searched the internet for clues. It looked like Akka might've had a seizure. And where there was one seizure, I discovered, there might be more.

Outside, the rain poured on. Water dripped from every piece of me, but at least the store had power, and it was warm. I pulled down my drenched scarf and wrestled my heavy pack to the floor. Akka was still weak, but our noses stopped bleeding. We were okay. For now.

I led us toward the back of the market, still trembling, still searching for survivors even though I knew I'd find nobody here. "Joe? Maryanne?"

Akka's nails clicked the tile floor loud as rocks on a tin drum, keeping pace beside me. I speed-walked past snacks and baked goods. A ladder still stood at the back of the store. The cash register at the deli was open, a bottle of soda and sandwich on the counter like someone was paying for them when the lights came, and they vanished without a trace. I ran a finger along the woman's wallet and read her ID. "Silvana Hector." Barely twenty-one, Silvana had a kind face and short blue hair. I didn't know her, but I was sad she was gone.

I pulled out the photo of me and Maple from last Halloween. I kissed that photo, wishing it were that day all over again. Wishing I were anywhere but here. Hoping somehow I'd wake up from this horrible dream.

I spied the landline phone. Slid the photo back in my pocket and tried it. I called number after number, but nobody answered. With every unanswered call, the knot in my chest grew. Akka pawed my leg as he did when my panic came—as if to say, *I love you. I see you're upset, but I'm here for you.* I took a breath and kissed his head. *I'm here for you, too.*

No reason to stay, we needed to get on the road. Keep searching for Grams. Pops. Maple. Nora and her family, and any other survivors. They had to be out there somewhere.

I had to prove we weren't the last ones alive.

As I walked the aisles toward the doors, the fluorescent lights flashed and buzzed. I spotted the bathroom and decided I better go before we went. I had nose blood all over me. Black dust, too. And I'm pretty sure I'd gotten my period along the way. I took Akka with me. Cleaned us as best as I could. Then grabbed some bottled waters. I found Akka a collapsible pet bowl and gave him water until he'd had his fill.

I hadn't realized how thirsty I was until I'd drunk enough to throw up. "Maybe we should eat, too." Even though I had zero desire for food.

The same thing happened after my mom died. Me and Maple weren't hungry for days. Pops and Grams got so worried, Pops set an entire strawberry cheesecake in front of us and said, "I know food is the last thing you want, but it's the only thing you need." He gave us all forks. "This was your mother's favorite, and she'd want you to eat. She'd want you to go on living. To eat cake and try to find any joy you can. So please. Let's all eat this for her."

I covered my face now, thinking of that awful day. I never thought anything could be worse. But losing them and Maple and Nora and having no human family to give me cake and forks and love was even worse. So, I did for Akka what Pops did for me. I found him the best food on the shelf, poured him a bowl, then grabbed a plastic spoon off the counter and searched for the one thing I could stomach right now. Not because of Pops, but because of Nora.

Ice cream.

Once, me and Nora watched *I Am Legend* after a bad day at school. I said, "How amazing would it be having the whole earth to ourselves. Free from terrible people like Daphne Black." Earlier, when Daphne, the biggest nightmare imaginable, found out I was attracted to girls *and* boys, she laughed and told me I was "confused" and to "pick a side." I was so shocked and angry, my mind went blank, and I left without saying a word.

"Forget Daphne. She is literal garbage." Nora handed me a vegan Ben & Jerry's Cherry Garcia. "But yeah. Having the world would be amazing. We could live in any house. Not have to go to school or take orders. We could be ourselves without worrying about what people might do or say. It could be just me and you forever, eating ice cream till we burst."

We laughed and clacked spoons like mini-swords. "It's a date."

I wished so bad she were here. *Nora, this one's for you.*

Me and Akka chose the best kinds of ice cream. "Cherry Garcia for me. Strawberry for you." Akka slurped ice cream from the container, wagging his tail. I set my back to the freezer, ate ice cream, and cried. Had it really been only one night since I hadn't seen my family? My heart ached like an open wound.

A sudden chill hit me sideways. Outside the front doors, "Blackbird" by the Beatles played.

My mom's favorite song.

The same one I heard in my dream.

Akka perked his ears to the doors. Could he hear the music, too?

I wiped my sticky palms on my jeans and ran to the front windows, thinking maybe someone's car radio was playing in the lot. But when I reached the doors, the music stopped.

Holy crow, wait. I dug my mom's journal out of my wet pack. I think I skimmed over something about music when I looked at it before.

I flipped through the book, past a section labeled, Dreams: "Inside the ship?" She'd drawn herself and other humans in a red-lit room. Humanoid beings towered over them—creatures Mom labeled, THEM. I shivered. The next page had a sketch of a metallic gold ball etched with a geometric symbol labeled, They were guarding this.

The next page was loose, but it held the line I was looking for: "A map in the music will guide you." A map in the music will guide you. What map was she talking about? I skimmed the journal but found no maps at all. Underneath the line about the musical map was another sketch of her in her car the night the "Dark-lights" came for her. "UFOs arrived after my favorite song came on the radio," she wrote.

Her favorite song.

"Blackbird."

I got chills. What if the "map" from the *map in the music* wasn't a paper map, but on her CD's playlist? Could the songs on my mom's Playlist for the End of the World be connected to the lights—to the UFOs?

I thought back to the lyrics of the first two songs on her CD. How they matched up with what I was doing at the time, and how eerie that was. Could the song lyrics be guiding me to something? But to what? Answers? My sister and grandparents? Other survivors?

I knew it sounded weird, but this clue was all I had, and I needed someplace to start looking for my family. Maybe I should listen closer to the lyrics of her songs? Maybe then I'd find more signs guiding us on.

Brattleboro was a long walk, but it was the way I told Grams and Pops I was heading. I had just grabbed Akka to leave when I caught another scent of my mom's orange perfume. It hung for a second, then vanished. Except this time, I know I smelled it. More goose bumps rose.

It felt like she was here.

I shook my head hard, jumped back to reality, and set my mom's journal in the pack. Then I grabbed more bottled water for the road, a pen, and a notepad, too. And while Akka lay at my side like an ice cream–stuffed sausage, I made a new plan. Because I knew me: without a list of goals, it was too easy to get sidetracked. Too comfortable for me to hide from the world. And no way would I let myself hide or forget why I was standing here now. Me and Akka would find Grams, Pops, Maple, Nora and her family, and, hopefully, the rest of those missing, too.

ISADORA WILDER'S EMERGENCY PLAN

1. Hike Route 30 to Brattleboro searching for G, P, & M.
2. Check the firehouses and hospitals first—find help.
3. Keep calling people and 911.
4. If you can't find help, others, or G, P, & M, keep going until you do.
5. Take what you need without guilt.
6. Watch for Mom's musical clues.
7. Keep Akka safe.
8. Do whatever it takes to survive.

I put the pen and notepad in my pocket. Checked outside for uglies but found only rain. All clear, I let Akka off his leash. He took off running like he had an itch he needed to scratch and went right to the dog toys we'd passed earlier. I smiled when the squeak-squeak-squeak of his new toy rang out a few rows down. *Dogs are gonna squeak stuff, apocalypse or not.*

While he was tossing his toy, I gathered supplies. A huge green backpack—one Grams and Pops could not have afforded to buy me. Actual masks—the kind Pops used for woodworking. Dry foods. Ziploc bags for clothes, period supplies, Mom's Discman, headphones, journal, water, and Grams's and Pops's phones. I shoved everything in my new pack. But before I put my grandparents' phones away, I called more numbers. Rechecked messages. And listened to their voices on their voice mails one last time. Hearing them was beautiful and horrible but helped me keep focused on finding them. I smiled at our Halloween photo once more before I packed it away.

As I struggled on my new pack, the rough amethyst on my necklace warmed like before. I spun in a circle, checking windows for uglies, and thought of something. Mom said she got the amethyst to protect her from the lights. But since the uglies came from the lights, could this stone help protect us from them, too? Maybe the stone heated like a warning when they were near?

"Akka, we should hi—" I glanced around, but Akka was gone.

"Akka?" I grabbed my bat and sprinted the frozen foods aisle but couldn't hear him. Mind racing, I skidded around the next corner and there he was, lying on the ground, chomping on a giant rawhide bone.

I slapped my chest. "Holy crow. You scared me." He gave me a look like, *What is wrong? This bone is not scary, Izzy.* I clipped his leash to his harness, gave him one of Grams's *Don't even play me, dog!* glares, and told him it was time to go.

I'd just started for the exit when something pounded the roof.

Akka dropped his bone and growled.

Uglies.

I pulled Akka behind an aisle not facing the windows, waiting for the monsters to leave. But the echo of limbs pounding metal only got worse.

BANG-BANG-BANG-BANG.

"Akka, to me." Boots squeaking the floor, I led Akka toward the back of the store. The ceiling lights flickered. Drywall rained from the roof. We hid behind the deli counter and waited, hunkered down, panting, sweating and scared. The movement on the ceiling paused. But those uglies couldn't fool me and Akka; we felt them tracking our moves.

After a minute that felt like three years, I peeked over the counter and peered through the front-store glass. A few gray uglies skittered down from the roof and stared inside. If they charged the glass, they'd be to us in a second.

Scanning for another way out, I spotted the side door. Grams used it once by accident. She'd been really confused that day. The alarms had gone off because it was an emergency exit, and when the entire store showed up to stare, I wanted to bury myself in Fritos and hide forever. But now, I'd have given anything to slap old Izzy's hand and say, *Don't you ever get embarrassed by her again. One day, you'll regret it.*

On the way, I spotted a raincoat on a rack and heard Grams shout in my head: *You better grab that rain slicker, Izzy, or everything you need to find us will be gone.* My breath hitched at her voice. Even when Grams wasn't with me, she was still with me.

When I dropped my pack to put on the coat, Akka growled. The glass windows at the storefront shattered, and the gray uglies pushed their long arms inside.

CHAPTER 8
DRIVE

"AKKA, RUN!" NO TIME FOR THE RAINCOAT, I grabbed my backpack and kicked open the emergency door.

Rain fell loud as thunder outside. I hurried Akka into the downpour, away from the grating alarm, and covered my ears against the sound. Gray uglies cried like a thousand banshees behind us. They thrashed and bounced off the walls, knocking everything down. I wondered if they hated loud sounds, too.

The side parking lot was clear. Four gas pumps stood before us, a vehicle parked at each. A black-and-yellow pickup truck, a red SUV, and two blue sedans. The truck was closest. I hesitated for a second, thinking the Izzy I was two days ago would never have stolen a thing. But I wasn't that girl anymore and this was a different world. Fight-or-flight juice kicking in, me and Akka raced through pounding rain to the truck.

Yes! The key was still in the ignition. The gas pump was still in the truck. With any luck, the tank was full.

I pushed water and hair off my face, then set the gas pumper thing on the hook. I opened the passenger door and hoisted Akka and my new pack inside, crossing fingers that the three driving lessons Pops gave me and the million hours me and Maple spent playing *Mario Cart* would get me and Akka outta here safe. I closed Akka's door and had just reached the driver's side when a baby ugly jumped off the roof and landed in front of me.

"Bork-bork-bork-bork!"

The baby monster opened its huge mouth a hundred and eighty degrees and wailed. I thought about grabbing Pops's knife but pulled the truck's handle instead. Akka went wild. The baby ugly snapped its razor teeth and lunged. I wrenched open the door and jumped inside. The baby ugly crashed into the open door and shrieked a mighty cry, but I was already inside, safe.

"Akka, it's okay! I made it!"

Akka growled at the glass. Every window fogged, I couldn't see anything outside, no clue where the uglies were. I searched for the defrost button and turned it on high. I fumbled for the wipers and twisted till they turned on, too. "I did it! You ready, Akka?" My co-pilot woofed and wagged his tail. "Good. Then let's get outta here."

I turned the key—and the truck rattled to life. "It works!" Akka barked like, *You are a fierce queen, and I love you.* Then I shouted a battle cry, put it in drive, and slammed on the gas.

The truck revved—but wouldn't go.

Why weren't we moving?

I peered out the unfogged windshield. A gray ugly dragged its body around the corner of the store through the pouring rain.

Uh-oh. It was missing a couple of legs. Dark goo dripped from its wounds as it pulled itself forward, shrieking into the rain. More uglies emerged from the store, jerking and writhing and coming for me. If I didn't figure this truck out, uglies would slurp us up like spaghetti.

I wiggled the gear stick thing around until I found the D for Drive. "Hold on, Akka, this isn't gonna be pretty." I floored the gas. The truck shot forward. I swerved away from the ugly too fast and the truck skid. Akka slipped on his seat. I pulled him back up, then turned the wheel this way and that till I shot us onto Route 30, no looking back.

"Woooo!" I turned to him. "Akka, we did it!" I spun the wheel by accident when I looked at him. I jerked the steering wheel back and Akka went flying. "Sorry!" Learning to drive was hard, but skidding away from monsters on a cluttered road in the rain was worse.

I glanced in the rearview. Again, the truck swerved with my eyes. "Shoot." I spun the wheel too hard, skirted a truck, and clipped the bumper of a car. Akka slipped off the seat and scrambled back, nervous. "Sorry, Akka. Trying to work my feet and hands and gas and brake is a lot and not remotely like playing *Mario Cart*." Akka panted at me like he knew I was doing my best, then stared out at the road. "Still, without this hero truck, we'd probably be swimming around in a monster's guts by now."

Hmmm.

Akka had a hero's name. Maybe this truck deserved one, too. "Akka, we should name the truck." This time, I kept my eyes on the road. "Who should we name the truck after?"

Akka farted.

I slowed down for a second and laughed. "Look, I love you, but that's not gonna work."

I focused on keeping the truck steady through deep puddles and thought about a character from my favorite books. Bob from the *Moonlight Society*. He wasn't rich. He had no fancy job. But he worked hard. He loved with every fiber of his being and would've fought a million uglies to save his family. Maybe Bob had no magical powers like the *Moonlight Society*, but in all the ways that counted, Bob was superhuman, too.

"What do you think about Bob?" Akka sneezed like I'd said something bonkers. "Well, it's a lot better than calling it Fart, so Bob it is." When I patted Bob's dash, a warning flashed through my mind. At the end of the *Moonlight Society* books, Bob dies.

The closer we got to Brattleboro, the more cars crowded the highway. I saw nobody else driving. No airplanes flying. No animals either. I scanned the road for Grams's familiar red coat and long brown curls. Pops's Carhartt jeans and plaid fleece jacket. Maple's blue coat and yellow Cons. For anyone walking Route 30. But all I found was a dying black world zooming past. And the whole time, my mind spun with thoughts about how my mom's music and the stuff in her journal seemed connected to things happening now. How I swore I heard "Blackbird" playing in the distance. How I could smell my mom's orange perfume.

Thinking about all this, I got distracted and almost hit a fallen tree. I squealed to a stop, slip-sliding all the way. Akka yipped, unimpressed. "Sorry, Akka."

Putting Bob back into gear, I spotted the radio.

The radio. Why hadn't I checked it earlier? Better late than never, right? Akka whacked his tail on the leather. "I knew you'd agree."

Thinking there might be an emergency broadcast, I pressed scan. But every station played static. I let it circle but only ever got white noise. Why weren't the radio stations giving warnings—broadcasting instructions on what to do? I gulped down a thick ball of worry.

Was it really just me and Akka on earth?

I squeezed the wheel, terrified of never finding anyone else alive. "Shake it off, Izzy. You've got a family to find, so stick to the plan and stay focused. You just have to make it to Brattleboro to look for help. How hard can that be?"

To keep me focused, I took out the photo of me and Maple and wedged it in a slit on the dash. I swallowed back the anxiety trying to rise and thought, *There. Now Maple's with us.* Then I thought of something else, too.

"Hey. We could play Mom's CD. See if we can find the *map in the music* to guide us." Akka blinked at me. "I know how it sounds. But maybe there really are more clues in the lyrics. Signs that help us figure out where everyone went and how to get them back." Akka grinned big as if to say, *That's the best idea I've ever heard*. And when he smiled at me, I didn't feel so hopeless. Like maybe we were right.

I leaned over, half watching the road, half fumbling into the backpack at Akka's feet looking for the Discman. "There you are." I glanced away for a second and nearly rammed into a van. "Ahh!" I swerved, overcompensated, and dipped into the ditch before getting straight.

I pushed Playlist for the End of the World into Bob's disc player and went right to track three. Tears came without warning when I heard my mom's voice. Akka cocked his head at the speakers.

"Song three of Annie's Alt. Mix. One of my favorites, 'Under the Milky Way,' by the Church." A long pause, then, "You are not alone."

Driving through tears, I weaved in and out of puddles and stalled vehicles, letting each note sink into the dark spaces inside me and light me up. And right when Akka pawed my leg to make sure I was okay, the guy sang about something shimmering and white leading you to your destination. Then I felt a cool hand press over mine.

"Ahhh!" I flung my hand off the wheel. Akka stood on the seat, hackles high as the song kept on, barking like he saw something I couldn't. The top of my hand tingled. My hair raised. And as the song hit its last note, I remembered what my mom said before the song played: *You are not alone.*

Suddenly, the CD shut off on its own and the truck felt winter cold. I stopped in the middle of the street. What was happening? Could that have been . . . ?

Mom?

No. It couldn't be. After she died, I tried contacting her spirit. Me and Nora even held a séance under a full moon. But my mom's spirit never came. It made me sad. Like maybe she didn't love me enough to come back, or maybe her spirit was just . . . gone. Eventually, I gave up. So, if she hadn't contacted me then, why would she now?

Thunder rolled across the overcast sky. Lightning struck a streetlight ahead. White sparks blew up from the blast and glittered to the ground. Then suddenly, the lyrics to the "Milky Way" song came back to me—about something shimmery and white leading you to where you needed to be. The song lyrics might be a coincidence. But they also might mean something. Either way, I had to check it out.

The Windham County Humane Society rose from the fog beside where the lightning hit. Puddles filled the lot. The lights in the building were off. The place seemed empty. But there might be animals trapped inside. Worried about animals without food or water, I accidentally pushed the gas. The tires screeched, and Bob flew—right into the fence. At that moment, a few things happened at once.

My mom's CD turned on. I spotted someone on the road. All the streetlights went out. And I thought I heard Maple scream my name.

CHAPTER 9

THE STRANGER

ONCE, MAPLE TOLD ME SHE KNEW WHERE WE went when we dreamed. That our spirits flew into other worlds and could contact other dreamers, too. That's how I felt when we crashed the truck. Like Maple's spirit was calling to mine as our mom's music played on.

"Song four of Annie's Alt. Mix, 'In-Between Days,' by the Cure." There was a silence. Then, my mom said real soft, "I never wanted to go."

Bob crashed as the drums began. I opened my eyes to a moonlit field. My mom was on a dirt road before me, circled in a halo of light. Grams, Pops, and Maple stood behind her, calling to me. Giant lights flared to life in the sky. A golden spotlight flashed down and took Grams, Pops, and Maple away as my mom pleaded, "Come back to me. . . ."

———

"Ahh!" I jumped awake, screaming. A rogue beam of sunlight hit my eyes. Blood leaked down my forehead.

"Bark!" Akka jumped in my lap. "Bark!"

"Ouch, Akka." I winced. Each bark was like a spike in my skull. "In-Between Days" blared on in the background (*Come back* . . .). My mind flew back to that dream. To my family calling to me before lights stole them away. To my mom saying, *Come back to me*, like the lyrics of the song. It was hard to tell what was real.

I shut the CD off and squinted at Akka through sunlight trying hard to break past clouds. "Thank goodness you're okay." My human family wasn't here. But my dog family was still with me. "Thank you for not leaving me, too."

Steam rose off the hood. The chain-link fence wrapped Bob's sides. The song ended. When it did, I realized Bob was still running. I turned Bob off, shoved the keys in my pocket, and remembered. Before we crashed, I saw someone on the road.

Suddenly, my skin prickled—like someone was watching me.

I sat up. Fog and black dust frosted the windows, and I couldn't see anything outside. I nudged my over-size lapdog aside, unbuckled my belt, and had just gripped Bob's handle when—

Knock-knock-knock.

"Ahh!" I nearly shot through the roof. Akka barked.

"Hello?" The stranger pushed close to the glass. I couldn't see their face for the condensation, but who-ever it was sounded young. "Are you okay in there?"

Holy crow. I wasn't the last person on earth.

Akka whined and wagged, excited—like the one knocking was a friend. But my brain wasn't so kind. *What if they want to hurt me? What if they want Bob or Akka?* I suddenly felt so vulnerable, all I wanted was for them to go away. I wiggled Pops's bowie knife from the sheath and held it before me, fingers tap danc-ing the hilt. When I rolled down the window, a tall, skinny kid my age waved back.

The kid was soaked.

"Oh, hey." The stranger blinked down at me, wild-eyed and nervous. Their eyes were the same amber shade as their jacket. Their hair, near black. Freckles dotted their tan cheeks and nose. The kid wore black jeans and a black backpack. "Sorry. I don't mean to stare. It's just. I wasn't expecting to find someone my age. You know . . . driving." I glanced away, unsure what to say.

Was I okay? I touched the blood on my forehead, head pounding. I didn't know. And what should I say about Bob? How should I answer anything? What are even words?

Akka nosed his way out the window and grinned at the kid for pets. The stranger pushed their wet mop of hair behind their ears; their baby-blue and pink nail polish flashed. "Oh, you're bleeding." The kid furrowed their brow with concern. "That crash looked pretty bad. I just wanted to make sure you were okay. But if you are, then . . . good. I'll just let you go."

"No, it's fine. I mean, uh, I have a headache. My lungs hurt. But my head stopped bleeding and my dog looks okay, too." I squinted into the sun. "So, yeah. I think we're all right."

"Okay. Well, good." They gave me a sorry half smile. "I guess I'll just get back on the road, then." The kid gave a still wave. Akka cry-barked for them to come back. Then the words my mom said when we crashed, which were the same as lyrics from my mom's playlist, returned (*Come back to me . . .*).

Holy crow, Izzy. What are you doing? This might be the last person besides you on earth. You might want to ask them to join you.

Maybe that song was a clue.

Akka growled, jumped into the back seat, and borked out the window. At the same time, my amethyst heated up fast. I unbuckled my seat belt as a high-pitched cry shook the woods.

The kid ran back to the truck. "The monsters. They're back." Clouds rolled like pirate ships across the sun-dappled sky. Akka borked louder as darkness draped the earth. "We might wanna—" Another shriek. "Run."

I glared into the woods. "Uglies."

The kid squinted at me, confused.

"Never mind." I grabbed Akka's leash and Pops's bat and led Akka from Bob. "Let's break into the shelter and hide."

"I like it! Let's go." The kid rounded the truck and raced to the Humane Society's door. A blackbird pin on their backpack flashed in Bob's headlights.

Blackbird. Like my mom's favorite song.

It felt like a sign.

"It's open, no bashing required." The kid waved us forward from inside the door. The distant trees shook. Shrieks filled the horizon as the three of us raced into the shelter.

We watched as three giant uglies moved on the tips of their long gray tentacle-arms up Route 30, toward Brattleboro. *Did they see us? Will they stop and break inside?* But they kept going. We watched until they were gone.

"That was close." The stranger limped toward the cages lining the walls. Their legs seemed in pain. "I think we're safe." They opened one of the cage doors. Blankets, shoeboxes, cat dishes, and fur. "Aww. All the cats are gone."

Akka sniffed the empty cat cages with a scared look. The shelter smelled like antiseptic, pet food, and love. But the kid was right. Every cage was empty.

"Yeah." My heart sank. No dogs barked, either. And outside, the usual natural sounds—peepers, insects, birds—hadn't returned. The silence of the earth felt heavy enough to crush my heart. If the wild creatures and domestic animals were gone, how was Akka still here? "What do you think happened to the animals?"

The kid knelt to give Akka pets and winced when their knees touched the ground. "The same thing that happened to everyone but us."

I bit my thumbnail and double-checked outside as Akka begged for more pets. "And what do you think happened last night? Why do you think we—" was all I managed to say before Akka shoved his snout into the kid's crotch.

"Oh—Haha. Hey there." Akka dug right in.

"Akka—no!"

"Wow, you're an extra-friendly dog." I could've lit a fire from the blaze in their cheeks.

"Stop, Akka." I pulled him away. But the second I let my guard down, Akka was back on the kid, sniffing, soliciting pets, and handing out more wet willies, too. "I am so sorry. He's not usually like this." Now, Akka was licking the kid's hands. A hot snap of anger rose in me and blew. "Akka, *enough*!"

My voice echoed through the empty shelter. I yelled louder than I intended and pulled a shamefaced Akka away, ready to burst into tears for yelling at my boy in front of what might be the last other human on earth. "I'm sorry. I shouldn't have yelled." I said it to Akka, and the stranger, too.

The stranger. I'd been so caught up I hadn't even asked their name.

"Hey, it's okay." The kid smiled till their dimples popped. "Really. Your dog is fine. Compared to Harry and Louis, yours is practically asleep." He laughed, but his smile fell fast. "My dogs lick me so much, it's like they're literally trying to eat me with love." Their eyes crinkled at the edges. "I haven't seen my mom or Harry and Louis, our corgis, since last night. You know. Since the lights came."

For a second, I thought they might cry. I twisted

my fingers, feeling guilty they lost their family *and* dogs, and I still had Akka. "I'm so sorry. My family also went missing lasterday."

Lasterday? Izzy, no.

I stood there, mouth open, panic rising. *Not yesterday or last night, but LASTERDAY? Why are you so embarrassing?* I pretended not to notice my mistake. The kid did, too, which put me more at ease. My scarf was suddenly too tight on my neck, so I wrenched it free and tied it looser before I freaked out. "Um, by the way . . ." I stared at my shuffling feet, banging my fist off my thigh. "My name is Izzy Wilder. My pronouns are she/her." Out of the corner of my eye, I saw the kid smile. "And the goofy dog licking your ear like there's peanut butter inside is Akka."

Akka side-eyed me like, *Let me live. I like ears, please let me have.*

When the kid stood, their knees cracked loud as Grams's. "Okay, first, it's good to meet you—Izzy and Akka—especially since I wasn't sure if I'd meet anyone ever again. Second, Wilder's a really cool name. And third, my name is Raven Barradell."

Chills dug in deep.

Raven.

Like "Blackbird" the song. Like the pin on their backpack.

Mom? Was that another sign from you?

Raven gave a slight bow, wet wavy hair falling in their face. "Oh, and my pronouns are he/him, at least for now. Thanks for including yours, too."

"Oh, uh. Yeah. Always. And thank you. About my name. I like it, too." Wait. Something just occurred to me. "Hang on. Your dogs are named Harry and Louis? Like Harry and Louis from One Direction?" I covered my mouth with both hands. "Don't tell me you're a—"

"Oh. Mmm, no. It's my mom. She's a Directioner for life." He covered his eyes, embarrassed. "Yup. She's a big Larry conspiracy theorist, too."

"No."

"Oh, yeah. She even has the One D perfume."

I laughed from the belly. It felt good. And when I did, Raven laughed, too.

"Your mom sounds like fun. Actually, I named Akka after a fire fawn from a fantasy series, so she's not the only nerd in town." Akka licked cat fur and sneezed.

Raven lit up like a little kid. "Are you kidding? Fandoms are the best! I'm a *huge* anime fan." He opened his jacket—and there was a *Fruits Basket* T featuring an extremely unimpressed orange cat called Kyo Soma. Raven ran a hand through his hair. "After a really hard couple of years, anime kind of saved me."

I nodded. Guess he'd been through some stuff, too. "Yeah. The *Moonlight Society* books did the same for me last year." Raven lowered his gaze with a hint of a smile. Like we shared something unsaid. Like he understood.

The lights in the shelter flickered. When I looked up, I noticed the clock. Holy crow. It was after five p.m. We'd been here way too long. Grams, Pops, Maple, Nora, and everyone else was still missing.

I had to go.

"I need to get back on the road and look for my family. I say we check the other rooms for animals and get outta here."

Raven glanced at his feet, hair veiling his eyes. "Oh. Totally. I need to keep looking for my mom anyway."

We searched the rest of the shelter for survivors but found none. I did find a few pollution masks for dogs, though, and grabbed them for Akka, as well as disposable masks in the surgery room for us.

We scanned the lot through the windows, making sure the coast was clear of uglies.

"See anything?" Raven asked.

"No. But the weird black dust is getting thicker since the rain stopped. We should put our masks on."

"Good thinking. The dust is crazy. Well, no crazier than anything else."

We donned our masks. Much to Akka's dismay, I put a mask on him, too.

We didn't discuss the gray uglies, dust, or UFLs—what they were or where they came from. I didn't know why, but I was almost afraid to talk about it. Like saying it out loud would make it too real. Raven didn't bring it up either, so maybe he felt the same.

"Then let's go." He opened the door for me and Akka, even did the flourish thing with his arm. "After you." His gentle eyes and blackbird pin gleamed in the sun.

Come back. My mom's words echoed to me like a dream. Like the sign I asked for. "Thanks." I smiled awkwardly through my mess of hair and led Akka, currently fighting with his mask, outside.

The breeze blowing off the road was damp and cold, layered with a stronger bleach scent than before. The sun was setting in a charm of pink and gold. Night was coming. All the streetlamps flashed on at once.

I realized then, I really didn't want to go into this dark world alone.

Akka raced out onto the black-dusted grass, shred-ded his mask into a thousand bits, and made the biggest, nastiest poop I'd ever seen. After Raven told Akka how impressed he was and Akka smiled back like, *I am the bestest boy*, I hurried up and made my move.

"Um, Raven?" I picked at my dust-covered nails. "Would you want to—" And of course immediately tripped over my undone shoelace and landed with my nose inches away from Akka's nasty poo.

"Oh my God. Are you okay?" Raven rushed to help me up. Akka lunged to slobber on my face because honestly, I think he thinks that helps.

"Thanks." I brushed myself off, embarrassed. "At least I didn't fall into Akka's—"

"Yeah. That would not have been good."

"No, not even a little." I dragged back my nerve as Akka licked Raven's shoes. "What I started to say was . . . do you want to join us on the road?" I looked everyplace but at him. "Um. Maybe search for our families and survivors together?"

Raven sprang a full grin. "Yes! Uh, I mean, yeah. I'd like that." He shuffled his boots in the dust. "Thanks. You know, for asking."

The parking lot streetlamp buzzed and blinked out over my head. That kind of thing seemed to be happening more and more since the lights came, and I wondered why. "Okay. I could use help with this guy anyway." I thumbed at my dog as he coughed out bits of torn mask.

Raven gave Akka pets, a sad look in his eyes. "I'd like that."

I motioned to the truck. "Maybe you can help me get Bob unstuck, too?"

Raven's eyebrows popped up. "Wait. Bob's the name of your truck?" I nodded as he walked over to Bob. "That is pretty much the best name for a truck I've ever heard in my life. And heck yeah. I can definitely help you with Bob." Raven glanced at me softly and smiled. "Let's see what I can do."

CHAPTER 10
LONG LIVE BOB

AS RAVEN ASSESSED BOB'S CONDITION, IT occurred to me that this strange boy and I would have to shelter somewhere together on the road. The thought made me so sick with anxiety, I bit my nail until it bled. Grams was always on my case about biting and picking my nails. But she knew, as one of my stims, it helped cool the live wire of nerves running through me.

Grams.

"Oh, I almost forgot!" I grabbed my pack from the truck. "There's something I need to do." Thinking of Grams helped me remember the spray paint I'd brought so I could leave notes for Pops, Grams, and Maple along the way.

"Sure." Raven popped his head up from under the

truck and pushed his damp hair out of his face. "You do what you need to do."

I nodded quick, then pulled out the yellow can of spray paint me and Maple used to coat my old desk. I smiled through worry as I shook the can and thought of that day.

"Ohhh, no," I told Maple as she poked her pretty head out from around the desk, paint can aimed at my bare feet. "Do not paint my—"

"What?" Maple replied. "I can't hear you over the sound of me painting your feet."

She sprayed my foot. "Maple Bonnie Wilder!" I shot up and chased her around my room until I did the same to her foot. Pops really let us have it, but we didn't care. We laughed until it hurt anyway and would have done it all again.

I choked back the memory. I was so tired of crying. I just wanted them all home.

Get it together, Izzy, and write.

So, on the brown brick wall of the Humane Society, I wrote a note in huge letters:

I'm sorry I didn't take the sweater.
Heading toward the Brattleboro firehouse.
I love you all.

By the time I got back to the truck, Raven had pulled most of the metal fence off Bob. "Okay." Black dust streaked across his cheek. "If you back it up, you should be able to get Bob free."

"That's great. Thanks." I put Akka in the truck as the last of the sun died. The earth and sky had turned the same shade, a bruised lavender plum. The parking lot streetlamps glowed lilac under a layer of dust.

The air was dirty. The whole world looked bruised.

Night had fallen at last.

Alien screams lifted from the horizon in a frenzy of wind. My amethyst warmed against my skin. I think I knew what that meant. I hurried to the driver's-side door. "We need to go."

"Normally," Raven said, hopping in the back seat, "I'd be nervous driving with a girl who just crashed a car, but crashing's the last thing I'm worried about right now."

I did a slow turn and eyeballed Raven as Grams liked to eyeball me. As if flames were ready to shoot from her pupils and burn down the world. Did he just insult my driving? Bad as it may be, me and Bob might be saving his life!

"You know there's actual horror movie monsters in the woods, right? Not to mention the giant, intelligent, unidentified flying lights from space that dropped them roaming the skies? And it's night? And this *girl* wasn't even going to bring you with me? So, unless you want to get sucked dry by the gray uglies in the dark, or you think you can drive better than me, don't insult my bad driving again. Understand?"

Oh no. Where did that come from? I'd never talked to anybody like that in my life. I glanced back at Raven, who looked terrified and impressed at the same time. I felt bad for unleashing on him. "Sorry. I didn't mean to yell. It's just . . . everything, you know?"

He nodded, rubbing his knees. "Yeah. I get it. And I'm sorry, too. That was rude of me. And insensitive. It won't happen again."

Before I shifted into reverse, faint notes of music played from someplace outside.

"Blackbird" again.

"Do you hear that?" The music seemed to be playing back toward home.

Raven shifted around, listening. "Hear what—the screams?"

Akka sniffed the air, ears swiveling. And then there it was again—a wave of my mom's orange perfume, and my arm hair standing on end.

"Music. Do you hear music?"

Right then, the "Blackbird" song stopped, and the scent of orange folded into that bleached ozone air. "Uh-uh. Just those awful screams."

Maybe I imagined it. I was so worried and anxious and embarrassed and confused about everything, I wouldn't be surprised. I needed to focus on my plan. First, make it safely to Brattleboro and see what or who we can find.

"Hey, Izzy?" Raven added, quiet and soft.

"Yeah?" I put the keys in the ignition, bouncing my feet.

"Thanks again. You know, for bringing me along."

I stopped bouncing and smiled under my mask. "Thank you for joining me."

Bob's front end was still a bit tangled in the fence, but when I turned the key, Bob revved to life. *"Yes!"* I whooped, Raven clapped, and Akka barked with excitement. "Better hold on to something." I shifted the truck into gear. Got it wrong, then, after some grinding noises, found reverse. "I am only a fourteen-year-old girl after all, and prone to crashing."

Raven grinned and might've blushed. "Yeah, number one. I said I was sorry about that. And number two. I'm fourteen, too. And number three. I guess I'd rather meet my end inside Bob with you and your awesome dog than get eaten by unbelievably ugly and ridiculously giant cosmic tentacle monsters from outer space."

I barely had a chance to react when the truck's CD player turned on full blast. "Song five of Annie's Alt. Mix, 'Never Let Me Down Again,' by Depeche Mode." I turned the volume down. It sounded like she'd been crying. "They fly high. And their eyes won't let you go."

An eerie feeling slipped over me. What she said sounded like code.

"Who was that?" Raven asked. In the rearview, he looked like he'd seen a ghost. Like her message gave him the creeps.

"My mom," I answered, and hit the gas. Synthesizers and drumbeats boomed. "Hold on!" Tires squealed. Bob ripped from the rest of the fence. Raven slid forward when Bob finally screeched free. "I said hang on!" I turned around and pounded the gas into the dark.

Bumping over asphalt and lawn, I drove toward Route 30. Raven grabbed the seat behind me and shouted over the music, "Turn the headlights on!"

"I forgot." I slowed and tried to find them. They weren't where they were in Pops's truck. "Where—I can't find them!"

I spun the wheel and slid on the pavement. I glanced around, pressing buttons and knobs. After a few brake slams and heart attacks, I found the head-lights and flipped them on.

"Oh no!" A shallow ditch illuminated before me. "Akka!" I thrust an arm out to grab my boy. We bounced and bumped into the watery ditch. On both sides, gray uglies shrieked from the dying black trees. "I'm going to get us outta here, hold tight."

Raven held Akka. I slammed the gas inside the ditch. Water splashed as the wheels spun. Burning rubber mixed with the toxic stink outside. The screams from the woods were louder and there was no time to waste.

Bob spun sideways in the muck. The CD shut off mid-lyric. When the back wheels caught solid ground, I revved the engine and hit the gas.

"Izzy, look." Tentacle limbs, small and gray, scurried from the dim water onto the truck.

Uglies.

"I see them." Their sharp teeth snapped as they focused their eyes on us.

"Bork-bork-bork!"

I swore and thought, *Sorry, Grams*, as Bob burst onto the wet pavement of Route 30 toward Brattleboro like a bat from a cave.

Raven jumped up. "There!" One scurried onto the windshield, blocking my view. One was at Akka's window, hanging on with its sharp claws while Akka borked. "We've got to get rid of them." Raven unbuckled, slid to the other window, and opened it.

"What are you doing?" I screamed, and swerved the road.

"Don't worry, just drive!"

I glanced back in time to see the baby ugly come for Raven. Raven punched it in the eye. I gasped, not knowing whether to laugh or scream as I swerved around a bike and watched the little ugly fly. "You did it!"

"Look out!" Raven pointed ahead. I almost missed the curve and turned fast, nearly hitting a tree.

Bob squealed sideways. "We're good. Just watch for my boy."

More babies were coming, and I needed this ugly on my windshield gone.

As Raven grabbed Akka's collar, I glimpsed Pops's bloody monster-crushing bat.

"Raven, see that bat? Give it to me, please."

"On it." He slipped over the seat as we bumped over something I hoped was just trash and passed me Pops's bat. "Do you want me to—"

"No. I got this. Just keep Akka still."

Akka let Raven hold him. When I opened my window, the baby ugly came after me. I tried to hit it and failed. The bat was too long.

"Izzy, do you need—"

"No!" I tossed the bat aside, grabbed one of the ugly's legs, and pitched the li'l sucker away. The gray ugly landed at the side of the road and scuttled into the woods.

"Yes! Nice pitch." Raven sounded amped. But I trembled like a leaf in the wind.

We closed our windows and let the last five minutes settle on the deep twilight road. Thankful for the houselights and parking lot streetlights keeping us from full dark.

"Well, that was . . ." Raven didn't need to say anything more.

"Yeah."

"At least Bob didn't die."

I caught Raven's gaze in the rearview. His hair was wild, his eyes were wilder. But the sheer relief on his face made me laugh out loud.

I plucked off my mask and skirted a wide, foggy curve. "Long live Bob!"

"Long live Bob!"

"Bark! Bork! Borb!"

"That's right, Akka." I laughed. "May Bob never let us down."

CHAPTER 11

DECOY

OUR TRIUMPHANT MOOD GREW DARK AS THE purple-smoke sky. We kept our eyes on the woods and the road as we searched for long limbs in the mist. Twice we had to pull Bob over to remove debris so we could pass. Twice we thought we saw shadows above the silver-blade clouds. And always, we felt watched. As Akka snoozed, Raven and I kept our thoughts to ourselves. I also had this nagging feeling we were going the wrong way.

I didn't know why. But something about the "Blackbird" song wasn't adding up. At first, I thought I heard it coming from Brattleboro. But after I met Raven, it seemed to be coming from the opposite way. And the more I thought about that vision I had of my mom after I crashed, the more I realized . . . In my vision, we'd been standing in the same field my mom was in the night she encountered UFOs. And the mountains in the vision looked like the ones behind our house, the same place I saw one of the UFLs fall. But those mountains and that field were in the opposite direction we were heading now.

Holy. Crow. What if we were going the wrong way? All my plans led to Brattleboro. I didn't want to turn around now. I really detested going back after I'd already begun.

Still, a small voice in me said, *Izzy, you have to find that field*. Most times, that small voice is hard to ignore.

"So," Raven blurted, jarring me out of my thoughts. "I see by your sweater you're into the *Star Wars*."

Wait.

No.

Did he just say *into the Star Wars*?

"My mom loves it," Raven continued. Seven more unholy words came from him next. "But I could never get into it."

Brakes squealed across my brain. "What?" I scrunched my face. "I've never heard those words put together that way before. What don't you like about *Star Wars*?"

Raven shrugged. "It's too unrealistic. And, uh, considering, you know, everything, that seems ironic now." Raven always looked kind of sad, even when he was smiling. It made him hard to read. He gestured to his *Fruits Basket* shirt. "Anime is just deeper, I guess? Less about good and evil and space, more about people and getting to the heart of things."

I slowed Bob and drove around a crack in the road. Akka bounced eyes between us like he was watching TV.

"That's what *Star Wars* is about, too. People in impossible situations doing what they think is right." *Izzy, calm down. He's allowed his opinion (even if it's wrong).* "I mean, yeah, maybe anime isn't in space. But look at the sky. We are literally *in space.*"

"Ha. Okay. I'll give you that. So . . ." That same haunted look fell over him. "If we were in a *Star Wars* movie, how would they deal with . . ." He gestured everywhere. "All this?"

I squeezed the steering wheel and slowed to avoid an overturned truck. "They'd go to the ends of the galaxy to save the world."

Talking to Raven like I knew him was so strange. Like things were normal, our families weren't missing, and our lives weren't in danger every second we were alive.

Raven clapped. "Then that's what we'll do."

I slipped a smile into the mirror and gave it to him. "Yeah, now you're getting it."

Out of nowhere, a light flared at our backs. We whipped around, thinking the UFLs were back. But it was just the moon pushing free of clouds, alongside a sky packed with stars.

I slowed down near an old Victorian house and snuck glances out the rear window at the starry black sky. "Is that . . . ?"

"Cassiopeia? I think so." He got out his phone and checked. "Yup. That's it."

Cassiopeia—the only constellation my mom ever remembered of all the stars in the sky. She used to point to it when it was out, lean real close to me, and whisper, "There she is, queen of the night sky." And we'd just stare at those big old stars and let them grab hold.

I snuck glances in the rearview and tried not to crash. "Weird how the song that was just playing mentioned *stars shining bright*?"

Raven worried his hands. "That is weird."

It made me wonder if this was another sign we should turn back and go toward the place that UFL crashed. I kept thinking about the lights as UFOs due to what my mom went through. I tapped my fingers on the wheel and wondered what my mom's abduction had to do with what was happening now. I'd been waiting for Raven to mention what he thought of the lights, and if he thought they might be UFOs. But he hadn't said a word. I guess it was like Grams said: if you wanted something done, you'd have to do it yourself.

"So I think the lights that made this mess of our world might be UFOs. I also think they beamed everyone into their ships. I know they don't really look like traditional *Star Wars* UFOs, but what else could they be?" The headlights flickered over a bump and my blurtations continued at light speed. "I'm not sure if they took the animals, amphibians, birds, insects, and every other living thing, too, but I haven't seen anything else breathing out here but us. Not even the plant life is breathing—it's all dying under this dust. And those monsters, or the gray uglies as I call them, I think they were dropped to destroy our earth. Maybe even to destroy us, too."

Raven nodded fast at me in the mirror, his eyes bright. "Thank you for mentioning UFOs. I didn't want to say anything because it sounded so unreal. Like, it doesn't matter that I literally saw what happened. It doesn't matter that I've been chased by monsters that look spawned from Jurassic Park on Mars. Even if this went on for three years, I still don't think I'd believe it. I mean, I didn't even like *Star Wars* because it was just *so much*. But now?" He waved his hands in the air. "We are literally living the *Star Wars* experience. So. You're right. The lights could definitely be UFOs."

I exhaled with relief. I didn't realize how badly I'd been waiting for validation. I didn't know why it was so important to me, but it was. Maybe my ideas were clearer than I thought.

"Hey, Raven?"

"Yeah?"

"Did you see the light, or UFO, if that's what it was, crash the night they came?"

Raven grinned. "Whoa. You saw that, too?"

I squeezed the wheel. "I'm glad you said something because I thought I might've imagined it. I think the one that crashed was the one over my house that night. The same one that covered Townshend, Newfane, and maybe Wardsboro." I risked a glance at Raven. His eyes were huge.

"I thought the same thing! I was on my lawn writing when I saw it fall and just . . . vanish before it crashed. I saw smoke from the woods after, too." I swerved around a car crash. "At first, I debated hunting down the thing that might've stolen my family. But something made me turn around and hike toward

Brattleboro." Raven glanced at me in the rearview. "I think that something was you."

My heart raced. "Actually, I had the same thought about you."

From the back seat, I felt Raven smile. "What do *you* think happened to everyone? And why do you think those monster things left us behind?"

"I don't know. All I know is every light-slash-UFO got away except the one over our town. And if it *did* take our families, what if they're on the ship with the rest of our town waiting for rescue? What if we're the only ones left to rescue them?"

Raven sighed heavy and nodded slow. "Then, we have to go after it and investigate. But . . . as much as I'd love to kick some aliens where the sun don't shine, how do we find the ship? And even if we found it, it's not like there's an 'aliens invaded and crashed in your backyard now what' manual. How do we defeat these gray ugly turd-burglars running our world and save everyone?"

Akka woke from his nap and yawned.

"That's what we need to find out. Plus, if we're gonna defeat an alien army, we're gonna need more help. So, I guess we go to Brattleboro first. If there are others left like us, that's where they'd be. We can explain our situation and swap stories with them, then all go on together."

Raven ruffled Akka's scruff and gave a hearty, "Agree."

"Good. It's settled."

I took my foot off the gas and slowed in the middle of Route 30. Grams's and Pops's phones buzzed in my pockets, then stopped. A bad feeling slipped over me. When I checked their phones, neither one would turn on.

Raven jerked forward. "Did your phone just buzz, too?"

"Yeah." I put Bob in park and tried to get them to work, but no luck. "My grandparents' phones are dead. Yours?"

"Mine, too."

I held their phones, breathing fast. Now even their voice mail messages were gone.

Akka climbed into the front seat, hackles up, and growled.

"Uh, Izzy?" An absence of sound hit. An inverted hush like seashells suction-cupped over your ears. My necklace heated. Raven pushed forward. "I'm not sure if you've noticed, what with driving and everything, but those lights we thought were stars? I'm beginning to think they're not stars."

"Bork-bork-bork!"

I swung around fast. Sure enough, the big bright

constellation was not Cassiopeia. 'Cause those sparkling gold lights were zooming right for us now.

The UFLs were back.

I slammed on the gas and skidded around a bend.

"Watch out!"

I crashed into a trash can. "Sorry!" It flew over Bob and kept on. I jerked the truck back and forth until I got Bob straight.

"They're coming too fast!"

Akka snapped at the windows. I worked to avoid everything in my path—bad thoughts, cars, trash, and Raven's back seat commentary—and catch a glimpse of the lights. "I see them." Five giant gold lights soared steadily toward us from the back of the sky. I sped up. My mom's necklace seared my skin. Panic came fast as the lights.

"Izzy! Watch out. There's a truck—"

"I see it." I swerved and skidded and stopped.

A semitruck had crashed on its side across Route 30. I drove Bob onto the pull-off before the crashed truck, rolled him into the bush, and hid under a canopy of trees. I turned Bob off and hopped in the back between Raven and Akka. That's when we heard them. The vibrational hum of the lights. Raven held Akka on the seat and whispered calm words in his ear as Akka cried. We stayed quiet as held breath until the golden lights flew overhead and passed us by.

"Well, that was close." Raven popped his head over Akka, eyes sparkling in the moonlight. "Good thinking hiding under the trees." Akka was panting heavily and crying. Our noses were bleeding, but we all seemed okay. "Yup. Those are definitely probably UFOs." He sniffed back blood. "Why do you think they came back?"

I shook my head in the heavy silence, thinking about the lights. How they came closer this time. Thanks to my mom's sketches, I had a good feeling I knew what they looked like beneath their shine. "It doesn't matter. All that matters is getting them gone."

Raven studied my face in the dark as I pictured my family in my mind.

I couldn't help thinking, somehow, I'd need those lights to get them back.

CHAPTER 12

STAY OR GO

I HOPPED OUT OF THE TRUCK, SQUINTING INTO the dust. The semitruck jackknifed perfectly across Route 30. Spilled boxes littered the road. The guardrail on one side, the forest on the other, we couldn't squeeze by. I stood in the quiet dark, sadness welling inside me. My world looked diseased. But under all the darkness and emptiness, the green heart of my earth still beat. I still felt it under my feet. *And even if it takes until I'm a hundred, I won't stop trying to fix my world until it's full of life and beauty once more.*

"See anything?" Raven called from inside Bob's cab. Akka grumbled to get out of the truck. But the dust was getting thicker. And because Akka wouldn't wear a mask, I needed to limit his time outside.

I turned and spoke through the glass. "Yeah. There's no way around the semi."

I wrapped my hands into my mess of curls, piecing out what to do. Maybe the blocked road was another sign we should turn back. I wrapped my sweater around me and bit my lip under my mask. Signs from the universe were helping at first, but now there were so many, it was hard to know what to do. And what if none of these "signs" meant anything at all? Maybe missing my family just had me desperate and grasping at stars, as Pops said. Pops, who always knew what to do. Pops. Missing with Maple and Grams and everyone else in the world.

Were we really on our own?

"So, what now?" Akka started barking. After a second, Raven set him free. "Do we go back, or"— he cringed under his mask—"possibly get eaten by excitable goth monsters as we do the zombie shuffle to Brattleboro on foot?"

That was so funny, I had to laugh. But my laughter didn't last long. I gave Akka water. Akka gulped it down in two seconds flat, then enjoyed a nice long pee on the black-dusted earth. "I don't know." I paced, tapping my thighs, biting my nails, and twirling my hair, all cylinders firing at once. "We could go on foot and look for another vehicle with keys and gas, but if we don't find one . . ." I glanced at Akka. He'd had one seizure already and refused his mask. Plus, the uglies. Akka trusted me to protect him, and I refused to risk his life. "Walking might be too dangerous."

Akka pulled toward the semi's open back doors and pawed one of the boxes. "Worf." Akka's *I know something you don't* word.

I opened the box. "Hey, check this out. This truck is packed with flashlights."

"Whoa." Raven grabbed one and turned it on. Everything lit in an eerie red glow. "These are infrared lights. Like amateur astronomers use while stargazing. See?" He shone it into the woods. "The red light lets you see stuff on the ground without blocking the light from the stars."

All at once I realized I'd left the crank flashlight at home. "These will definitely come in handy." I shoved one in each pocket. "We should grab a few for the road."

"On it." Raven stuffed a ton of them into his backpack. I watched with understanding. I was about to do the same. Raven glanced up at me. "Yeahhh, I have anxiety." He threaded a curl behind one ear, stood, and winced in pain. "I like to know I'm not going to run out of anything, you know?"

I nodded. "I know all right. I have anxiety, and other stuff, too. So yeah. We should definitely take more." Raven smiled like he could see right through my anxious heart. I felt a bit better now. Closer to Raven, too.

While we stuffed flashlights in our packs in the middle of the highway, I realized I'd never seen Raven around. "Hey. What school do you go to? I don't think I've seen you at Leland and Gray."

"Oh, right." Raven zipped his pack. "Me and my mom moved to Townshend a few weeks ago after we inherited my great-aunt Frida's house. We used to live in Norway, Maine. You've probably never heard of it. It's small. Anyway. I'm homeschooled. Have been since kindergarten. Funny story. My mom planned to homeschool me right away. But I pitched a massive fit and she let me try traditional school." He laughed. "Well. I wasn't even there a day before I snuck out and walked home alone because . . . uh, I was bullied for wearing a skirt." My blood fired up on Raven's behalf. He aimed his amber eyes onto me. "I don't get what the big deal is. Why people push gender onto colors and clothes. Anyway, I decided I didn't want to go to such a dumb school and never went back."

"I don't get it either." I crunched my teeth and squeezed my fists tight. "I'm sorry that happened to you, Raven."

Akka plopped down at Raven's side. "Yeah." Raven

stroked Akka's ears. "My mom's the best, though. She told me I should dress how I wanted and to never give anyone the power to tell me who I am or want to be. Ever."

Goose bumps. That was something Grams would say. "Your mom sounds wise."

Raven sniffed back sudden tears. "She is. And listen . . ." He stepped real close to me. "I'll walk this entire planet to find her, and your family, too, and won't stop until I do." He beamed through the red light and dust. "You and Akka can count on me."

Strange noises cracked the still night. Akka jumped up and growled.

"Did you hear that?" I cinched up Akka's leash. I'd heard the same noises earlier.

"Yeah. It sounds like the earth breaking in two."

Suddenly, the semi's horn started honking and all its electronics flashed on.

"Bork-bork-bork!"

"Raven?" I covered my ears. Static howled from the semi. "That's going to attract—" Screams bleated between honks, from the direction of town. "Uglies." My necklace was outside my sweater; when I gripped it, it was hot.

Music broke through the static inside the semi's cab. It was a song I knew from Pops. "Paint It Black."

Electric guitar wailed into the night. The music crackled with static. Then another song my mom loved cut in: "It's the End of the World as We Know It (and I Feel Fine)." Another one by R.E.M. Orange perfume whipped up out of nowhere.

Mom.

Under the music, the ground shook. Crumbling stone and cracking earth echoed through the mountains. Akka jumped and yipped at the ground. Then the shaking and music, and whatever electrical surge caused the chaos, stopped. And the earth went quiet.

"What the what *was* that?" Raven glanced in every direction. "It felt like an earthquake."

"Yeah. And did you hear those uglies scream?"

"Mm-hmm. And what about that song? The lyrics were . . . appropriate." I got more water for Akka, which he drank like it was the last on earth.

"Yeah." They sounded like something from my mom's CD. "The end of the world and everything painted black. Sounds about right."

Raven kicked around an old side-of-the-road shoe. When he spoke, he sounded nervous. "So, what do you think we should do? Go on foot or go back?"

"Before we decide, I need to know what those sounds were." I glanced from the semi to the moon lighting the road. "Take Akka? I have an idea."

I scaled the giant tires of the semi and climbed up onto the flat side, facing up. When I stood and stared toward Brattleboro, I almost fainted with fear.

Three enormous uglies blocked the road ahead. They swayed in the center of Route 30 above the dark-hilled horizon like the biggest, ugliest daddy longlegs you ever saw, driving the tips of their sharp-pointed legs into the road and earth. Breaking up pavement. Ripping down trees. Digging up soil.

"Izzy . . ." Raven called from below. Beside him, Akka pawed the semi, trying to get to me. "What do you see?"

I didn't answer. I was too transfixed. At least twenty more uglies climbed the overpass. Their limbs pulled upward onto the bridge, shadowed against the city lights. My blood ran cold. They were destroying our earth.

"Izzy? Are you okay up there?"

"Yeah, hold up. I'm—" One of the uglies turned my way. I ducked. My mom's journal dug into my belly. I remembered something I'd read inside earlier. A memory of me from when I was five:

Izzy melted down at the park when I forgot her favorite cup and we had to go back to get it. One of her big peeves is going back the way we came. But I told her, "Listen. All our lives we'll be going back. Back to forgotten cups. To places and people and things we forgot. But if you pay attention as you go, you'll see things you missed the first time. And sometimes, these are the most important finds of all."

Oh, Mom. I wished so badly I could just talk to her. She knew me better than anyone. And even back then it was like she was preparing me for this moment. Maybe she was trying to tell me that if we went back the way we came, we'd find the most important things of all.

"Sorry. I'm coming." I scrambled back down the truck, coated in a layer of dust.

I was prepared to worry about my filthy self later, but Raven pulled a colorful rag from his backpack and gave it to me. "Take it. Everything in my pack is wet anyway."

"Thanks." The rag wasn't even a rag. It was a wet, white T-shirt with a rainbow over a thunderstorm sky.

"So? What was going on out there?"

I wiped my hands and took Akka's leash. "See for yourself."

The uglies called to each other. A *t-t-t-t-t-CHHH-HHHH* shriek like the loudest cicadas you ever heard. The road shook and rocks crashed against stone. A minute later, Raven returned. "Yikes. That's . . . *not good.*"

I paced, fists hitting my thighs. "I know."

"Is there any way around them? Like back roads?"

"Raven? I think we should go back." Black dust gusted harder. My throat felt charred, and I coughed. "Find another way to get to the truth and save the people we love."

Akka jumped up, paws on my chest. "I'm okay, bud. Promise." I ruffled his big furry head, then grabbed Raven's sleeve and pulled him toward Bob. "Come on. We need to go." I hopped in the truck. Akka scrambled into the front seat, panting heavy, his tongue and eyes caked in dust. Raven slid into the back with a furrowed brow but didn't say a word.

I coughed again, a sour feeling in my gut. I slipped down my mask and checked myself in the mirror, to see something. Just as I thought. My face and mouth were slick with dust. The inside of my mouth, too. Raven's was the same. We spit, then wiped our tongues. I cleaned Akka's as best I could, then found us new masks from my pack.

"Here. Hope you like sunflowers or daisies. It's all they had at the River Bend."

Raven wiped dust from his face. "Daisies for me, thanks. They're my mom's favorite."

I smiled sadly and donned my new mask, then wrestled Akka's on, too. "You *will* wear your mask,

Akka. Do *not* take it off, you hear me?" Akka seemed to sense Grams's fire in my voice and kept it on. "Good boy, now let's go."

I turned the ignition. The air felt heavy and electrically charged.

"So where to?" Raven rested his head against the window, closed his eyes, and yawned. "Are we going after the crashed UFO?"

This time, I found Bob's reverse on my first try. "We go to one of the houses up the road and lay low for the night. Eat, clean up, then sleep on it." I coughed into my mask. "We need to be on top of our game to find our people. And I need rest if I'm gonna think, never mind drive."

I stepped on the gas, heading away from Brattleboro, battling every worry-thought in me. On the way, I whispered a mind-message to my mom, not knowing if she'd actually hear me.

If you're here, help us. Give me another sign. Guide me to answers that'll help me find Grams, Pops, and Maple. Please, Mom, show us the right thing to do.

A shock of electricity brushed the top of my head. A quick whiff of orange circled the truck. A cozy warmth flooded my chest, and I knew she was here.

Suddenly, all the power in the city flickered. The city lights sparked and flashed. The gray uglies chittered, swarmed, and howled.

That "Paint It Black" song started up in my mind as every light in the city went out.

And the world went black.

CHAPTER 13

ALIENATION

"THE LONGER THE NIGHTMARE WENT ON, THE easier it was to believe." My favorite author wrote that in book two of the *Moonlight Society* series. At first, I thought she was talking about a nightmare you had in sleep. But as we stared down the darkened ruination of our world, I wondered if I was wrong. If she meant that the most terrifying nightmares were real. And if you stayed inside them long enough, you grew so accustomed to the dark, the nightmare was the realest thing of all.

Monsters bellowed from every direction as I drove away from town. The earth was black. The sky was black. The houses, stores, and hillsides faded to black when the lights went out in Vermont. I didn't stop driving, though, because thankfully, Bob's headlights still worked.

Akka twisted up out of his snooze and pressed his nose to the glass. The entire outdoors looked painted black.

"Raven? Are you awake?"

Raven shot up at once. "What? Did I fall asleep? Wait. Why is it so dark?"

Alien cries rang from the mountains like midnight wolves. Our eyes met in the mirror. No way were those wolves.

"All the power to the city just died."

"Oh no. That's . . . bad."

"Yeah." I swerved around a giant branch in the road and nearly slipped into a ditch. "That means everything's going to stop working. All electricity and houselights. Fridges and stoves. Heat to keep warm. But also water pumps, and gas pumps for Bob. City lights and streetlights and phones and outlets and . . . Oh no." I instinctually felt for the phones. "We won't be able to charge them. And landlines won't work either." A suffocating panic gripped me. "How will we communicate to others? How will we know if anyone's out there with no phones?"

The river beside the road roared and looked ready to flood. The bleached stench of our new world grew.

"Right. And even if we found working phones or laptops or whatever and wanted to look anything up, the internet still wouldn't work."

This was really bad. "What do we do? How will we gas up Bob? Without street lights and the glow of city lights, it'll make the uglies so much harder to see." A million frenzied thoughts plowed through my brain at once. How would we do anything without light?

Raven caught my attention in the mirror. When he smiled in his gentle way, it helped soothe my mind. "We do the only thing we can do. We keep going, and rock the heck on."

I almost slammed on the brakes. "Wait. What?"

"Nothing like some good old eighties music to wipe our worries away. Music saaay like from your mom's CD? I mean, it might help us relax to hear anything other than the flock of starving alien cryptids shrieking in the dark, right?"

"Raven"—I grinned and tapped the wheel—"that is honestly the best idea ever."

As we drove toward the mountain range sketched in my mom's journal, where we saw the UFL fall, I pressed play on Playlist for the End of the World. There was so much to worry about, but when my mom's voice came on, it felt like maybe everything would be all right.

"Song six of Annie's Alt. Mix, 'Never Surrender,' by Corey Hart." I knew this song. She used to play it for me when I was sad. But now when her voice came through the darkness and said, "Find the light, Izzy. And don't give up," I choked on my chills. "This song is for you."

My heart leapt with joy.

She is talking to me.

The music came on and we listened in the great wide dark. The lyrics made me cry. Thinking of how lost I felt. How sad Mom sounded. How I'd never hear her real live voice again, and how badly that hurt. How I didn't want that to happen to Grams and Pops and Maple, too. I could just see the photo of Maple and me, wedged in by the speedometer. I touched her happy face and thought, *If I lose them, too, my heart might be too broken to recover.*

But as the lyrics unfolded around us, it really was like my mom was here. Telling me to take courage and fight. (*Never surrender . . .*)

Find the light, Izzy.

All these little messages meant something.

Wait. *A map in the music will guide you. . . .*

Maybe I was right before when I thought the *map in the music* referred to the song lyrics on her CD. But what was she guiding us to? Did *Find the light* mean find the crashed light that fell from the sky? Maybe emergency people—police and ambulance and fire, maybe even the men in black—were already at the crash site? Maybe she was trying to lead us to them, so they could help? Or was I missing something? The key to finding Grams, Pops, and Maple?

I wanted to believe, like the R.E.M. song, and the words in Mom's journal, and that stop sign sticker said (*Do you believe?*). I had to believe we were on the right track. So, I allowed myself a hopeful ray of sunlight feeling to shine out of me. Hunting down the UFL/UFO was the best lead we had, and no way would I surrender. I'd fight every ugly on earth to bring my family back to me.

The song ended. I took a sharp curve as the next one began. "Song seven of Annie's Alt. Mix, 'True Colors,' by Cyndi Lauper—"

Bump-bump-whack.

Bob hit something and the CD shut off.

"What was that?" Raven gripped the back of my seat.

Akka barked like he was possessed.

"A pothole, maybe?"

But looking closer, I saw jagged lines crossing the road. I slowed down. The closer we got to the lines, the more the headlights revealed. The lines were cracks in the road. We drove over another crack and Bob hit hard. Suddenly, the earth trembled under Bob's wheels. Bob shook like a tin can in a quake. Behind us in the pitch, gray uglies cried.

"Izzy . . ." Raven leaned in close to my ear. "The monsters are breaking the roads. We're driving over gaps in the pavement."

My necklace heated up fast.

Oh no. Not good.

I slowed but didn't stop. I couldn't. Because now, pointed tentacles pushed from the trees like thick, windswept hair. Red eyes shone from the forest on both sides of the road. Then I saw it. A gaping crack crossed the pavement, ten feet ahead.

"Holy crow. Holy crow." I slowed down. The cement peaked up like a ramp—too wide to cross. Uglies trapped us both ways. There was no way out.

I caught Raven in the mirror. Saw the fear in his amber-gold eyes. Thought about his mom and dogs waiting for him. And about Akka, the fur-boy who owned my heart, looking at me, and I made my move. "Hold on, okay?" I grabbed Akka's collar. "I'm jumping it."

"Wait—"

"No."

I pressed the gas harder. The way was clear. Raven flew backward. I tried to hold Akka, but I needed both hands and had to let him go. Raven grabbed my boy's collar and held as I floored the gas.

My mouth opened. For an instant we actually flew. "Ahhhh!"

Bump-bump—bump-bump. The front wheels touched down. The underneath scratched pavement. The truck bounced. We flew off our seats and skidded sideways along with Bob. Akka cried and slid the seat. Raven reached for him and screamed as I spun the wheel hard to get Bob under control.

"Izzy, watch out!" Another massive pothole loomed straight ahead.

"I got it! Hold on!" I spun the wheel hard. The tires squealed. I finally got Bob facing straight. And just like that, we were clear and speeding away.

"Woooo!" Raven howled. "You and Bob the God did it!"

Akka hopped around like a puppy, wagging and barking with glee.

"We did it. But we're not done yet." I pushed the gas and swerved to avoid an uprooted tree. Raven and Akka slammed sideways. We almost crashed.

"Bork-bork-bork!" Akka scrambled over the seat

to snarl and snap out the back window.

Raven peered out the glass beside him. "Izzy, they're standing right behind us."

"*Bork-bork-bork!*"

The necklace fried my already burned skin. I floored the gas. The giant old farmhouse I'd spotted earlier stood on the right, just ahead.

"Let's get to that house and hide. I don't think we can outrun them this time." The truck spun on a slick of rainwater. Akka stopped borking and scrambled to stay on the seat. The gray uglies galloped behind us fast as a train. A dirt road ahead branched off to the left. I wasn't sure where it went, but there were uglies all over it.

I slammed the brakes and jerked the wheel too fast. Two tires lifted off the ground, then slammed right back down. Red eyes big as Frisbees streaked in the dark. The monsters were coming at us on all sides.

"My gut says stop." Raven nodded. "We should definitely stop."

Tentacles slapped into Bob's side, nearly knocking us off the road.

"One's got us!" I pressed the gas, but Bob didn't move.

The ugly wrapped Bob with its tentacles and picked Bob up with us inside.

"Bork-bork-bork!" The gray uglies glared at Akka through the windows. We were hovering midair.

"Izzy! We can jump. We're only a few feet off the ground."

"But then we'll lose Bob! And what about Akka?"

A giant red eye stared through Bob's windshield. I panicked. Bob jostled in the ugly's grip. I froze and might've died; it was hard to tell. I was lost in its stare. And I swear, when I gazed into the monster's eye, "Blackbird" played.

Raven grabbed my arm, screaming. Akka pawed the dash, trying to get at the ugly. A quick whiff of orange filled the cab. Akka flipped the switch for the radio. I thought I heard my mom say, *Izzy*, right before the radio blared on.

Feedback screamed through the truck. White-hot pain shot into my skull. Akka cried. Raven shouted. I couldn't hear anything but feedback and screams. The ugly shrieked. Bob lurched—for a second, I thought the ugly would toss Bob into the trees and we'd fall.

"Akka, to me!" Frantically reaching for Akka, I hit a knob under the dash. My head was pounding with radio feedback when, suddenly, a burst of bright red floodlights hidden underneath Bob flipped on. Every monster surrounding us screamed. Their tentacles flew back. I grabbed Akka's collar. Raven clutched my sweater. Then Bob crashed to the ground.

The radio shut off. Bob's red floodlights flickered but eventually stayed on. The gray uglies fled to the outer perimeter, hovering just outside the bubble of red light. Sharp tentacles stabbed toward us, crossing the red bubble shine. But when their limbs hit that glow, they shrieked and snapped their limbs back fast.

Akka lay limp and stared unfocused, like he was stunned. "Akka." Drool laced with red and black leaked off his tongue. I shook him. "Akka, look at me?" In a beat, he rolled his eyes onto me. Then licked my cheek. "Good boy!"

The gray uglies called to each other from the woods. Alien words I couldn't understand but that felt like they were making a plan. Raven slid down the back seat. I whipped around to him slumped in the corner. Head bleeding, out cold.

"Wake up!" I crawled into the back seat. Akka scrambled into the back and jumped in his lap and snapped him awake with a bark in the ear. "Raven! Are you all right?"

"Mmm. What happened?" Blood dripped from his nose. I checked me and Akka; blood leaked from our noses, too. "My head. It's . . ."

"Pounding. Same. But we have to go."

Bob's red lights flickered. I was terrified they'd go out.

Most of the gray uglies had scattered. Only the two biggest stayed. They eyed us from the shadows outside the red, waiting for their chance.

"Where did the red lights come from?"

"From Bob—a button hid under the dash—but this is no time to chat. We need to decide if we want to keep driving, or hole up in the farmhouse for the night. I'd thought hide in the farmhouse, but they might just bust in there, too."

Raven sat up, eyeing the woods. "Those uglies don't like the red lights, do they."

"No. And right now, they seem like the only things keeping them away."

"Pretty wild we found all these infrared lights, right?" Raven hooked my gaze. There was something unsaid in his eyes. "Almost like it wasn't a coincidence."

A willow of truth tickled my spine; that was my mom's spirit at work. I guess I was holding back a few unsaid things, too.

"Yeah. Thank goodness we did, because with the road cracks so hard to see in the dark, if we try to leave and hit another hole, Bob might die. And if the lights keeping those ugly butts away go out, we'd have to make a run for it, and we might be too slow to out-run them on the road." I coughed hard from talking so fast. Deep breaths were getting harder to find.

"Okay. You're right." Raven petted Akka's black-dusted head. He'd just started to say something else when Bob's infrared lights flickered and died.

All at once, the wild darkness swallowed us whole.

I clenched the steering wheel. "Raven. What's—"

Something moved outside the truck. Branches snapped in the distance, but I couldn't tell from which direction. Raven grabbed my sleeve and I jumped.

"Sorry." Raven met my eyes and let go.

Akka growled close to the glass.

"There's uglies out there, Raven. I can feel their eyes on me."

Raven and I grabbed on to each other and stared into the dark. "What do we do without any—" We didn't even have time to scream as the uglies crashed through the brush and sprang.

"Only one thing to do."

Run.

"Raven, Akka, we gotta go, now!" I grabbed my backpack, twisted the two flashlights from my pock-ets, and turned them on. "We can use the flashlights as cover to get inside the house."

"Yessss. I'm with you." Raven scrambled on his pack, grabbed the box of flashlights from the back, and flipped two lights on. The gray uglies shrieked as I jumped out the door.

Raven raced up the farmhouse driveway. Me and Akka followed close, two uglies hot on our heels. Raven rushed the door and shouted, "It's open, hurry!" When I glanced over my shoulder, I tripped and slammed into the ground.

CHAPTER 14

THE FARMHOUSE

I'D READ ABOUT PEOPLE'S LIVES FLASHING BEFORE their eyes. I'd seen it in movies, too. Honestly, though, the concept never really made sense until I experienced it for myself.

I tripped over the farmhouse walkway on the way to the door. My cheek bounced off jagged cement. Black spots stole my vision, and memories flooded my mind. Walking the woods with Akka. Thrifting with Maple. Laughing over bad jokes with Grams. Woodworking with Pops. Nora and me holding hands under the stars. Me and Raven working together to save earth. I needed to get up. I needed to . . . fight. I needed . . .

I burst awake to Akka licking my cheek and Raven calling my name. "Come on. I've got you." Raven grabbed the red lights and shone them at the uglies heading our way. They opened their jaws wide and hissed, then backed away from the light. Raven scooped me up out of the dust, took Akka's leash, and hurried us to the door.

We stumbled inside the pitch-black farmhouse and slammed the door. Raven locked it, then hunched over coughing on the living room couch.

Still wobbly, I sat at Raven's side. "Are you okay?" Akka got between us, anxious and pawing our legs. Red light from our flashlights filled the room with shadows and a creepy horror movie vibe. The house was late-September-in-New-England cold.

"I will be—" He coughed. "How are you?"

I halfway smiled and grazed my scraped cheek. "Alive, thanks to you."

Bang-bang-bang. Uglies on the roof. Akka snarled and galloped to the hall window. He'd ripped his mask off. Black dust gusted inside.

"Uh-oh." The window was open.

Red eyes flashed by the window outside. Raven staggered to his feet, flashlights in hand. I grabbed mine and shone the red lights at the uglies.

I raced toward Akka. He snapped at one ugly's

arm and missed. The monster screamed, limb smoking inside the red light. I led Akka away from the window as Raven slammed it tight. The gray ugly recoiled to the lawn, then ran into the woods.

Raven heaved himself back onto the flowery couch and adjusted his mask. "Do you think it'll be back?" Old-fashioned wallpaper covered the walls. The downstairs was carpeted. It didn't seem like anyone was home. "There were two uglies before. I distinctly remember—"

Bang-smash.

"Bork!"

A window broke in one of the back rooms. The other ugly was here.

Me and Raven jumped up, him slower and wincing in pain. We flashed our lights at every window we could, but we didn't have enough flashlights. I squeezed my fists tight. "We're gonna need that box in the truck."

"Yikes." Raven swung to the front door. "We have to get it." Glass smashed to the ground in the back of the house. The creature chattered like it was talking. More banging on the roof. "I have a bunch in my pack. Maybe that'll be enough."

"I have more, too."

I dumped my backpack. Shoot. I'd forgotten Pops's

bat in the truck. Raven emptied his on the rug in the near pitch-red dark. "Hey, what's that?" Mom's Discman, alongside her journal. "Is that a Discman?"

I didn't answer. This wasn't chitchat time. This was saving-our-lives time. More glass shattered upstairs. And real far away, Akka yipped and cried. Me and Raven met eyes.

Akka was gone.

I grabbed what red lights I had and sprang toward my boy's cries.

The house was like a maze. I flashed red into every room until I found stairs. I wanted to scream for Akka but didn't want the uglies to know where we were.

"Bork-bork-bork!"

Raven limped after me up the creaky stairs, and there was my boy, growling out the hall window into a pair of wicked red eyes. Tentacles stabbed inside. Goo dripped from the ugly's head as it pushed through the broken-glass window, teeth first. "Akka!"

We pointed our lights at the ugly. It screamed so loud my eyeballs shook. The ugly shuddered away and crashed to the ground.

"Akka." I grabbed my boy and hugged him tight. "You brave and naughty good boy."

Raven looked out the window. Black goop slicked the house's side. "It's gone."

We slunk to the floor with exhaustion. I was having a hard time catching my breath, which was one of my triggers for a panic attack. And like the precious boy he was, Akka shoved his head into my lap and calmed me until my breath returned.

Raven groaned beside me, rubbing his knees. Akka went to him next and decided licking his eyeballs would cure his sore knees.

"Hey. You all right?" I stood and aimed the flashlight out the window, just in case.

"Me? Yup. I'm always okay." Raven pushed back his long hair and threw on a grin that said, *I'm strong and trying, but maybe I'm not all-the-way okay.*

I knew those grins. I handed those out sometimes myself. "Okay."

"Okay."

A black-dust wind gusted through the window, shaking the grayed curtains like ghosts. I moved out of the way. "We should put red lights in every window to keep the uglies away."

"Yes." Raven finger-gunned me like a dork. "On it."

We perched red lights out each window in the house, then found our way to the kitchen. China plates covered the walls. Porcelain birds perched on glass shelves. This was some cute old person's house, but it looked so scary in the red light. "We can keep watch for a while. Make sure it's safe, then try and sleep."

I gave Raven a thumbs-up and set Akka up with food and water. I think I nodded out, because I didn't even notice when Raven placed two cans of SpaghettiOs, a jar of peanut butter, and two cans of Pepsi on the table. "I wasn't sure what you'd like, so I guessed." He handed me a spoon.

"Thanks." Akka curled up on the cat bed under the table—half-on and half-off—and proceeded to snore and kick up his heels. I worried he'd have another seizure. I bounced my legs under the table, hoping his seizures had stopped. "There's a lot of food I'm sensitive to, but somehow you picked foods I like and can actually eat."

Raven nodded with a sweet, shy grin. Then we opened our SpaghettiOs and Pepsi cans. And wow, did they taste good. If it weren't for the red glow, it might almost seem like normal.

"So," Raven said, and covered his full-chewing mouth. The house was so quiet, though, and my ears so sensitive, his chewing was loud enough to hurt. "What do you think is causing that bleach smell outside?"

I'd just loaded my mouth with Pepsi. I swallowed so fast my nose burned. "At first, I thought ozone. Maybe from the lights. I don't know, but it keeps getting worse." It was hard to focus on what Raven was saying because his chewing only got louder. I almost said something. But he'd just saved my life and fed me, so I didn't want to seem rude.

Raven's eyes rolled back with ecstasy as he stuffed his face with food. "Can I ask you something weird?" He wiped his face with a napkin from the holder on the table and chewed, and chewed, and chewed.

I balled my hands into fists and fought the instinct to cover my ears. "Ask me something weird? Sure. Everything is weird light now anyway."

Oh no. I did it again. I said *light now* instead of *right now*. I wanted to become a sea cucumber and drift off to sea. Again, if Raven noticed, he didn't say anything.

"Okay. So, I have a theory." He leaned across the table, chewing sequence complete. "What if the dust is alien spores? Like that Stephen King book where space dust grows inside people until aliens pop out."

"Oh, heck no. It better not be." I read that book, too, and thought of that earlier but didn't want my mind going down that particular Anxiety Road. "The last thing we need is aliens popping out of us." I had another horrible thought. "But what if the dust gives us monster DNA and we end up uglies, too?"

"Uhhh, okay." Raven stood. The wood chair dragged the floor. "I don't like these theories. Let's forget they exist." He yawned. "But what was up with that feedback from Bob's radio earlier?" He picked blood off his neck. "What kind of sound makes ears bleed?"

"I wondered that, too. It definitely seemed like the uglies were hurt by the sound." I filed that information away for later. "As fun as this whole topic is, we should check for a basement and see if there's a safe place to hide for the night."

Raven yawned again and answered in a sleepy voice, "It's on like *Donkey Kong*."

I raised my eyebrows at him.

"Ha. Something my mom always says."

I nodded, echoing his sad smile. "Akka, come on, bud." Akka raised his bleary-eyed head and got up slower than usual. I hugged my boy close. "I'm going to keep you safe, okay?" I got a big old sloppy kiss in return. *Don't worry, Izzy. I will keep you safe, too.*

I carried a candle down the creepy, dungeon-like basement stairs. Without heat, the house was cold. The cluttered basement was finished. Rug. Board games. Woodpile, stove. Tables of junk. Freshly made twin cots with a coffee table between. The cots smelled like grandparents. Grief bit to the marrow of me. The basement smelled like home.

"Hey, what's that?" Raven dropped his pack beside one of the cots and shone his light at a table in the corner. "No way." He turned to me, excited. "It's an old transistor radio. Probably been sitting here for years." He flipped it over and fiddled with the hatch on the back. "Oh! It's still got the battery inside. We might be able to hear other people in the area with these." My heart skipped a beat. "Let's turn it on.".

Raven turned a knob, and the radio crackled to life. "It works!" Static whined through the speaker, but that was it. "Hmm. We should bring it with us. Maybe I can get it to work."

"Sounds good." But it didn't sound good. A dark slither of sorrow snuck up on me and I felt myself losing hope. That familiar worry slithered back into my mind:

We're the last people on earth.

Fighting panic, I dug fresh clothes and period supplies from my pack. Toothbrush, too. Red light glowing before me, I found the basement bathroom and peeled off my disgusting, monster-gut clothes. The bathroom was dingy. The water ran for a second, then stopped. The pumps always stopped when the electricity went out. I didn't bother with my caveman hair; unless I showered, there was nothing to be done. I studied my reflection. Who was this person staring back at me? By the time I left the bathroom, I felt like an alien to myself.

After Raven had his turn to get clean, we aimed a couple of flashlights at the small basement window and covered it with a sheet. Another shone up the stairs. I didn't know why the infrared light bothered the uglies, but I didn't care as long as it worked. I just hoped it was enough.

My mom's journal was still stuffed into my jeans. Pops's bowie knife was still on my belt loop, too. I'd almost forgotten about them. It's like my head gets so busy with worries and details and trying to do so many things at once, my thoughts want to shut down. Akka crawled beside me on the cot. There wasn't much room. But I always made room for my boy. Plus, I might like Raven, but sleeping next to a near stranger still made me really nervous.

"Good night, Izzy Wilder," Raven whispered as his cot springs creaked.

"Good night, Raven Barradell." I pulled the covers around my neck and rubbed the flannel fabric, trying not to think of the uglies and UFLs outside. Of no adults around to protect me. Trying not to worry about Grams, Maple, and Pops. Nora and her family. The animals and trees. Bugs and seas. And the whole wide earth.

"And good night to you, Akka, Fire Mage."

Akka scratched the end of the cot to get comfy and worfed.

"Akka says good night to you, too."

I pressed play on my mom's CD player but got nothing back. I forgot the CD was still in Bob. Sudden tears welled inside me and overflowed. Funny how you could be surrounded by people and dogs and still feel so alone. To help dispel the gloom rising in me, I let my family come and sit, smiling, on a couch inside my mind. Because somewhere out in the dust, they needed me. And I'd die before letting them down.

When I ducked under the covers, I shone my flashlight to the middle of Mom's journal. The first page I turned to about broke my heart.

> My doctor said he visited Paris a few weeks ago. I told him he was lucky. I've always wanted to go and keep telling Izzy and Maple I'll take them one day. But now, after everything, that feels like a lie. I don't know how much longer I'll survive.

I sobbed in silence so Raven wouldn't hear me. Then I curled my legs to my chest, thinking about all she went through. How she'd fought cancer. How she'd been taken repeatedly by UFOs. And even when they didn't take her, she had recurring nightmares about the end of the world. I wanted so badly to jump through the journal and tell her how much she was loved. I wished, more than anything, I could go back in time and hold my mom until she felt loved.

After a minute, I wiped my face on the musty pillowcase and went back to the book. Immediately, the sketch of a symbol caught my eye.

Under the sketch, Mom wrote: "Purple means something. Investigate."

Purple means something? But the symbol wasn't even purple, what did she mean? The date on the page said Feb. 22. Only a few months before she died.

On the next page she'd drawn the purple amethyst necklace. I wondered if the purple she was talking about referred to the amethyst. But what did the amethyst have to do with the symbol? Clues were so confusing. There was no way to know if you were right until you'd solved the mystery.

I flipped through the rest of my mom's journal, all the way to the back, where my mom wrote: "They come for me when I sleep. When I'm with them, I see what they're planning. Things I'm afraid to write down. I need to stop them before they hurt the people I love. And everyone else, too."

As if that weren't scary enough, on the last page, my mom had scribbled my name over every centimeter of space. "IZZY, IZZY, IZZY"—until the bottom, where she'd written: "I'm sorry. Forgive me." My stomach sank. Why would she write that? She hadn't done anything wrong.

I wanted to think about what all the clues my mom had given me meant, but my eyelids kept dropping closed. So, I tucked the blankets up tight at my neck, slipped hope like a charm in my pocket, and fell into a fast sleep.

I dreamed of music, blackbirds, and stars. Of Maple dressed in purple.

Perfectly everyday things.

CHAPTER 15

WEST

I WOKE TO THE SCENT OF ORANGES AND AKKA'S tongue in my ear. In the back of my mind, a single word called out from my fading dream.

West.

I rolled over on the creaky cot in the dark and wiped Akka spit from my face. When I sat up, Akka went for my mouth. "Bleck. Akka, no." I gently nudged him away. For a second, I couldn't remember where I was. But when the cot springs creaked, I remembered real quick.

The farmhouse.

I squinted into the pitch. A cold shower of fear descended.

All the flashlights in the windows were out.

I hooked Akka's collar and listened. I heard nothing and saw no light. Barely awake, I felt for my flashlight under the covers, found it, and turned it on. Raven was gone.

"Raven?" I whispered. Akka sniffed his cot. Where did he go? Then my mind did its favorite trick and dug into my basket of fears. Maybe something had snatched him away. Maybe whatever took him would take us, too.

Akka whined and pawed my thigh like he did when my panic came. I knelt to pet him and realized the basement was warm. The woodstove in the corner crackled and popped with the scent of fired-up oak. I still wasn't sure I was safe until Raven opened the basement door.

"Izzy?" he called softly into the basement. "You awake?"

Sunlight beamed downstairs. "I'm up." I exhaled with relief. I really did like having Raven around. Akka galumphed upstairs to his new friend. "And here comes Akka to lick you now."

"Oof." There was some banging around at the top of the stairs and happy nails scrabbling the kitchen floor as Raven fended off Akka's *hello, hooman* attack of love. "Okay, I surrender my ears! Good morning to you too."

When a smile hit my lips, I trampled it down. This

was no vacation. No time to be taken off guard. We were at war. It was morning. Time to save the world.

"I made breakfast," Raven said. He was framed in the doorway at the top of the stairs. I rubbed my face and squinted up from the bottom of the stairs. Morning light shone all around him. Like the gold light around Mom in my dream. "I figured with the power out, we should probably use whatever food we could before it went bad."

My stomach grumbled. "Right. Thanks. For the fire and food. I guess we do have to eat."

Wait. I suddenly remembered the red lights were out. I raced upstairs. "Are the flashlights out up here, too?" I ran around checking. Every one of the flashlights we left on all night had burned out. "Did you look for uglies?" My amethyst was cucumber cool. All the curtains were open. "Shouldn't we keep the curtains closed just in case?"

Raven glanced up from the eggs frying on the old-fashioned kitchen woodstove and shrugged. "I checked but didn't see any monsters. I actually feel like they don't like sunlight? I could be wrong."

I scanned the windows for uglies, but nothing in the dust stirred.

"Okay. Sorry." I felt bad for snapping. "I just get anxious is all."

Raven gave me a sympathetic nod. "No reason to be sorry. Even if I didn't have anxiety, I wouldn't fully trust you if you weren't freaked out by, you know, actual monsters." He set the table and sat. "Oh yeah. I had a bad dream."

"Oh no." I gulped down OJ. "About what?"

Raven glanced into his hands. "I won't bother you with . . . all that. But. It's weird. I dreamed about going west."

I dropped my glass and it crashed to the floor. "West?" I rushed around cleaning up glass. That was what I dreamed about, too.

"Yeah. Weird, right? And here. Let me help." Raven found a hand broom, got on his knees, and swept. He was so close I could smell his (pine?) deodorant.

"Thanks. For helping. But . . . Raven?"

"Yeah?"

I paused. "I dreamed about going west, too."

All the blood drained from his face. "What?"

"I know. What are the odds we'd dream the same thing?" *Is this a clue, too?* "Do you think it's a sign? Like from the universe or something?" *Or from my mom?* I thought to myself.

Raven swept glass into the trash, a haunted look on his face. "I guess we'll find out."

He looked like he was holding something back. But

instead of questioning him further, I addressed the purple elephant in the room. "So. Where did you find that shirt?"

Raven smiled. "What, this old thing?" He laughed. It was a loose-fitting lilac blouse with ruffles. "I found it upstairs in the closet. I feel bad taking it. But it's nice? Very 1970s chic. But don't worry. I'll bring it back as soon as we . . ." He paused to slip Akka some scraps. "When everything goes back to normal, I swear I'll bring it back."

Silence settled as we ate peanut-butter sandwiches, eggs, and OJ and fed Akka—currently living his best life—an entire thawed ham. And goodness, how he danced for that ham. Raven took extra care not to chew so loud this time, almost like he knew it set my nerves on edge.

When we'd finished, Raven and I cleaned up, gathered our flashlights, any batteries we could find, and the transistor radio from the basement. Then we masked up, grabbed our packs, and stepped into the sun.

No signs of life met us outdoors. No uglies, no people, nothing but black dust and dead-looking trees and a crispy cool wind. We stood beside the truck, guarded against the dusty wind, and stared at the daytime highway. As far as we could see, the pavement was busted. Puckered and cracked as parched earth. I didn't know why, but the uglies were busting up the ground. The black pods along the ditches were empty as deflated balloons. The baby uglies growing inside them, gone.

Akka worked to push off his mask. I gave him Grams's stink-eye and he stopped real quick. I hoisted him into Bob, which the uglies hadn't touched, thank goodness. Then we spray-painted notes on the pavement in front of the farmhouse in case our families came by.

WE'RE HEADING BACK WEST.
GOING TO STAY ON ROUTE 30.
Izzy and Raven

Bellies full, hearts heavy, we got back on the road.

"So, do we have a plan for going after the UFL? Or are we just gonna wing it?" Raven picked his nail polish nervously in the back seat. Akka left my side to sit with him in back.

"I had a plan. But a lot's changed." I turned Bob's red floodlights on. If our theory of gray uglies avoiding sunlight didn't pan out, maybe Bob's red lights would keep them away.

"Well, then we should make a new plan." Raven's

voice got real quiet. "We need a plan so no one gets hurt." He petted Akka until his worry flipped into hope. "We could call it the *Izzy, Raven, and Akka Save the World Plan*."

I swerved around a huge pothole. "Wow. No pressure."

"Nope. None at all. Why would saving the entire human and animal population and the earth alone cause any pressure, amiright? Anyway, on to the details."

Raven still seemed anxious, but his smile was real, and I couldn't help smiling back. "Okay. New Save the World Plan. Step one: Drive Bob west. Step two: Look for help. Step three: Find the UFO." I almost said, *Follow Mom's music and journal for clues*, but changed my mind. I wasn't ready to share all that stuff yet, so I kept those clues to myself. "Step four: Do whatever it takes to keep each other safe. Want to add anything?"

Bob bumped over rubble I couldn't avoid. More sinkholes and cracks, too.

Raven cut a hard look outside. "Yeah. First, we need to take extra-good care of old Bob here. Because . . ." He picked at his nails. "Well, if anything happened to the truck . . . I don't know. If Bob dies, what would happen to us? Would we make it on foot?" Raven continued loving up my dog. "I guess I'm just worried someone's going to get hurt." He shook his head. "Sorry. I just—really like you both."

My heart gave a wild beat. "Yeah. Me and Akka really like you, too."

Dark clouds slid over the sun. Raindrops hit the windshield as we entered Townshend—my hometown. Though now, with everyone gone, Townshend didn't feel like home.

"Hey." Raven coughed and cleared his throat. "Would you mind if we checked the radio again? Maybe whatever disturbance we hit before is gone."

I nodded and fumbled for the knob. "Good idea. Here goes nothing."

I pressed the button. Static and feedback shrieked through the truck. Akka yipped and leapt into the front seat. I winced and changed channels. But the same feedback wailed through every station. I turned the radio off and coughed. "There goes that idea."

"Wait. Do you hear that?" Something whined inside Raven's backpack.

I whipped my head around and swerved. "Yeah. What is it?"

"Hang on." He rummaged in his pack and lifted something out. "It's the transistor radio."

The transistor screamed just like Bob's radio. Akka whined and panted heavily. Pain stabbed into my skull. Raven shut the shrieking thing off as I screeched to a halt.

"Izzy, your nose."

"I know." I wiped the blood away, my head ready to explode. "Yours, too."

He wiped his blood on the filthy rainbow shirt in his pack and stuffed it away. "It's weird. Now the transistor is jammed onto one station."

A tingle of cold swept my neck. "What station?"

"Umm, 95.1."

95.1. The numbers from Mom's journal. That couldn't be a coincidence.

But what did those numbers mean to my mom? Were they referring to the radio station, the UFLs, or something else?

"What do you think the feedback is?" Raven put the transistor away.

I swerved past downed power lines and wished I had a better answer than, "I don't know."

"I know. I don't either. Like . . . why did the power go out? And what's jamming the radio frequencies? What's up with the infrared light—why does it seem to keep the uglies away?" He leaned forward. "I feel like we should research alien abductions. See if we can find clues on how to beat these monsters. Maybe we could even figure out how to *not* get abducted, which would be super great, too." Raven's hands fluttered like excitable birds. "I mean, I did research some stuff before the internet went out. Like what might be wrong with the air and what the dust and those disgusting black pods were before, you know, they ripped open and baby monsters flopped out. But I couldn't find anything that made sense." His hair fell over one eye. He didn't push it away. "Basically, we need more information. About everything."

Akka stirred beside me. I stroked my boy's ear and set eyes back on the road. "I agree. I looked some things up too but got nowhere fast. So much doesn't make sense."

"Right? And you know what else I thought of? Maybe the monsters, black dust, and even the UFLs were created by some weird covert faction of the government. Like, what if somebody made the tentacle turds and dust as weapons to wipe out parts of the world."

I nodded. "I wondered if the lights might be some secret government thing, too." Still, nothing explained why the three of us survived and everyone else was gone. Not even aliens or an evil government faction explained that.

Raven wrapped his jacket around his fancy blouse. "I also just need to mention how nervous I am about purposefully hunting the UFL." He worried his hands in his lap. "I mean . . . what if government agents *are* guarding it or something? What if someone is watching us on satellite and we get in trouble? Or worse, killed."

What he said had weight. What if Raven was right?

Raven squeezed the bridge of his nose. "Sorry. I'm just so scared, you know? But for sure, we definitely need to keep going west." He clapped his hands and startled Akka. "Oh, sorry, buddy. And yeah. No matter what, we need to find the light that dropped out of the sky and take on whatever men in black and/or monster aliens try and stop us. We need to get things back to the way they were. Right?"

Raven looked at me, almost pleading for me to give another option. And the last thing I wanted was to put Akka, Raven, or myself in danger. But we had no choice. We might be the last people on earth. "Right. As my pops says, do what you need to do to survive."

"Your granddad's a smart guy."

I swallowed hard and pictured his kind face. "He is. Now, all we need is more information and answers to our growing list of questions so we can figure out how to get him, and everyone else, back."

As we drove through Jamaica, Vermont, the infrared light under Bob circled us in eerie red shine. The dust was so thick here, everything looked burned. Sinkholes speckled the landscape. Whole homes had sunk into the ground. And now, every few minutes, a low rumble shook the earth. But all I could think about was the symbol from my mom's journal ☿, and the words she'd written right after it: "Purple means something. Investigate." I tapped my fingers on the wheel. A cold creep of a feeling washed over me, like I was missing something. Had I seen that symbol before? My hand gravitated to my mom's amethyst. What was I—

Holy crow. It finally hit me where I'd seen that symbol. I grinned and screamed with joy. "Raven! I know what we need to do."

CHAPTER 16

PAIN

I HIT THE BRAKES BESIDE THE JAMAICA GENERAL store and screamed in Raven's face, "You said we needed more information if we want to beat the uglies and find our people, right?" Akka got up real slow, his mask caked in black. "Well, I know how to get it."

Raven looked at me, scared. "Okaaay. Tell the class your secrets, Isadora Wilder, we're waiting."

Dusty winds wailed over buildings and junked cars. "The library! We go to the library in Manchester. Then we find all the mental ammunition we need to figure out how two kids and a dog can save the world."

Raven smacked his forehead. "I can't believe I forgot the library. Of course, that's where we'd go." He massaged his shoulder and blinked at the view—houses torn apart by uglies. Dead grass and flowers, trees rotten at the root. The look on his face told me he shared my sadness about the earth. "I just hope when we're done, there's a world left to save."

"Me, too." I let Akka out to do his business, and before hitting the road, we ran into D&K's Jamaica Grocery for more snacks and water. We also found earplugs for the feedback in case we needed them. In the back room was a half-eaten bowl of dog food and pictures of a shepherd on the back of a motorcycle, goggles, helmet, earmuffs, and all. I said a few words for the sweet dog and his owner, hoping, wherever they were, they came back safe and sound soon. I spotted the dog's gear on the desk and liberated them for Akka. I wished we had goggles for us, too.

Raven held up a finger like, *Hang on*, and swallowed a mouth of who-knows-what food. "Sorry. I'm just so hungry. Anyway, that dog gear is perfect. Too bad Akka will hate it all."

I nodded. "To the core of his sweet doggie soul." Akka saw them and ran.

Raven twirled his flashlight nervously. "The earplugs will make the ugly turds hard to hear."

"True."

Trying not to stress about that, we snarfed more food and hit the bathroom. When I pushed out of the bathroom, I had a coughing fit and couldn't quite catch my breath. Raven hurried over to me.

"Here." He pulled something out of his pocket. "For your lungs."

An inhaler. Maple had asthma, too. I nodded, tears rimming my eyes. Usually, I wouldn't take anyone else's prescriptions, but I used Maple's once while hiking and it worked. And it worked this time, too.

"Better?" Raven hovered over me, soft eyes and concern.

My heart thundering, I nodded and gave Akka some love. "You have asthma?"

"Yeah. My body isn't the easiest to get along with sometimes." Raven's smile was heavy with history.

"I'm sorry." I tried getting the goggles on Akka, but it was a no-go, so I wrestled his mask on instead.

"Whoa. Check it out." We still had Bob's red lights blaring, but Raven found some red holiday lights, too. "I got us nine boxes of battery-powered lights, just in case." He grinned all proud. "I even got extra batteries."

Not a minute after we got back on the road, Raven shouted in pain.

"What's wrong?" I slowed the truck and peered at Raven through the mirror. His face was puckered and strained. "Are you okay?"

"Sorry. Don't stop. It's just . . ." I slowed around the boulders clogging the road. "I have Lyme disease. Got it a few years ago and it kind of messed me up. And I don't care what some people say, once you have Lyme, it's in you, especially when you're stressed. You know, like when space lights the size of stadiums steal the people of earth and leave a parting gift of monsters that want to eat you alive." He almost laughed, but not me. Pops had Lyme disease, too.

"Does it hurt your joints? They hurt my pops so bad, sometimes he can barely think."

"Pretty bad. My knees are swollen, see?" His knees were big and red. "It's hard to walk sometimes. My shoulders and back get angry, too. But it won't stop me from figuring this out with you." He got real quiet. "I promise I won't slow you down."

"Hey." I pointed my finger at him in the mirror and almost drove us off a cliff. "You *never* have to apologize for your illness. Not to me or anybody, ever. I've got physical stuff, too. Autoimmune mostly. But then the mental stuff. Depression, anxiety, intrusive thoughts, and I'm autistic, too. I get being different." I met his kind eyes and was pretty sure my cheeks were red as lobsters when I looked away. "I think we're gonna do fine."

Raven half grinned into his twisting hands. "That

sounds good, then. Thanks. It's been so hard since my mom, you know, since the lights took her and my dogs. My mom's my best friend, so it's . . . hard."

My hand dug into Akka's fur. "I know. I can't think too much about everyone I lost to the lights because my thoughts explode out of control. Plus . . ." My fingers white-knuckled the wheel. "My mom died last year. She was my best friend, too." I swerved around a dead motorcycle in the road. "I miss her. I miss everyone so much it hurts."

"Oh. Sorry. I didn't mean . . . Uh. We don't have to talk about it, but was that her? Your mom. On the CD before?"

I nodded fast. "Yeah. I found the CD a few days ago with some of my mom's things. I hadn't listened to it till I left home the day me and you met. She died of cancer."

Raven pulled closer to the back of my seat. "I'm so sorry. That's awful."

"Yeah. But sometimes, it almost feels like she's still with me."

There, I said it. I hadn't wanted to, but saying it made it feel more real.

He smiled big and sweet. "Really? I feel the same way about my grandma. I even get little signs she's around me. I made the mistake of telling my dad that and he . . . well, let's just say he wasn't very open-minded about it."

"Oh." I bit my lip. "Sorry."

"Don't be. The last time I saw him, he told me I was worthless after hurting me in public, and I haven't seen him since."

"Oh, Raven. That's horrible. I . . . don't even know what to say."

"It's all good. You don't need to say anything. My mom believes me, though, about my grandma and her signs. And I believe you, too." I smiled and was about to share my mom's journal when Raven spoke before I had a chance. "Would you mind putting on your mom's CD again? I mean, if you want. If you don't, I totally under—"

"No. I don't mind." Maybe she'd even give us more clues. "I love her music, too." I pressed play as we passed a humongous sinkhole in a field to the right. I checked the field in case it was the one from my mom's book, but the mountains behind it were wrong.

Then, to the west, a rainbow appeared as my mom's voice came on. "Song seven of Annie's Alt. Mix, 'True Colors,' by Cyndi Lauper." I knew this song, too. She used to play it when me and Maple were little. My mom continued, "This song reminds me of a rainbow arched over an ugly gray sky." We both gasped. Like Raven's rainbow T-shirt and the rainbow in the sky now. "Look for the rainbows, okay? When you see one, know I'm with you."

My hands shook. I tried not to crash as the singer sang about being brave, not hiding your truth, and letting the beautiful rainbow that is you shine. When the song ended, I shut the music off and just breathed. Akka sniffed the speakers, then rested his lovely head on me.

"Hey, Izzy?"

I sniffed. "Yeah?"

A pause. "Your mom. She's special, isn't she. Like *she knows something about all this* special." It wasn't a question, but a knowing from Raven's deep-down soul.

Finally, everything I'd been holding back flew out of my mouth. "Yeah. I didn't say anything because I was afraid you'd think I was making it up or something. But since the lights came, it's like the invisible layer separating the dead from the living disappeared with everyone else, and she's always around giving me cryptic messages. Sometimes, I even smell her perfume. I know it sounds weird. But then there's the music on this CD. Some of the lyrics have been guiding us where we need to go, even when I didn't want to listen. And her talking straight onto the disc? It feels like she's talking to me right now. Like she's telling me something." A whole minute went by without Raven saying anything. I suddenly wished I could get out and walk. So I could get the million watts of energy coursing through me out.

"I think you're amazing, and that's amazing, and I am glad you told me that." I exhaled hard. "I mean, the rainbow thing has to mean something. And the songs from earlier. 'Never Let Me Down Again'? When it talked about the stars shining bright right as we saw those stars, or UFOs or whatever, that's when I started writing lyrics down."

"You've been writing my mom's playlist lyrics down?"

We'd just entered downtown Manchester. It must've been late afternoon. The buildings were all dark and empty. No signs of life other than us.

"Yeah. Look." He held the notebook up while I drove. "'Never Surrender,' by Corey Hart. A few minutes before it came on, I was doubting every unbelievable thing happening. Really getting in my head, you know? Wondering if I'd ever see my mom again when your mom said, 'Find the light, Izzy.' I mean, obviously she was talking to you. But when she said, 'Don't give up,' I don't know. It almost felt like . . .

maybe she was talking to me, too."

An arc of sunlight shone through my window. "Yeah." I smiled. "That seems like something she'd do."

"Nice. Oh, and before that, the lyrics to 'Never Let Me Down Again' by Depeche Mode—when they were singing about the stars shining bright. And your mom said something like 'They fly high and watch you' or something. Then seconds later, a fleet of UFOs flew over us and I was like"—he made the sign of his mind being blown—"these songs are signs. And if we wanted to fix things, we needed to pay attention to the songs and your mom's words."

"That's how I feel!"

The library came up on the left. And when I turned into the lot, my mind blew all over again. That symbol from my mom's journal was painted above the library's front doors. I couldn't help wondering if maybe my mom had been researching here, too.

I parked Bob. "Before we go in, look," Raven said, and passed me his notebook. Akka scrabbled on his seat and fogged up the glass as I opened it up. The page was framed with blackbirds, and the lyrics to "Blackbird" were scribbled inside. I gasped. "The reason I turned toward the Humane Society wasn't coincidence. I kept hearing that song and followed it right to you and Akka and poor, crashed Bob." He smiled softly. "Then, when you opened your eyes, 'Blackbird' stopped."

Chills. "I wondered if you'd heard the music, too." I wondered where the music was coming from. Maybe it was my mom leading us together. Maybe she didn't want us to be alone.

I handed Raven back his notebook and noticed the cracked eggs doodles on the cover. I meant to ask him about what they were, when uglies cried, not far away.

I grabbed Pops's bat from my pack and gave Raven my knife.

Armed with flashlights and weapons, we left Bob behind. And as I smashed the library window in with Pops's bat, the lyrics to "Never Surrender" circled my mind. I realized then. My mom's *map in the music* had been guiding me all along.

CHAPTER 17
THE LIBRARY

THE LIBRARY WAS DARK AND QUIET. DUST BLEW through the broken window and into our lungs. But under the toxic layer of bleach, I could still smell the books. Their scent reminded me of afternoons ticking away between pages. Of falling between pretty covers, getting happily lost inside someone else's dream. But there was no need for fiction now. I'd already fallen between the pages of my own alien world.

"So." Raven dropped his backpack on the long table, slick with new dust. "Where do we start?"

I twirled a spiral of hair and paced. "If we're going to find our people, we need to know what or who we're up against so we can outsmart them. Look for books on aliens and abductions, like you said. Invisible force fields, too. Like what might've made the light that crashed disappear. Figure out what's going on with the black dust. And what's making the radios go wild. Oh, we could research Area Fifty-One. Because what if the UFLs *are* government crafts or something. For all we know, we're in some kind of apocalyptic war." I didn't say anything else, but I was also anxious to research psychic phenomena and supernatural contact with spirits to understand what was happening to me.

Raven pulled out his journal and started writing things down. "Oh. And how about electrical surges and electromagnetic energy. And some out-there history books to see if anything like this has happened before. Because in this crazy world, you never know."

I nodded. "That's one hundred percent of the truth."

Raven disappeared down the nonfiction aisle. "I'll start with radio frequencies and the power of light. Let me know if you find anything."

"Sounds good." I pulled my mom's Discman out and slipped the headphones on. I'd grabbed the CD from Bob before leaving the truck. "I'll check out aliens and government stuff. See if there's any books on abductions, too."

"Good luck," Raven said from a distance away, leaving me and Akka alone.

I climbed the staircase, Akka at my heels. I stopped once to catch my breath, and a memory winnowed me back in time. Me and Maple, in this very library, years ago.

"Izzy?" six-year-old Maple asked, all giant eyes and cheeks.

"What?" I answered, chewing the life out of my shirt collar, nose in a book.

"Do you like me?" Maple asked.

I remembered staring at her like the question didn't make sense. "Yeah, I like you. You're my sister."

She twisted her lips, unsatisfied. "Okay. You promise to always like me, Izzy?"

Maple looked about to cry. And when she told me her best friend at school didn't want to be her friend anymore, I took her pudge-hand in mine and told her, "I promise to like you and love you to the moon and back, always and forever."

As I stepped onto the top floor, I ran my fingers along the spines of the books, in the aisle where me and little Maple sat years ago. I put my face in my hands and sank to the floor, crying. Wondering if Maple could hear my heart calling to hers. "I love you, Maple. Always and forever. And I promise to bring you home."

When I stood, right in front of me was the section

on extraterrestrials, alien abductions, and UFOs. Like we were led to this very spot. The faint scent of oranges wound my neck like a scarf. My hair raised, and somehow, my headache vanished at once.

"Mom?" Out of nowhere, the red flashlights in my pockets turned on. Akka peeked around the corner and ran to me, excited, then sat beside me, staring at the air at my side. "Akka. She's here, isn't she?" Akka glanced up at me. "Can you see her?"

Chills slipped over me as the Discman turned on by itself. "Song eight of Annie's Alt. Mix, 'I Think We're Alone Now,' sung by Tiffany." Chills, even stronger than before. I broke into the shiniest grin. There she was. Talking to me. "There's no one else around. And in this quiet we are found."

The bouncy music started. When it did, I glimpsed the book Akka was sniffing on the bottom shelf. A red book called, *In This Quiet*.

I gasped into my hands and opened the book as the song played on in the background (*I think we're alone now . . .*). I flipped through the book, confused. It must not have been in the right section because it was a book on depression. "Mom? If you led me here, why are you showing me this?" Akka's eyes didn't move from the space beside me. I held up the book. "Is this how you felt when you got cancer?"

I listened for an answer but heard only the beat of my heart. Before finding her journal, I never knew she had depression like I did—nobody ever mentioned it. In my memory, she was always smiling. Always my funny, beautiful mom. But I guess I knew better, didn't I. Sometimes even at my saddest, I was smiling.

The journal fell out of my jeans when I crouched on the thin blue carpet. It opened to the page that said, "I'm sorry. Forgive me." Beside it was the sketch of a gold ball and geometric symbol labeled, They were guarding this. This meant something, but what?

I flipped through the library book on depression, searching for the geometric symbol and gold ball, and found nothing. I didn't know what she was trying to say.

I pocketed the book on depression and grabbed as many as I could carry on UFOs. Coming around the aisle, I tripped over Akka and slammed into a push-cart full of books and almost dropped the books on his head. "Sorry, Akka. I didn't mean to—"

Wait. The cart was packed with books on cancer. And dying. Science fiction and mental health. Even one on paranormal activity.

I staggered back. How could this be real? Even in a book or movie this wouldn't fly. Like if I wrote this in English class, Ms. Avery would write in her big red pen, "Too heavy-handed. Rewrite."

Suddenly, the CD skipped to the middle of the Tiffany song. (*I think we're alone now | I think we're alone now | I think we're alone now*—) Akka put paws up on me like he was saying, *She's here, Izzy. She's here.*

"You okay up there?" Raven called upstairs, and I jumped. Then, the music stopped. "I heard a crash."

Everything got real quiet. I slid my headphones down, shaking to the bone. "I'm fine!" I shouted, aware of how loud my voice was. "I just tripped. I'll be down in a sec."

"Okay." Raven sounded like he didn't believe me. But I couldn't worry about that now.

I pulled a few books off the cart and sat on the rug with Akka. The first book, *Seeing Through Dreams*, said some people gained special abilities after trauma. A car crash, a near-death experience, psychological events so scary they altered the brain.

Was that what was happening to me? How I was sensing my mom's spirit? Was it from the lights shining on me? Or the trauma of losing my family? I wanted more concrete clues, not just drawings and lyrics and poems. I needed to find something solid to tell us exactly where we needed to go. Something to show us our families were still alive and how to bring them back. I wanted to talk to her in person. I hated that she was gone. That she hid so much from me. I wish my mom had trusted me to help with her cancer and all the UFO stuff before she died. That she'd confided in me like a friend. I thought we were close as two sheets of paper stuck together, but maybe I didn't know her as well as I thought. Still, maybe if I kept following her beyond-the-grave clues now, I could find our family and solve the mystery she couldn't while she was alive.

Thinking about that gave me hope.

The next book was *Angels: A History*. I read that from every walk of life, angels have come to humans with messages of hope and fear and the apocalypse. That some humans could pass on and become angels. Akka curled up on the rug beside me. He snored away in his mask, and I thought, *Maybe Akka is an angel, too.*

I searched for books about ghosts and contacting lost loved ones from the other side but found only more mental health books—and one other: *Unexplained Phenomena in Vermont*.

The cover showed a photo of a UFO over the Green Mountains at night. I turned page after page, reading how strange things occurred in the Vermont mountains. Vortexes. Caves that sucked people in until they were gone. Creatures from bigfoot to pig-men, winter zombies, and the windigo of indigenous legends. How Vermont had the most reported UFO sightings and abductions out of anywhere in the USA. But that's not what blew my mind. According to this book, there was a place called the Bennington Triangle not far from here, where a bunch of people vanished without a trace. "Holy crow, Akka. This might be it."

Some said it was UFOs who took them. That mag-netic energy, not just in the triangle but in all of Vermont, had been drawing extraterrestrials for cen-turies.

Wait.

I flipped back to the book's cover. My heart jumped. The cover showed the same mountain range we were chasing. The one my mom sketched in her journal. The one by the field where she was abducted by a UFO. "Holy crow, holy crow, holy crow."

I put the sketch my mom did of the field and the mountains in the distance, and the photo from this library book cover, side by side and almost cried. They were identical. On the inside of the book, the photo credit claimed it was taken of Mount Equinox.

Mount Equinox in Manchester. The town we were in now.

I had to know more. I flipped to the section on Mount Equinox. It had more photos of the road leading to the mountain. The road was called Three Twelve Road. My mom had written 312 over and over in her journal. I almost died right there, my heart was beating so fast.

"Akka." I grabbed his sweet face. "Maybe the missing UFO crashed on Mount Equinox." Akka groaned and flopped back down, unimpressed with my findings. "I gotta tell Nora about this." Akka was already up when I realized my mistake. "Not Nora. Raven. Because Nora's gone."

The words sounded so final, I regretted saying them the second they flew. But you couldn't catch words once they'd been said. All I could hope was they weren't true.

Slipping my mom's journal back down my pants, I noticed Akka's muzzle coated in drool. Black foamy bubbles leaking to the ground. I opened his mouth. His gums were bleeding. "Dust." I tightened my mask and put Akka's back on, sick with worry. "Sorry, bud. I'm gonna figure this out. I promise."

"Izzy?" Raven called from the bottom of the staircase. "Come see what I found. It's important."

"Okay. One more second." I just needed to check

one more thing. I needed to find the symbol on the gold orb my mom drew in her book.

I had searched every book about symbols I could find—hieroglyphs, planetary and astrological symbols, Greek and other ancient markings—but hadn't found any like this.

"Hey." Raven snuck up behind me. I jumped about nineteen feet in the air. "Oh, sorry. I didn't mean to—"

"No. It's fine. I'm always really jumpy." Akka rushed around the corner to his new friend. Raven had a bowl of water for Akka and a stack of books. "So, did you find anything?" I took Akka's mask down and he slurped that water down fast.

"Did I ever. Come. Let's grab a table." I slipped Akka's mask back on and followed.

Rain pinged the windows. Shadows grew long and dark inside the library and out. I suddenly got a real bad feeling like we'd been here too long. I passed the last aisle before the table and caught a misty figure with long wavy hair out of the corner of my eye. When orange perfume circled me, Akka barked. The apparition looked right at me and said, "Open, open . . ." The books I'd been carrying fell from my arms.

It was her.

CHAPTER 18

SIGNALS

MY MOM RAISED ME TO SEE LIBRARIES LIKE OLD friends. A quiet place to be yourself. To know you aren't alone. So, when I saw the white mist in my peripheries, when I heard her speak, I knew the ghost-spirit was my mom. That even when I couldn't see her, she was with me. And I was never truly alone.

"Izzy?" Raven dropped his stack of books with a smack on the table and came after me. "What happened?"

The word she'd said to me wedged in my head and wouldn't let go. *Open* just kept rerepeating on a loop. My mom had given me a message, but I wasn't sure what it meant. Open—open what? Akka scratched the ground my mom just drifted past. Raven stared at me, waiting for an answer, but I was deer-in-the-headlights stunned. My processing disorder sometimes made it hard to answer questions, especially when I was taken by surprise—and seeing my mom's ghost definitely took me by surprise.

"Um. Sorry." I shook off the sighting of my mom and focused on the books I'd dropped. They were scattered everywhere. Raven helped me pick them up. "I thought I saw someone," I finally answered. "Over there. But—"

Raven shuffled off to duck down aisles but came right back. "I couldn't find anyone." He crouched over to catch his breath. Dust blew hard through the broken window downstairs. The stink had gotten worse; it was like breathing fumes. "Should we check the rest of the library?"

Me, Raven, and Akka weren't looking so good.

"No, it's all right." I smiled. "I might've imagined it." My chest clenched inside that lie. I knew without a doubt I'd seen and heard my mom.

"Okay then." Raven tightened his mask. I adjusted Akka's, too, before he wandered toward the next aisle. "Let's compare notes and *check out* these books." His eyebrows flipped up. "Get it? *Check out* the books. Because this is a library?"

I paused, so amazed at his dad joke, I laughed till I

coughed. "Wow. I didn't know you were such a *fungi*."
I pointed to the book on top of his stack—*Fungi from Around the World*.

Raven cringed. "I guess I had that coming."

Akka returned—maskless—with a book in his mouth. "Akka! What? Where's your mask?" Akka ambled over real slow, dropped the book, and woofed. Raven and I read the title together: *Cosmic Dust, and the Clouding of Earth*.

We looked at each other like, *Whoa*. "Nice find, Akka." I ruffled his head, then opened his book. "Okay. It says cosmic dust, space dust, and/or extra-terrestrial dust falls to earth every day from stars, meteors, and comets. This dust can grow new stars, create new planets, and even . . ."

"What?"

"Help a dying star or planet die quicker."

"That's . . . not good."

"No." I twisted my hair and bounced my leg. "What if the black dust is here to eat earth? It's already changing the air, killing plant life, and—" I glanced at Raven's red eyes and coughed. "What if it's trying to kill us, too?"

My mouth tasted like blood.

Raven exhaled extra slow. "If that's what's happening, we need to find as many people as we can, build a bunker, and, I don't know . . . filter the air or something. Gather an army and take back our earth from these stupid, deadly aliens."

"Agree. And speaking of finding people . . . I forgot to show you this." I passed Raven *Unexplained Phenomena in Vermont* and opened it to the section on the Bennington Triangle. "Did you know Vermont has been plagued by monsters and vortexes, off-the-charts magnetism, UFOs and alien abductions, and other unbelievable things for centuries?"

Raven rubbed his eyes. "No, I did not."

"Me either. But I think we have to go to there." I tapped the cover photo. "What if the strange phenomenon circling the Bennington Triangle caused the UFL that almost certainly abducted our families to malfunction and crash. What if the top of Mount Equinox is where the craft landed?" I forced my jittery legs still. "Raven. What if the UFO is up there and our families are still inside?"

Raven stared into his twisting hands like he was thinking the right words to say. "Izzy. I hate to say it, but if our families were inside when the UFL crashed? I mean . . . what if we get there and we don't like what we find inside." He wiped his eyes and turned away. "What if we find something in the ship that hurts more than keeping the hope of finding them alive?"

I nodded, eyes on the ground. "That crossed my mind, too. But sometimes, and I'm gonna sound like an old lady here, you have to do what you have to do, even if it's scary."

Raven glanced back at me with a glint in his eye. "You do sound like an old lady."

I smile-glared at him and thought of Nora. "Okay, okay. But listen. True story. Last year I told my best friend I had a crush on her."

Raven blasted out of his funk fast. "You did not."

"Yeah, I did. That was *rough*. But I had to do it. If I hadn't admitted my feelings for her, I'd have wondered if she felt the same way every day until uncertainty broke me apart." I picked my nails. "I owed it to our friendship to know the truth, no matter how hard it was hearing her tell me she didn't want a 'love thing' to get in the way of our 'best friend thing.'"

Raven sighed and twirled a bracelet I hadn't noticed before. "I hear you. And sorry." He glanced at me, freckles peeking over his daisy mask. "Crushes are the worst." When Raven shifted in his seat, I noticed something hanging off his belt.

"Uh, Raven? What's that thing?"

"This? Yeaaah. That would be my dad's Taser I forgot to mention." Raven's tone went cold. "He's a cop. I liberated it from his private stash a while back thinking I might need it."

"Wait. You had a police-issue Taser on you this whole time? When those uglies were hunting us?" I perched my hands on my hips like I'd seen Grams do a million times. "And you didn't mention it?"

He cringed. "Sorry. I don't like this thing. Or my dad, for that matter. And the Taser only has one use." A shadow dragged over him. "My dad used to threaten me with it."

I startled like I'd been pushed, and every bit of me fired up mad. "Did he . . . hurt you?"

Raven focused on Akka, who'd come to sit at his side. "Sometimes. But not with this." He stroked Akka's ears. When Raven glanced at me, I saw a vulnerability I felt in my core. "Yeah, he's a bad guy. He never really liked me, you know?" He gestured to his stolen blouse. "The way I dress. My nail polishes. That someone's gender doesn't stop me from like-liking them." Raven gave a sad laugh. "I never understood it, though." He hid behind his hair. "All I ever did was try to please him."

I squeezed Raven's hand. "I don't talk about this much, but me and my sister have different dads. Neither of them wanted anything to do with us. So, I might not understand your exact situation, but I know the hurt of thinking you aren't enough for someone. My mom used to tell me and Maple that some people's bodies grow, but their minds stay small all their lives. And she was right. You can't let garbage people define you because they don't even know you." I glanced up at him and smiled. "I'm sorry your dad can't see you for the wonderful person you are. But Raven?"

He blinked fast at the ground. "Yeah?"

"I see you."

Raven grinned, tears in his eyes, and nodded. After a few seconds, he looked at me and said, "I see you, too."

I blushed hot as a volcano and let go of his hand. One of Raven's books caught my eye. "Hey, what book is that?"

"Oh." Raven opened it. "This one is on ley lines. Do you know about ley lines?"

"Yes, actually. They're like an energy grid that runs through the earth. My mom taught me about them before she died, which is interesting now that I think about it." I curled my legs up on the chair. "Maybe she told me about them because of all the stuff we're going through." Raven shifted in his seat until our arms touched. Normally, I'd have moved over. But not this time.

"From what I know about your mom, that tracks.

Oh whoa. Look. This section's about southern Vermont. Ley lines cross under the Green Mountains? I had no idea." Raven glanced at me. "What if the cosmic dust, gray uglies, or UFOs supercharged the ley lines somehow?"

I coughed. "Maybe that's why the electricity went out and the radios are going bananas."

"Exactly. And then there's this." A book on Area 51. Raven tapped a photo of a fedora man in 1952 who worked for the real men in black. "This guy admits the U.S. government made a deal with the grays—the aliens with big heads—to let them experiment on us if they stopped trying to take our earth. Others from Area Fifty-One say they learned how to make UFOs fly."

"No way."

"Mm-hmm. I admit this is all *Star Wars* fan fic, but, ha"—he ran his hands through his mussed-up hair till it stood—"I'm starting to come around to *Star Wars* not being *full* fiction. There are too many stories here for it not to be true. But none of this is going to help us find a possibly invisible UFO or know how to save everyone if we do find—"

The ground shuddered like an earthquake. A purple book fell face-up onto the floor.

"What was that?" Raven glanced over his shoulder.

"Uglies destroying our earth, probably." Akka raised his head under the table. "It's okay, bud. You're safe." Akka flopped back down to sleep. When I picked up the fallen book and set it on the table, Raven looked like he'd seen a ghost. "What's wrong?"

Then I saw the book's title: *Into the Darklights*. I shivered.

Darklights.

"Izzy? Why do you look scared?" Raven clutched the collar of his frilly blouse.

I'd been thinking about the purple lights from Mom's UFOs she called Darklights. And about seeing her ghost. But that didn't explain why he was rattled, too. "I could ask you the same thing."

Raven scooched over. "Sorry." He waved his arm at the books. "This is all just a lot."

"Yeah. But we got this, okay? We can't let ourselves lose hope."

"Right. Of course you're right." Raven smiled. "Now, let's see what *Into the Darklights* has to say."

The book was about those who've seen UFOs beam their loved ones away. Some abductees claim to remember their time inside UFOs. Some watched spaceships disappear at close range, like the ships had invisibility shields.

Raven smacked his palms on the table. "Yes. Like the light that disappeared."

"Yeah. And this couple, Hugh and Linda Carlson, said when UFOs stopped over their farm, every light exploded, and their animals busted through fences, running for their lives. Oh, and this Mark Ness person saw a UFO on his way home, stopped the car, and when the UFO shone its lights, he froze and couldn't move. The lights messed with his radio, too, and . . ."

Raven passed glances between me and the book. "What?"

I touched my mom's amethyst. "Mark Ness said the lights made his amethyst ring heat so hot, it burned his skin and didn't cool until the UFO had gone." I turned to Raven. "I never told you this, but look." I showed him the spot the amethyst fried my skin.

Raven cringed. "Ouch."

"Yeah. When the uglies and UFLs are close by, my crystal heats up, too."

"Whoa, whoa, whoa. Wait. Amethyst. Heat. Izzy! I read a book for school last year, *The Hidden Properties of Crystals*, that said something like amethysts can absorb and reflect energy from anything putting out heat. That they act like superconductors—and can even emit forms of infrared light." Raven blinked.

"Infrared light. Like the flashlights and lights under Bob that keep the uglies away. Oh my God. Amethysts get overloaded with alien energy and overheat."

"And infrared light interferes with whatever energy these aliens emit."

Raven watched me pace. "My mom says our bodies are big meaty batteries that make actual energy. It's why when you run your socks across the carpet you make static electricity."

I pointed at him. "My pops says that, too. It's like the reason I can't wear a watch. No matter what, they always die on me."

"Really? Same. Watches, and also when I walk under streetlights, they just . . . go out."

"That happens to me, too." I slowed my pace and wrung my hands. "Maybe that's why we're still here. What if our big, wild energy mixed with the ley line energy, or cosmic dust energy, or UFO energy, and protected us from being taken by the lights. That might even explain why Akka wasn't taken. I was holding onto him when the lights came . . . I know it sounds silly—"

"No. It sounds amazingly accurate and absolutely possible. Especially since Louis and Harry weren't anywhere near me when the lights came . . ." Raven adjusted his mask with sad eyes. "But we can't be the only ones with bizzarro energy. There have to be more people like us, which means—"

I grinned. "We aren't the only survivors." Then, like an avalanche, all this new information started adding up. "Holy crow, Raven. Maybe energy is the key to everything. If the power of Mount Equinox is big enough to lure aliens to earth and crash a UFO, maybe we can find a way to channel that energy onto the aliens and off of us and make them leave."

Raven pumped his fists in the air like, *Yes!* "And bring our people home."

Energized with possibilities, I darted back into the aisles. "If we're going to climb a possessed mountain full of aliens, vortexes, and monsters, then we are going to need a map."

"Cool. You find a map." Raven started upstairs. "I have one more thing to do."

Akka followed me to the back of the library. As we snaked aisles searching for maps, the vision of my mom and her saying *Open* looped back into my thoughts. Then a song my mom used to love popped into my mind. "Open Your Heart," by Madonna.

I stopped in my tracks.

Open your heart . . .

Open. Was the Madonna song a clue? Did the lyrics have to do with finding our families—to finding everyone?

I went over the lyrics as I looked for maps, but all I could remember was the line about locks and keys, the tune, and the title. I was humming the song to Akka when I found a map of the area. The second I opened the book, the song in my head shut off, and Raven returned.

"Check this out." Raven coughed, paused to catch his breath, then handed me a small book. "Radio frequencies. Talking about the jammed radio signal made me wonder what was causing the evil feedback on 95.1." Raven pointed at the page. "It says radio waves have the longest wavelengths in the spectrum of sound waves. Some are as long as a farmer's field, some are longer than earth. So the sound on 95.1 could be coming from space, ooor from close by."

Raven smiled big and put something in my hand. I choked on my spit when I saw what it was. "Raven."

"This was inside the radio signal book."

"No way." It was a flyer for hikers advertising Mount Equinox. It had a trail map and— "Wait." I'd forgotten what sat at the top of the 3,855-foot mountain. "The radio towers!" I shouted louder than I'd intended. "I forgot about the radio towers at the peak."

"Uh-huh. And one is WVTQ, on guess what station."

"95.1, holy . . . crow."

"Holy crow is right." Akka walked over, tags jangling, and dropped a ball at Raven's feet, which Raven promptly rolled across the floor.

"Okay." I twisted my hands. "What if the UFO is jamming the radio signals? Or sending a signal of its own?"

"Yes." Raven rubbed his shoulder like it hurt. "We are definitely on to something."

I took Akka's ball, let him kiss my nose—his favorite—and rolled his toy. "Raven?"

Raven piled the books neatly and grabbed his pack. "Yeah?"

"We need to go up Mount Equinox. We need to see what's up there for ourselves."

That same fear I saw earlier shadowed Raven's face. But this time, it didn't stay. "After what we've read, and everything with your mom . . . yeah. If there's even a small chance my mom, Louis, and Harry are in that UFO, or if it can lead us to them somehow, then I'm all in. No more fear. We do what we have to do."

I smiled, happy. Akka dropped his drooly ball and woofed. "Good. I'm glad. Because it's hard finding a friend at the end of the world."

Raven blushed down at his boots. "Yeah. It sure is." He shouldered his backpack and furrowed his brow. "Weird the flyer was in the book, though. Like someone left it for me."

A cold chill crept over me. "Um, where did you find that book anyway?"

"The first aisle upstairs. Why?"

I swayed, light-headed. The same spot I thought I saw my mom's ghost.

Open, open, open . . .

Open your heart.

"Hey, you okay?" Raven almost touched my arm to steady me, then pulled back.

I took a slow breath—then smelled a hint of orange. *Mom.* "Uh, yeah. I'll be fine."

The wind intensified. Dust smacked glass and whistled through the broken window. The light inside had turned mauve. Night was coming.

It was time to go.

CHAPTER 19

DON'T MAKE A SOUND

OUTSIDE, THE WIND HOWLED, AND DUST BIT LIKE A sandstorm. Even wearing masks, we choked our way to Bob, parked just out the library door. I didn't know if the black dust was spores seeding the world with who knew what. Or something to choke out any survivors left behind. But there was more of it now. So much, the air was thick. And if it didn't stop coming, it really would kill the earth and us with it.

"Where'd all this new dust come from?" Grit needled my skin as I fought the winds to the driver's-side door. Lightning cracked a tall oak nearby and started a fire, but the dust put it out. Bob's lights flashed. Our radios whirred. The earth hummed with energy. Almost like it was moving beneath our feet.

Raven held an arm over his eyes. "I don't know!"

Akka barked at the wind, disoriented by the storm. "Akka, to me!" I cracked Bob's door. The wind hooked into it and threw it open, nearly tearing it off. "Load up, good boy." Mask over his muzzle, goggles on, he choked and slipped when he jumped. "Akka!" I caught him and hoisted him onto the seat.

Raven came up behind me, coughing so hard, he doubled over in pain. "Is he okay?"

"I think so." I coughed into my mask and pushed Akka's butt across the seat. Raven and I hopped in and slammed the doors. I fumbled in my pocket for keys while scanning for red eyes in the storm.

"This is bad." Raven wiped his eyes. Black dust smeared his eyelids like kohl. "This dust will make it hard to see uglies." He took a napkin from Bob's dash and wiped his mouth under his mask. Sure enough, it was streaked with blood. I felt under my mask. My fingers came away bloody, too.

A few barely legible words from my mom's journal echoed in my head.

There will be blood.

When they come, don't make a sound.

"It's gonna be hard to drive in this dust, too." I turned the keys. Even with the headlights, I could barely see the road.

"Izzy, don't forget the red lights." A cold dagger of fear clipped Raven's words. A second later, my amethyst heated up fast.

"Oh no." Akka pushed up on his seat and growled. When I flipped on the red lights, shrieks erupted from all sides. "The uglies are back."

"Yup—go, go, go!"

"Holy crow, holy crow, holy crow." I thrust Bob into reverse. Two limbs stabbed through the black cloud ahead. I stomped on the gas going backward. I hit something, then rolled over whatever it was.

A still shape lay in the road in front of Bob. Raven peered out the windshield. "What was that?"

Red lights pooled around us like a blood mist. Whatever I hit was in the center of the road, but in the dust, I couldn't make it out. "I don't know. What if I hit someone?"

"No way. We haven't seen anyone this whole time."

Akka snapped at the windshield, spit flying. There had been two uglies ahead of us, but now there were none.

Then I saw it. Small tentacles loomed out of the red-lit dust. "Oh no. It's a baby ugly." It was injured. Maybe dead. Steam rose from the body. It was already coated in a layer of dust. A whoosh of guilt whipped up in me. Even though they were taking over our world, I felt bad for hurting it.

Raven leaned close to my seat and said real soft, "Come on. We should go. Before its parents come back."

Akka hadn't stopped borking, but we couldn't see the other uglies. So, I put the pedal to the metal, drove around the small ugly, and got back on the road.

The closer we got to Mount Equinox, the more the ground trembled like a minor earthquake that never stopped.

"You see anything?" I pushed forward, darting around debris and potholes, avoiding the cracked streets of residential Manchester.

When we bumped around a huge crack, guttural cries wailed under the earth.

Raven and I shared a glance. Raven pointed at the buckled road ahead. "The cracks and holes. Maybe the uglies are underground."

A low hum rose through the storm. The same *vv-vvvv-VVVVV* hum we'd heard before.

"Izzy, look." Huge dark shadows lowered over the mountains ahead. I kept driving as waves of fresh black dust released from the sky. "The lights are back. Maybe we should shut our lights off, so they don't see us."

"Right." I shut Bob's lights off and drove under a large tree, onto someone's lawn. Total darkness blanketed Vermont. The deep hum kept getting louder. So loud, it drilled into my skull.

The dark oval shadows sailed above us, just over the clouds. Moonlight glinted off their metallic surfaces and windows, blocking out huge chunks of night sky. Seeing them this close, I knew there was no denying they were UFOs.

Akka borked. I huddled him close and told him to hush.

"They're coming," Raven shouted in a panic. "They're coming for us."

"It's okay. Stay quiet. Trust me." I remembered what my mom said: when they come, stay quiet. But Raven wouldn't hush.

"We have to go!" Raven shouted louder. He held his Taser before him, ready to shock anything that moved. Akka scrambled and cried, a wild look in his eye.

I grabbed the dog helmet and earmuffs we found in the Jamaica general store and shoved them onto my boy. I wished I'd remembered them sooner to help block the rising sound. The closer the ships came, the stronger their sonar signal vibrated through the atmosphere—like they were listening for something below.

Like they were listening for us.

I pulled Akka close, jammed earplugs in my ears, and passed some to Raven as the vibration from the UFOs screamed.

Five ships stopped directly overhead, above the dust and low clouds.

"Izzy." Raven's eyes were so red. "We should go." His nose bled. Mine and Akka's, too. Bob rattled and shook. "If we don't go, they'll see us." I wished I could tell him what my mom's journal said, but there was no time to explain now. The ships were right above us. "Izzy. The noise. My head!"

The ships lowered. The humming intensified. I had to help Raven calm down.

My notebook. I scrambled for a pen and paper as quietly as I could. Akka blinked at the ships, stunned into silence and awe. Raven was about to say something when I put my finger to my lips and wrote on the notepad I brought from home: "Stay quiet and I know they'll go."

Bob shook harder. My insides felt torn apart. Raven put his palms over his ears, gaze bouncing between the ships and the note, and nodded.

VVVVVVVVVVVVVVVVVVVVVVVVV—

The three of us huddled together inside Bob as five ginormous spacecrafts rolled past. When they were gone, whatever was shaking the ground stilled. The winds died. The dust fell. And the world felt flat as the dust-covered road.

We sat in the truck to catch our breath. We wiped blood from our fur and skin. My ears rang something awful. Like an endless chime. I flipped Bob's lights back on. Then, we drove. Because night was coming, and when the night came, the uglies came with it.

"What do you think they want?" Raven asked. "The spaceships. Do you think they know we're here?"

Akka trembled beside me. I stroked his cheek until he found calm, then glanced at myself in the mirror and saw fear staring back. But surprisingly, I also saw hope. "Maybe they're looking for us. Or maybe they're trying to find the same thing we are—the crashed UFL." My lungs hurt and my headache was worse. My sweater was a holy heckin' mess I wanted to clean before Grams word-whipped the life outta me. Grams. I was so tired and over all this. "But you know what? I'm sick of wondering what *they* want. This isn't about them. It's about us. And our people." My fingers squeezed the wheel so tight, my hands felt like claws. "This is *our* earth. *Our* home. Our families and our lives. I say we forget about what they are and talk about what really matters. How we're going to find our people and send them and their monsters home."

"You're right. And hey. I'm sorry about shouting before. I wasn't shouting at you. I hope it didn't seem that way. The shaking and noise. It hurt. Made me think thoughts I didn't want to be thinking. Bad things. Worry things. Anyway, I'm really sorry. I hope you're not mad."

I drove around an oil truck, then over the curb to keep following the signs to Manchester center. I felt exposed on the main road, but the main road was the only way I knew would get us where we needed to go. "It's okay," I told Raven. "I'm sorry about letting loose on you, too." I smiled. "You should see my grams when she's yelling at me. You could light a fire with the look in her eyes. But behind it, there's a lotta love."

Raven nodded. Then he asked, "Hey. Can I ask you something?"

"Sure."

"How did you know to stay quiet? When the UFOs went over us."

I sighed. This was it. If I was going to share my mom's really personal journal, the scary things inside and her beyond-the-grave hints, the time was now. All of a sudden, a cold chill blew past my cheek. And the scent of orange entered the cab.

Mom was here, giving me the courage to go on.

"Okay. So . . . Can you smell anything *different* in the truck right now?"

"Ugh. I'm so sorry! I know I stink like teen boy and wet dog. Apologies, Akka." He looked so sorry my heart bottomed out. "No matter how much deodorant I put on, it's like my sweat burns through it in two seconds, and—

I almost laughed. "No, goofy. Besides your BO and Akka's funk."

"Oh. No. Why? What do you smell?"

I thought about what to say to get it just right. "If I tell you something personal, would you maybe consider . . . not laughing?" A fireball of heat swirled in my chest—a fireball of old pain from people laughing at me. "Because I want to trust you, okay?"

Raven put up his hand. "I swear on my first-edition *Sk8 the Infinity* manga, and also on my honor. I'd never laugh at you for any reason. And when we find everyone—and we will!—please lead me to the garbage people who laughed at you because I will tear them a new—"

"Okay, okay, you don't need to tear anyone's anything," I said, laughing. Somehow, in all this darkness, Raven made me laugh. "But I am going to share something with you I've been scared to for obvious reasons. So . . . I smelled oranges. So strong, I couldn't even smell bleach."

Raven's brows raised. "Oranges?"

"Mm-hmm." I focused on my cuticles. "Um, I told you my mom died last year. And her favorite essential oil was oranges. She always wore it. So, ever since the lights came, I've been sensing her near me. Like her spirit or ghost or something. I've had other signs she was around, too. Numbers—Three Twelve. Like the road leading up Mount Equinox? And the other Three Twelve on—"

"The stop sign we just passed." Raven looked stunned. "I saw it, too. And there was an orange. On the sign."

"Yes!" I slammed the wheel and Bob jerked. I coughed after shouting. "And other things, too. Song lyrics, like 'true colors' and 'driving with my best friend.' I even had a dream of her when I crashed into the Humane Society and passed out."

Raven pushed forward, suddenly serious. "A dream?"

"Yeah. Like she was telling me something important. Like the dream we shared telling us to go west. And I keep hearing music, too. Mostly 'Blackbird.' Real soft, but there. Like at the edge of the universe but also inside my head, playing in the direction I need to go. I don't know. It's like she keeps showing me things. Leading me places. And sometimes, I think I figure out what she's trying to say. But other clues I don't get."

Raven picked a loose thread on his sleeve. "I asked you before if your mom was special. If she knew things. Do you think she was psychic or something? Like she left that CD and . . . I don't know. Do you think she knew this was going to happen before she died?" He waved his hands before him. "Ugh. Sorry. You don't have to answer that if you—"

"No. It's okay." A cold sweat slicked my brow as I snaked through downtown. My skin felt electrically charged. Like the closer we got to Mount Equinox, the thicker the energy in every molecule of the world grew. "If she was clairvoyant, she never mentioned it. But . . ." The journal in the belt of my pants rubbed my belly and suddenly felt too big to keep to myself. I thought back to Raven's blackbird pin, and the timing felt right. "She did leave something behind besides the CD. Something I've been reluctant to share but think it's time to show you now."

Raven blinked eagerly in the rearview. "What kind of something?"

A crumbling inn appeared to my right. Somewhere

ahead, "Blackbird" played, and I knew the right thing to do. I stopped in the driveway of the old inn, slid the journal from my pants, and handed it to Raven over the seat. "My mom's story. Something that might save our lives."

As soon as he took the tattered book, Bob's dashboard clock flashed a bunch of numbers, then stopped on 3:12.

My mom's favorite number.

CHAPTER 20

WHAT IS HIDDEN COMES TO LIGHT

I'D CONSIDERED SHARING MY MOM'S JOURNAL with Raven bunches of times. But sharing my mom's private journal wasn't like sharing personal stories of my own. Something about it felt weird. Like without her permission, something about it just felt wrong. So there was that. But also, if someone I barely knew told me their ghost mom was abducted by aliens and had written a secret book that held clues about the apocalypse and burned a CD of old songs that might combine to make a cryptic map leading to their family, who'd also been abducted by aliens, I'd think they'd eaten bad eggs and were hallucinating. I'd held out sharing her journal, but after getting to know and trust Raven, I didn't think my mom would mind. I finally felt okay about sharing my mom's story. If roles were reversed, I bet he'd have done the same.

I turned on Bob's interior light as Raven opened my mom's journal carefully, like it was a delicate treasure set to break. He read the beginning and smiled.

The first page was all about me.

Well, here I am!

This is my new pregnancy journal! I'm hoping that I can fill this book up for the baby (baby Isadora Bellamy Wilder!) growing inside me right now. I cannot *wait* to meet you, and I hope we will have as strong a bond as my mom and I have. I love you, sweet angel girl.

Raven read stories of me and Maple fighting.

Well, Izzy pushed Maple down this morning and gave her a nice egg on the head!

And laughing.

Omg, journal. Okay, Maple just called Izzy a juice bag as an insult (because it sounds a whole lot like another more vulgar insult!) and honestly, Maple's is better. . . .

Raven read the hopes and wishes she had for us growing up to be fierce, gentle, and strong. And the day-to-day dreams of a loving human walking this world. Raven grinned as he read my mom's entries. But when he got to the parts where she was sad—the pages and pages of writing through her depression— Raven's smile didn't last.

Every day, I try to be strong. For Mom and Pop. For the girls. For everyone expecting me to always be here, for everyone depending on me. This sickness, though . . . this monster in my head has taken so much from me. The lights have taken so much from me. I can't help worrying, when all is said and done, will there be any of me left?

Then, when he came to the sketch of her in the field the first time she was taken, he gasped so loud I jumped.

"What? Your mom saw UFOs a year ago? Wait." His eyes bugged as he flipped a page and stopped. "Your mom was abducted by UFOs."

I lowered my chin and picked my nails. It hurt to

think about her that way. "Yeah."

"And are the mountains she drew *these* mountains?"

"Looks like it."

"And are these the songs and lyrics from the CD?" I could practically see Raven's mind-wheels spinning as he puzzled things out. "She must've put the music together between her abductions. But why? It's almost like—"

"She knew this would happen." I tapped my thighs and bit my nails with nerves. "And when she told people about it, nobody believed her. She got so depressed, maybe she didn't even believe herself. But I swear, she guided me to her journal, like she guided me to you. I think she's here to help us stop all this like she never got to do." Akka licked my hand with love, and I smiled back the same. "I know how this sounds, but it's the truth. That's why I'm showing you this. Because maybe you can help figure out some of her clues."

Raven landed on the page of the gold orb. He squinted at it and mumbled, "What's this thing? I never saw this in . . ." He paused. "I mean, I can't imagine what it is or why she drew it."

"I know. I can't imagine either." I bit my lip. "I was hoping you had an idea."

Raven looked closer at the sketched orb. "I literally have zero idea. But her drawings. This journal . . ." He shook his head. "How is this possible? Why did this happen to us?" He shoved a hand through his hair. "I mean, what good is it knowing the future if we can't figure out how to fix it?"

The air hummed. The atmosphere pressed in around us. The black dust fell like snow.

"And this headache," Raven continued, "it's so bad I can barely think."

"Same." Akka sat beside me, a low growl in his throat. Maybe he had a headache, too. Suddenly, Bob's interior light flickered and died. "Weird."

And that hum I kept feeling every which way around us was worse.

Raven pulled a red flashlight from his jeans, and I got mine. Akka climbed into the back seat. I followed and sat between Raven and my best boy. And when Raven shone his light onto my mom's journal, he squeaked with surprise.

"Uh, Izzy? Look at these pages. Did you know these other drawings were here?"

When I scootched over and set eyes on the page, I couldn't believe what I saw. Hidden under her charcoal sketch of UFOs shining over Vermont, she'd drawn, in what must have been invisible ink, several familiar shapes lowering inside the beams. The shapes had giant red eyes, gaping mouths on humongous heads, and tentacles with pointed tips reaching across the page.

Uglies.

"No." Mom hid secret pictures under a few of the originals—drawings you couldn't see unless you were looking with infrared light. "Holy crow. She knew about the uglies, too."

Raven's eyes glittered like he was impressed. "Invisible ink. It's genius." He ran agitated hands through his long, dusted hair and moved even closer to me. "I bet this isn't the only hidden message either. We should go back to the beginning and look for more."

Suddenly, Raven and Akka were too close. I couldn't get enough air. I was too hot. All my clothes felt too small, and I was about to jump out of my skin. I slipped my mom's headphones and Discman off too, but it wasn't enough to feel free. "Akka, please move." He backed away fast. "And Raven, back up. Please."

And he did. Right away. "Sure." Raven glanced away. "Sorry." I felt bad making him feel bad, but mostly, my impulse when people got too close without invitation was to push them away. And I was taught that honoring my body and self always came first.

"No, you're good. I'm just stressed and need space."

"Totally understand." Raven smiled, which helped

release a few nerves.

After some deep breaths, I relaxed. I held the journal between us, flipping pages, red light shining down. Dust hit Bob's windows as the dust storm raged on. "Hey, I found something." I'd stopped on the page I thought was just shaded gold. I figured she'd drawn the gold lights. But there was more hidden underneath. At the top of the page she'd hidden two half orbs, drawn in invisible ink, side by side like upside-down bowls. Golden light beamed from the one on the left. Ultraviolet light beamed from the one on the right. Human and animal shapes hung suspended in both the gold and ultraviolet lights.

"Oh my gosh." I swallowed and covered my mouth. "Look at all those bodies. Do you think . . . maybe . . . could those be the missing people and animals? The ones the lights took?"

Raven's stunned expression curled into a grin. "Holy. Freaking. Potatoes. The missing life forms of earth." He pumped his fists. "Yesss. But why in the gold beams are their shapes amorphous, or whatever that word is? They're clustered at the top of the page like they've been broken into particles of light. But in the ultraviolet beams, their bodies are more solid and nearer the ground. What do you think that means?"

My mind spun like a motor on high. The Madonna

song started up inside my head. I ignored it and stared at Raven, hoping to get my thoughts out. "What if everyone was beamed up through the gold lights? And this half-orb thing was the button that beamed them into the ships? Obviously there are so many people and animals that their bodies would have to be broken down to beam into the ships, right?"

"Right. I like where you're going with this. . . ."

I thrust a hand into my nest of curls. "Okay. So do you remember what we were talking about in the library? How amethysts absorb *and* reflect energy?" I touched my crystal necklace, then tapped the page. "What if that orb thing works like a crystal? What if the orb *is* a crystal? What if the orbs are like buttons on the UFO's bridge that can lift a lot of people at once? Up through gold lights, and down through purple lights—the same way they dropped the uglies?" *Purple means something.* "If we can find the crashed UFO and figure out how to work the orb, we can reanimate everyone and everything they took aboard the crashed ship."

The whole time I was talking, Raven was nodding and quiet, clapping excitedly. "Yes, yes, yes. If the aliens can manipulate and shrink people and animals and stuff, and the orb works like a transporter, maybe everyone they took from our area isn't life-size anymore." I gasped and grabbed his hand. Raven nodded and squeezed back. "Maybe the crashed UFO still has our families inside the orb."

"Raven?" I stroked Akka until my racing heart calmed. "You read my mind."

Raven squirmed nervously and took back his hand. "Purple means something, right?" He flipped the page to my mom's words. "Maybe that's what she meant. Maybe purple, like the amethyst and ultraviolet light, is what brings our people home."

"So, if we're right, and the light from the orbs is powerful enough to turn the bodies of everyone and everything into pure energy, and also return that same energy back to material form . . . and these orbs are aboard each UFO . . . and the crashed UFO is on top of Mount Equinox, then, Raven, I think we have ourselves a new plan."

Raven smacked his hands together as the wind and dust outside roared. "I am one hundred percent on board with the *Ghost Mom, Izzy, Akka, and Raven Save the Earth Plan.*" Raven got gum from his pack and handed me a piece.

Spearmint. Grams only chewed spearmint gum.

"I'm glad we agree. And thanks. For the gum." I put a piece in my mouth and sighed. It tasted like memories. The dust was thicker, and night would be here fast. "We should go."

Raven flashed his long lashes at me as I climbed into the front seat. "Thanks for sharing your mom's journal with me. It means a lot that you trust me."

Akka, my forever co-pilot, scrambled up to my side. I buckled in and smiled. "Of course." A flutter of belly moths swirled in a you've-got-a-crush-coming tornado. *Vader's tears, Izzy, this is not the time for crushes, so stuff that feeling in a galaxy far away and drive.* "I'm happy I shared it with you, too."

We left Manchester and drove up Route 7A toward Mount Equinox, hunting the spot the UFO fell. The scrub brush along the rural road looked dead. Sharp rocks littered our path. Lawns were punched with holes, like uglies had tunneled underground. And as nightmare after nightmare zoomed by, Raven took the Playlist for the End of the World CD out of the Discman I left in the back seat and passed it to me. I popped it into Bob's CD player and started it from the beginning. Then Raven and I talked about how we both loved poetry and dogs. About our lives and homes. His garbage father and mine, and our amazing best friends. We told each other what we'd do when we saw our families again. Until Mount Equinox came into sight and our conversation stopped.

A red-and-black-dusted sunset lit the horizon

like a bad omen. Mount Equinox loomed above it all. I slowed Bob in the center of the two-lane road and turned the music down so I could think. A few notes of "Blackbird" played in the distance. Akka's ears swiveled toward the song. I was sure Akka heard it, too.

A wind/solar-powered road sign appeared to our right. The bright sign read:

INVISIBLE TURN ONTO EUFORA ST AHEAD

Except the E, R, and A in EUFORA were flashing like they were about to die. A second later, the E, R, and A, and the TURN ONTO and ST, blinked out, leaving three words shining through the dust.

INVISIBLE UFO AHEAD

A second later, all the letters blinked out.

"Uh, Raven? Did you see that sign, or was I dreaming?"

"No. I totally saw it." Raven pulled close to my seat. "If you're dreaming, so am I."

The air turned heavy as cement. Akka's hackles went up. My best boy leapt to his feet and borked like the devil at Mount Equinox. I squinted at the mountains.

Something wasn't right.

"Raven. Look." I pointed toward the peak of Mount Equinox, so tall you couldn't see the top for the clouds. Except— "Do you see that spot the dust and clouds aren't hitting? That oval-shaped emptiness like a big, invisible egg, bulging on the peak?"

Raven unbuckled and squinted out the windshield. "Oh my God. I can only see it if I look a certain way. But yeah." He coughed and blinked his wild eyes onto me. "That sure looks like an invisible UFO to me."

CHAPTER 21
THE TRUTH

I'D SEEN THE ALIEN MOVIES. READ ALIEN INVASION books on the end of the world. I'd learned about invisibility shields from *Star Wars*. How space bends around the ships, hiding all kinds of evil inside. But staring up at what might actually be a crashed UFO, I wondered how much fear a person could take. If we made it inside the ship and found something too horrible to comprehend, would we be able to take it? And what about my family; how were they surviving since they vanished? Was Maple's anxiety out of control? How was Pops's heart holding up? Was Grams confused and lost in the UFO? Was Nora with her family or battling monsters alone? I wondered if Raven, Akka, and I could conquer our unimaginable fear. Or if, like so many before us, we'd crash and burn before making it out of the story alive.

"Could that really be it?" I was talking to myself, but Raven answered anyway.

"I guess there's only one way to find out."

I nodded and twisted my hair. "It's probably another hour's drive to Equinox, having to skirt all the junk in the road. So we better hurr—"

The lights on the dashboard surged and flashed. The air crackled with static, my hair stood on end, and the music burst through Bob's speakers. "Song nine of Annie's Alt. Mix, 'Radio Ga Ga,' by Queen." A sudden whoosh of icy air entered the truck, even though all the windows were closed. Akka stopped growling and wagged his tail, smiling at the space between me and Raven.

Mom.

"Izzy? Did you, um, feel that?" Raven shivered. "And maybe smell oranges, too?"

I grinned. "Uh-huh."

(Radio ga ga . . .).

We listened until the end of the song, then shut the music off, and continued toward Mount Equinox in silence. Toward the Bennington Triangle, where all the UFO sightings occurred and all those people over the years went missing. I kept the headlights off and drove by Bob's red lights only. Less light, less of a target on us. The closer we got to the mountain, the thicker the dust became. It piled in the streets like black sand and buried crashed cars. And hid the gray uglies, too.

The transistor radio whined from the back seat, even though it was off. Same with Bob's radio. And whenever my mom's Discman wasn't playing her CD, a wave of ever loudening feedback streamed out of that radio, too.

"Where do you think the uglies went?" Raven's face had turned a sickly color. His eyes were as blood-shot as mine.

I gripped my amethyst tight. "Maybe under-ground, like you said."

The earth trembled for a few seconds, then stopped. My mom's amethyst burned, but again, we couldn't see any uglies.

"Raven, we should—" I coughed and wiped dust from my eyes. "String Bob with the holiday lights from the store for extra protection, just in case."

"Yes." Raven picked dust boogers from Akka's eyes. "I love that for us. Let's do this."

We strung Bob with more lights, kept our flash-lights close and Pops's bat and blade closer. Raven seemed extra nervous. Akka, too. So, when we got back on Route 7A, I pressed play on my mom's CD again, hoping it would help keep us calm, and maybe give up some more clues.

"Song ten from Annie's Alt. Mix, 'Pictures of You,' by the Cure. The best song from the best album." My mom paused. "I had all my best days with you." That time she was definitely crying. Did she know my heart would be breaking over losing everyone I loved? Did she know her family would be nearly wiped clean of this earth when she made this CD? I stared down the dusty road and let the song sing to me—like the lyrics came from her. It was like she wanted me to feel what she was going through before she died.

When the song ended, I shut it off—then something hit me. All this time, she'd been trying to tell me she was sorry for leaving. That she never wanted to go. That she loved me. She was still here, and I wasn't alone.

Mom. All my best days were with you, too.

"Blackbird" played up ahead, toward Mount Equinox. I smiled over my trembling chin.

Then Raven said out of nowhere, "You hear 'Blackbird' again, right?"

"Yeah. I hear it. It's coming from Equinox. I'm sure of it."

Mom used to sing me and Maple to sleep with that song. But until now, until I really listened to the words, I never thought of it as sad. Maybe those who'd never been this hurt couldn't understand this song until they'd been hurt this bad, too.

Lightning flashed over the mountains. When "Blackbird" ended, it started over. I had a terrible feeling I couldn't shake and was so caught up in the lyrics and what they might mean, I nearly crashed into a boulder in the road.

"Heads up!" The tires squealed. I caught Akka before he slipped.

Something hit the ground in the back seat and Raven jumped. "Oh no."

"What?"

"Your mom's Discman slipped off the seat and it fell." He cradled it like a baby. "Sorry. I couldn't catch it in time."

"It's okay. Is it broken?" I rounded another corner, Mount Equinox in full view. The wind ripped dead leaves from trees. The air shook with a thrumming pitch of noise, a backdrop of vibrational sound that got more intense every minute.

"I don't think so. I put the batteries back in. But did you know there's something taped to the inside of the battery back cover thing?"

My heart thumped. "No?"

I slowed down. Flags popped out of the dust cloud

ahead, snapping fast. Right after, the entrance sign for Mount Equinox appeared.

We were here.

I pulled Bob into the parking lot in front of the main building. Half the gift shop had collapsed into a sinkhole in the ground. The pavement was pitted and broken. Nobody else was here. It felt like the calm before the storm.

"Can I see the paper?" Raven handed the battery cover to me with such a forlorn look, I felt sick. "Thanks." But I didn't know why. "Blackbird" looped the air outside.

As the soft music played, dread blew through me like mist over a grave. I peeled off the Scotch tape and found a small, folded note. I recognized the paper. It was the last page ripped from my mom's journal. Another note from my mom. Dated May 8 of last year.

The day my mom died.

Dear Izzy and Maple,

I'm so sorry. I can't do this anymore. I've been so sick for so long. I am just so tired. Tired of fighting. Tired of being afraid. Tired of walking through the world like it's already ended and feeling like I'm letting everyone down. The Darklights have gotten inside my head, and they won't stop coming for me. But please know this isn't your fault.

I didn't want to go. I tried with my whole soul to fight this, but one day, all my fight was gone. So take my journal. And my playlist, and all the love I have left—it's always been yours. Don't blame Grams and Pops either, okay? I left them a note too. I asked them to keep the actual cause of my death a secret from you girls. To tell you I died some other way. Keeping this from you was my final wish. Maybe that was wrong, but I don't know if I know what's right anymore.

I never wanted this for either of you. I hope you can feel that. But in the end, there was just me. I didn't know what else to do. But, sweet Izzy and Maple, if you can, try not to remember me as your mom who died by suicide. Remember me laughing on my best days and smiling just for you. And that wherever you are, I will be by your side.

I love you to the Milky Way and back.

Always,

Mom

My blood ran cold.

No.

My body went numb.

No.

Akka stood and tried licking my tears through his mask. I latched on to him like I was drowning and he was the only life raft in the raging sea.

"No."

"Izzy?" Raven scootched toward me and touched my shoulder. "Are you okay?"

"Don't touch me."

My brain just kept saying no as I replayed those three words:

Died by suicide.

My brain froze. My body was not my body. My mind was not my own, but I felt everything and nothing at once. Sadness. Emptiness. Pain. I cried and shook so hard I couldn't stop.

Raven whispered something, but all I heard was, *Suicide. Suicide. Suicide.*

She could've come to me. Confided in me. I could've helped her. Been there for her when nobody else would. I wanted to reach through time and hold her and tell her I was with her. That I believed her and would do anything to help her be okay.

But she was gone. So gone. And all I had now was her ghost.

"Izzy, please talk to me." Raven stared at me, aglow in a shift of red light. "I want to help. If I can. Even if you just need to vent or whatever, I'm here, okay?"

I glanced at Akka beside me. Soft fur. Soft eyes, wanting to wipe my tears away. I couldn't answer Raven. My mouth felt foreign to me. There was so much inside me, I didn't know what to do with it all. Grams and Pops told us she died of cancer. Of a brain tumor. They lied to me and Maple? Inventing a story about cancer felt so wrong. Why would Mom make them do that?

My whole life felt like a lie.

Mom.

I tore my hands from my hair. My mom didn't die of cancer. She died of suicide. I pounded the steering wheel. "What did she do?" When I thumped the wheel, another song started on her CD. "I Am by Your Side," by Corey Hart.

Her note said she'd always be by my side. And all at once, the cracks in my heart I'd been trying to keep together from losing her and Grams and Pops and Maple and Nora got too big to hold, and my heart broke apart inside me and shattered to the floor.

"Izzy? Are you okay? Do you want to talk about it?"

"No." I couldn't get the word "suicide" out of my head. *(I am by your side . . .)* I banged my fists against my ears to stop the thoughts. Mom left us. On purpose. Mom didn't love us enough to stay. In my heart, I knew this was wrong. I knew Mom couldn't help it. I knew suicide was a disease stemming from mental illness. That it wasn't her fault, like my depression and anxiety wasn't mine. I knew this like I knew my family couldn't help being taken by the lights. But sometimes what you know and what you feel are universes apart and you get lost in the space between. "I'm sorry. I gotta get out of here."

I was so tired of losing the people I loved.

"Wait! Don't go out there alone. It's not safe—and look at the dust!"

"I just need a minute. Please, I don't want to be in the truck." I needed to move my legs. Get all this wilding energy out of me.

"Bark!" Akka got on me and pawed my arm off the door handle. "Bark! Bark!" *Izzy, do not go out there because it is not safe and I love you*, Akka's brown eyes said.

I ruffled my best boy's fluffy jowls and decided to stay in the truck, knowing Raven and Akka were right. "Fine, whatever. Just don't talk to me right now, okay?" I flapped my hands in front of my face. "Just for a second and . . ."

Tears welled up again. After fourteen years of

being Isadora Bellamy Wilder, I knew there was no running from the real me, tears, explosions, and all. So, I rocked until I got that word out of my head. Petted Akka until I calmed.

"Sorry." I touched the photo of me and Maple on Bob's dash, crying and snotting like a professional. "Can I get a Kleenex, please?" Raven passed me one from the back. "Thanks."

"It's okay." Raven gave me a caring smile. Akka jumped all over me, mask off, licking my face dry. "Whatever you need."

I folded up my mom's note with the same frozen feeling that came each time I lost someone I loved. But I had my best friend at my side, and a kind new friend. Maybe I could open up and let Raven in, too. Because even though it felt like it sometimes, I wasn't alone.

So I held on to Akka and told Raven everything. About how my mom really died. About how my grandparents told me and Maple she died of cancer. And he listened. To how, in a matter of minutes, everything I thought I knew about my family went up in flames.

"Thanks for staying, Raven."

He looked about ready to cry. Like he understood how it felt to be the loneliest person in the world.

"Thank you for letting me stay."

Suddenly, the ground rumbled. Bob rattled and Akka borked. "Blackbird" played on a faraway wind. And then too many gray uglies rose like demons from the ground.

In the darkness, my mom's words flew back to me: *Wherever you are, I will be by your side.*

My mom was with me even if her body wasn't. And I swore to her then, as red-eyed monsters surrounded our truck, I would not let her down. I would finish what she started. I would survive. And no matter what, I would bring our family home.

CHAPTER 22
THE FIELD

THEY SAY WE CAN GET USED TO ANYTHING. THAT humans were built for change. And they're right. I was no longer shocked by the gray uglies pushing arms through the broken earth. Wasn't surprised at their red eyes staring from the tops of the trees. I was used to seeing UFOs and the whirling nightmare of dust. I'd accepted the burn on my chest from the amethyst heating my skin. But just because you were used to fighting with all you had to survive each day didn't mean you shouldn't do all you could to get gone. To escape. To battle your nightmares and win.

And I intended to win.

"Bork! Bork! Bork!"

Gray uglies surrounded the truck. I whipped out

Pops's blade. Akka dove at the windows, spit flying at the glass. Raven grabbed the bat and blared his transistor radio until the windows rattled. We scrambled the cab for the flashlights and shone as many as we could outside. Uglies hissed and lunged from the dust, teeth first. And when I twisted Bob's radio on high, I'd never heard anything so loud in my life.

Bob shook. The ground shifted. The truck slipped sideways into a hole. Everything inside the truck moved. Raven was screaming, but I could barely hear him over the feedback. The uglies shrieked and tore at the sides of their heads. Some ran off, the braver ones stayed. The red light burned their limbs. Black goo leaked from their eyes and skin, but they kept coming back for more.

"Akka's helmet—where is it?" Akka cried at the radio frequency. I searched Bob's back seat. When I moved, the truck tilted even more sideways, and our flashlights fell to the floor.

"There—" Raven pointed under his pack, currently pressed up against the passenger-side door, slowly sinking into the cracked ground. I slipped Akka's helmet over his mask, and this time, he didn't fight me.

"Izzy, look ou—!" One of the uglies stabbed a hole through the back window and went after Raven. But Raven bashed the ugly's limb with the bat first. Already fried from the red light, the ugly's limb snapped off and dropped outside. The monster shrieked, then raced back into the night. I cradled Akka and cried at the pain in my ears as Bob sank deeper into the cracked road. "Put these in!" Raven screamed over the noise. Earplugs. Right.

Veins popping, blood pounding, I hollered, *"Hold on!"* Akka borked as I slammed on the gas. Bob's left-side wheels spun. Smoke billowed from the tires and under Bob's hood. The bleached air filled with smoke. The red eyes of more uglies closed in. And just when I thought we were doomed, I forced Bob out of the rut and onto the last part of unbroken road.

We were free, but for how long? Even though we got away from all the uglies before, more would come. No matter how many red lights we shone, or how much noise we made, they weren't ever gonna stop.

"Turn it down!" I couldn't hear Raven, just see his mouth move in the rearview. When we had gotten far enough away, we turned the radio to a bearable level, took out our earplugs, and listened, but all we heard was the echo of feedback ringing in our ears.

"Do you see anything?" I wiped dust and dried tears from my face.

"No," Raven shouted extra loud. "I think they're gone."

Cold wind howled through the broken back window. I coughed from the incoming dust. Raven rummaged for something in his backpack, pulled out a shirt and roll of pink duct tape, and quickly covered the hole. "There. That should hold for a while."

I nodded and mumbled my thanks. A second later, my thoughts turned back to my mom.

I'd stuffed her final note in my pocket without even knowing it. I removed it carefully, like it was the most precious of all things, and smoothed out her words. Somehow my brain fixed on just three: *Secrets. Lies. Suicide. Secrets. Lies. S—*

Izzy, stop. But my mind kept repeating those words.

I wished so bad Grams were here. That I could bury myself in her soft chest. Or have Pops wrap his strong arms around me. Make me feel like I wasn't lost but found like he always did. Be the strength I needed to go on. I wished Maple would hold my hand like she did when she was scared and help still the words and thoughts and fears looping my mind.

But they weren't here.

Even with Raven and Akka, I felt so alone.

Suddenly, my heart pounded so fast, I lost my breath. Black flowers bloomed behind my eyes, and nausea hit next. I swayed in my seat, and coughed, so dizzy I thought I might puke. I slammed the brakes in the center of the road. "Raven. I don't feel so good."

Raven unbuckled and leaned forward. "What do you need me to do—drive? I don't know how to drive, but, I mean, maybe I *could* drive if you needed me to?"

My nose started bleeding again. Instead of answering Raven, I grabbed a Kleenex and shoved it up my nose. Teeth clenched, stomach sour, feeling suffocated by every last thing, I rocked back and forth, an angry leviathan thrashing hot and wild inside me. Akka pawed my thigh and whimpered. Then he forced his head under my arm, like he did when a cyclone of emotion and worry thoughts carried me away.

"Izzy. You're scaring me. Please. Let me help you."

"No." I wiped my face and couldn't stop crying. Like all the adrenaline that got us away from the uglies had gone and left an ugly poison behind. "No one can help me." I clutched my mom's last note to my chest, all mess, no shame. I rocked and ignored Akka nudging me. I cried and suddenly all I wanted was to run fast and away. I didn't want anyone looking at me. I didn't want to be here. I didn't want this to be my life. I didn't want any of this.

I felt like a beast in a trap, ready to bite.

"Maybe I can try and help, if you let me?" Raven twisted his bracelet and stared outside. "I'm a good listener. And I bet I could drive."

The stink outside got stronger. The dust just wouldn't stop. Everywhere I looked, a blackened wasteland looked back. My amethyst warmed, but I was too mad to care.

A sudden chill filled the truck. Akka growled behind his helmet. The earth shook. The dashboard lights flashed, and a new track played through Bob's speakers. "Song eleven of Annie's Alt. mix, 'Ceremony,' by New Order." She paused. And I swear, I could feel her here with me. "Listen to the strength inside you. It's loud and fierce, and beautiful. So go into the darkness and show no mercy. I'm always by your side."

I shouted a strangled cry and squeezed my fists. I knew this song, and I didn't want to hear it. Didn't want to be strong. I didn't want to hear the lyrics telling me any darn thing. I couldn't do it—the song, the shaking earth, the uglies, Raven's and Akka's worried eyes. "I'm tired of music and clues, Raven. Sick of the world and the truth. Sick of the pain in my lungs and the dust and all we still have to do. I'm sick of putting you in danger. Sick of being angry and sad. Sick about all my mom went through alone. Sick of not having my family with me." Akka snarled and got in front of me. "I'm just so tired."

I curled over the wheel and heaved. My legs were

cramped. I couldn't stretch them out. Couldn't move with the seat belt. I was ready to leap out of my skin. "I'm sorry." I unbuckled my belt. "I have to get out of here. And this time, please don't try and stop me. Akka, stay." I felt like the worst person in the world.

"Wait—what?" Raven hopped into the front seat.

"Please. I can't." I jumped out into the dust.

"Izzy, wait! I'll come with you."

"No! Just keep Akka safe. I'll be right back."

I slammed the door behind me and ran. Akka barked and scratched the driver's-side glass. I cried harder, sucked the black bleached wind deep into my fireball lungs, and stopped at the side of the road, leaving the red lights behind.

At the edge of a dark field, fifteen feet from Bob, I fell on my knees, and sobbed. I let the world fall away. The uglies keening from the woods. Akka and Raven. The ground trembling under me. I took a minute, and when I slid my face from my hands, it hit me.

The field across from me was the field from my mom's journal. I hadn't noticed it before because she'd sketched it from the side facing Mount Equinox, currently behind me. I got up and rushed into the field to check my theory. Sure enough, I was right. The ridgeline was identical.

This was the road where they took her. The place

my mom went into the lights. I fixed the field to memory. Tried to imagine her here, alone in all that fear, and felt an overwhelming sense of quiet. A wave of warm air washed through me until my worry and fear were gone.

Mom.

I couldn't believe I actually found it. The field where my mom was abducted. The place that changed our lives. The smallest hope twined my heart like a rose. If I found this field, I could find my family, too.

Out of nowhere, the ground shook so hard, I fell. I fought to find my footing, but before I could, the earth cracked and buckled and peaked like a volcano twenty feet ahead. Rocks barreled toward me off the rising peak. I had just scrambled out of the way when a fifteen-foot ugly broke free from the mound and screamed.

I thought about running back to the truck. But if I did, I'd lead the ugly to Akka and Raven, and I wasn't about to do that.

The gray ugly straddled the broken mound of earth on long, pointed arms, opened its massive maw, and hissed. Black goo dripped from its sharklike teeth. Its eyelids blinked sideways like a snake as it held me in its cold gaze. I froze for a moment before I slid out my knife and forced myself off the ground.

"Izzy!" Raven called from somewhere behind me. "Hold on!"

From the truck, another song came on. I must've forgotten to turn the CD off. My mom was saying something, but the only words that came through were "'Fight,' by the Cure."

Then the music blared.

I stared the monster down (*Fight, fight, fight!* . . .). Music boomed through every piece of me. Raven shouted. Akka borked. But all I knew was the bowie knife in my fist, my heaving breath, grit in my eyes, and all the anger and sadness in the universe rising inside me. *(Fight, fight, fight!* . . . *)* When the ugly scrambled toward me and screamed, I screamed back. "AAAAAAAAAAAAAA!" I sprinted to meet it, knife high, but Raven got to me first. He stopped beside me, Pops's bat in one hand and the transistor radio in the other, volume on high.

The feedback blare wailed through me so bad, I didn't know if I'd survive. But when the ugly came at us again, no way was I letting it stop me.

Nose bleeding, head pounding, I ran at the ugly and shouted, *"Go away! Get away and leave us alone!"* The monster staggered and shrieked at the noise but didn't back down. I slashed the long knife in front of me, crying and howling out my pain and shock and sadness. All the lies and grief I didn't want to carry, I wanted to put on the monsters that stole my family. I lunged at the monster, ready to fight.

But when I went after the creature, the transistor radio wailed at a level it never had before. I fell to the ground in pain. *(Fight, fight, fight! . . .)* Raven collapsed behind me as the power lines above us sparked and burst.

"Izzy!" Sparks showered over us as the radios screamed. The pain was too much. The truck shook at our backs, too.

The ground buckled and bounced. My mom's CD burst on and off, then back to on. A power surge hit the truck. *"Bark-bark-bark—"* The red lights under Bob flared. The headlights shone brighter than a new star. Then, suddenly, Bob fizzled and died. The protective red lights went out. The moment screeched to a halt.

And all went silent at the end of the world.

Akka whimpered inside the truck. The gray ugly pushed itself off the ground and chittered a signal into the woods. Others howled in answer in the distance. Red eyes popped between branches a ways away, then streaked forward fast. Holy crow. They were all coming for us.

Raven jumped up and past me faster than I'd ever

seen him, determined and angry as me. "They're gonna get Akka. You should get him. I'll be right back." He had Pops's bat. The transistor radio, and his dad's taser, too.

"Wait. Stop! Raven, where are you—"

Akka cried from the truck. A gray ugly had found him. Tentacled limbs rocked the truck. Akka howled to get free, eyes on me.

"Go, Izzy!" He raised the radio. "I'll hold it off, you get Akka—I'll be right back!"

I shook my head and growled, "No you don't, Raven Barradell. This is my fight, too!"

Vermont hushed as Raven ran at the gray ugly, screaming.

"I told you, I'll be right back!"

Leia's buns, did I move fast. Heart flying, I raced to Bob and freed my best boy. "Akka, to me!" I helped him out of the dead truck. The ugly lunged on the tips of its arms, headfirst, at Raven. Raven swung the bat and hit. He had the transistor tucked in his jeans. I grabbed my flashlight and shone it on Raven to cover him. More uglies appeared but wouldn't come near the infrared lights or radio shriek, but not this ugly. It wanted us and wasn't gonna let anything stop it. But Raven was the bravest kid I'd ever met. When the big ugly swung, Raven tased one of its arms. The thing propelled backward, into the trees. No time to waste, me and Akka ran to him.

"Raven, are you okay?" Another power surge ripped through heaven and earth. Bob's engine suddenly started back up. The truck's dashboard sparked, and red lights flared back on. At the last minute, I grabbed my mom's CD from Bob's player and stuffed it into the journal in my jeans. The transistor radio shrieked, and for a second, the volume turned off. More gray uglies flew over the tops of the trees toward us. Raven was in front of the truck, his back to the headlights, trying desperately to turn the radio back on when the transistor fell and jammed. Raven picked it back up, but it wouldn't turn back on.

"Bork-bork-bork-bork!" Akka dove toward Raven. Three gray uglies galloped out of the trees. Raven stuffed the radio into his jeans, muttered a curse, and raced to us, shouting, "Run! Get in Bob and go!"

But I wouldn't leave him. I ran at the ugly, blade high, and Akka followed. My best boy circled the ugly, lunging and snapping, distracting it. But with his mask still on, he couldn't bite. The gray ugly chittered—*tchh-chht-chht*—long limbs undulating in the twilight gloom when it lunged at Raven's back.

Raven, almost to me, reached out his hand to mine. I'd just touched his fingers when the gray ugly whipped a long, seal-slick arm around Raven, raised him up, and sprang toward the trees. In the blink of an eye, they were gone.

"Bork-bork-bork!"

The world hit pause. Nothing moved as I fought to understand what happened.

"Raven!" I howled, coughing into the black wind. Akka pulled toward the woods. "This isn't real." I choked. "It didn't happen." But it did.

Raven was gone.

Sometimes when I got caught in the web of surprise, I couldn't move for the shock. When too much was happening at once, my brain synapses shut down and I froze. I wanted to move but couldn't. I wanted to race off after Raven, but inside the freeze of shock, what I wanted and what I could do were miles apart.

"Raven!" I turned in a circle. All the other uglies had vanished. I smelled a quick swirl of orange. Then I gripped Akka's leash tighter and forced my feet to move.

Raven was gone.

And I was the only one who could get him back.

CHAPTER 23

TAKEN

"BORK-BORK-BORK!" AKKA CALLED AFTER RAVEN and the ugly that dragged him into the woods. My first instinct was to follow. But chasing Raven on foot was foolish in all that dust, uglies all around. We needed protection.

We needed Bob.

Me and Akka raced back to Bob, choking on dust. I tripped over Pops's bat sticking out of the dirt. Raven must've dropped it when the ugly carried him off. I grabbed the bat and Akka and loaded them into the truck. All the while, Raven's screams got farther away.

I slammed on the gas and sped through the field. We circled the mound left behind by the ugly, bumping over rocks and debris, as monsters wailed like orcas from the trees. I spotted a logging road ahead and took it. Branches slapped the windshield. Akka jostled and cried in his seat, eyes pleading for his new friend. "Hang on, bud. We're gonna get him back."

Akka growled and borked behind us. Sure enough, more uglies were coming up fast. Tentacles snaked through the dust toward Bob. I threw my burning-hot amethyst over my sweater, distracted for only a second when one of the uglies smacked the truck. Bob skidded sideways over the field. The monster latched on to Bob's back bumper and shrieked like it was dying. Its limb fried in the red lights and finally let go.

"Akka, get down!" Mask gone, motorcycle helmet on, Akka lay down. "Good boy!"

I sped toward the logging road's end. And there was Raven, twenty feet ahead, in a clearing of trees, coiled in the gray ugly's arm.

The large gray held Raven around his waist, ten feet off the ground. Ugly babies circled below. Raven screamed and fought, but the ugly only held tighter. The transistor radio lay in the dirt under the ugly, volume off. More uglies slipped out of the night woods, red eyes on Raven. I drove Bob as close as I could, but a pile of logs blocked Bob's way. The gray ugly swung its giant head toward me and stared into my eyes. I could've sworn it smiled as it raised Raven to its open mouth.

I glared at the monster ugly and shouted, *"Raven, cover your ears!"* Raven nodded quick like he knew I was about to roll down the windows and blast 95.1.

I'd set the volume only to medium, but feedback screamed loud enough to shake the stars. Akka pawed his ears. I clenched my teeth against the noise. Baby uglies writhed and fled into the trees, black goo pouring from their mouths. The giant ugly holding Raven contorted and shook but wouldn't let go. Raven jerked up and down with the ugly's flailing limb. I could barely think with the ear-piercing sound, but I had to do something fast.

"Bork-bork-bork-bork!" Akka scratched the door to get free. I scanned the area and spotted a small space on one side of the log pile. If I'd gotten good enough at driving, I might be able to squeeze Bob past and drive into the dumb monster and set Raven free.

I stomped the gas in reverse and backed up, then pulled forward and slipped through the space like I'd been doing it all my life. I gave Raven a thumbs-up, raced Bob to the big ugly's feet, and turned the volume on high.

The noise was worse than anything.

Blood gushed from my nose. My eyes shook in their sockets like dice. Raven held his ears tighter, and I held my best boy closer. But the massive gray got it worse.

The ugly screeched into the dust. Bob's infrared lights hit the ugly's sharp-tipped back feet until they smoked, caught fire, and burned. Black liquid dripped from its eyes. It got disoriented. And when the ugly stumbled backward, Raven punched it in the eye. The ugly screamed in Raven's face but wouldn't let him go.

The feedback wasn't enough. I needed to try something new.

Flashlights! I grabbed all the flashlights I could and shone them out the window, onto the monster's belly. It hissed when its stomach caught fire and whipped a few limbs at the truck. "Holy crow, holy crow, holy crow—" One second before the ugly eviscerated Bob, I slammed Bob into reverse and peeled backward out of the monster's reach.

Smoking and bleeding, the gray ugly scrambled into the trees still holding Raven but dropped him inside the woods. I scanned the area for danger. But all the uglies seemed gone.

"Raven!" Me and Akka ran into the forest after him. I left Bob's feedback on low and shone my flashlights over us, hoping it kept any uglies away. Raven's amber jacket appeared through the dust. Akka arrived first and licked his face. I knelt at his side.

"Can you hear me?" I couldn't hear my voice over my ringing ears. I could barely breathe with my throat clogged with dust. "Are you okay? Please answer me."

Raven rolled over and groaned. He had a bump on his forehead and a gash on his cheek. But somehow, he looked happy to see us. "Izzy? What happened?" I helped him sit. Akka wagged, whined, and licked Raven clean. "Akka . . ." Raven coughed, picked leaves from his hair, and gave Akka pets. "I'm happy to see you too."

I was so thankful Raven was okay—but my relief faded fast. I finally knew how Grams felt when I put myself in danger. Because right now, I wanted to throttle this boy smiling at my dog like he wasn't almost a monster's snack. "Why did you do that?" I jammed my finger at his chest. "Why did you go after that ugly by yourself?" Raven opened his mouth but never had a chance to say a word. "Don't you *ever* scare me like that again, Raven Barradell, do you hear me?"

Raven leaned back like I was a hot wind blowing. "But you did the same thing? And Akka—the uglies. I—" But I kept coming, finger stabbing, Akka looking at him like, *My new friend, you are doing the right thing backing away because she is small but fierce.*

"But nothing. You could have died! You could have been *eaten*! You could have been . . ." My voice trailed off at the end. "You could have been taken and not given back." I turned away, on the verge of tears.

"I'm sorry." He looked sorrier than anyone ever. "I thought if I could distract them, you'd have a better chance of escaping." He coughed and took a whoosh off his inhaler. "But you didn't escape. Why didn't you leave when you had the chance?"

"Because." I twisted a ringlet of hair. "We're survivors. We can take a break to collect our thoughts if possible. But we can't run from the hard stuff." Colder winds blew. "We have a job to do. People who need us to fight—for them and us. And no matter what's happened, I won't let them down. Not my grams. Not my pops. Not my sister or friends. Not your One D—loving mom, or your dogs." Raven's mask was gone. I pulled another from my pocket—a rainbow one I found inside Bob—and passed it to him. He nodded and put it on. "So as my sister says . . ." I paused past the lump in my throat. "Suck it up, buttercup. Because I need you. To help me battle uglies, and to be our friend." I met his eyes. "Friends are hard to find at the end of the world."

Raven let me help him up. "Yeah, they sure are." Heat climbed into my cheeks as he stumbled, and I held him close. "Sorry. My knee is really bad. And my stomach where that ugly jerk grabbed me isn't great either."

"Okay. Lean on me if you want." I worried it would be awkward because I was short, and he was tall. But when Raven wrapped his arm around me and we started walking, it felt like the most natural thing in the world.

The forest was pitch except for the two flashlights. As I kicked rocks and sticks out of our path, my foot hit something metal: the transistor radio. I picked it up and handed it to Raven. "Oh my God. You found it!" He turned it on, and this time, it worked. "Yes, Izzy, thank you." Raven kissed the radio. "And thank you, radio. We're gonna need y—"

An out-of-place sound of metal crunching metal echoed from the clearing ahead. A low groan of earth ripping open followed. Akka pulled forward and barked. Raven and I looked at each other like, *Huh*, as the feedback from the truck radio suddenly shut off.

We hurried arm in arm toward Bob and the strange metal-crunch noise. But when we got to the clearing, our beloved Bob was gone.

Akka howled into the black wind. Me and Raven stared in disbelief. A massive crack had opened in the earth and swallowed Bob whole.

"Bob!" Me and Raven stared down into the crevasse, wide and long as a bus. And there was Bob, five feet down, headlights up, wedged tight in the earth. "No." I glanced at Raven, on the verge of tears. "Our hero is gone."

Gray uglies shrieked and called like alien baboons in the jungle. Raven turned on the transistor and set the volume to low. I cast eyes into the trees, puzzling out what to do. "Our backpacks, food, water, clothes, extra flashlights, and phones are all inside Bob. How do we get them if the doors won't open?"

"The trail map from the library was in my pack, too." Raven scoured the ground like he was looking for something. "But I remember most of it. We can follow the paved road to the top. As for our stuff, if we tried to get it, we might get sucked down."

I coughed harder, each jag getting worse. "I know. But Bob was one of us. I don't want to leave another family member behind." I just realized that photo of me and Maple was still inside. I squinted into the swirling dust. "Plus, you know what losing Bob means, right?"

Raven looked to the top of the mountain. "Unfortunately, yes. We have to climb that ridiculously big, cursed mountain on foot with our dusty lungs and my bad knees, not to mention monsters literally everywhere." He handed me a bottle of water he'd picked up off the ground and brushed off some dust. "This must've fallen out of Bob. It should last at least until we get to the top."

Akka flopped at my feet, black strings of drool hanging from his lips. He had no mask. I poured water in Akka's mouth, then ripped a sleeve from my shirt and fashioned Akka another mask. "It's not great, but it'll do." Akka didn't even fight me. He suddenly seemed too tired to fight.

A wicked gust howled past. We faced the apocalypse wind.

"You ready?" Raven found a decent-size walking stick at the tree line and used it like a cane. "As you can see, I'm dressed in my best and ready to hike a mountain to see a UFO and kick some aliens in the junk," Raven said with a flourish, arms out. I smiled at his shenanigans, then almost cried. That flourish was Nora's signature move.

I shook off my sad and replaced it with mad. "Yeah. Let's take these monsters down and bring our people home."

We stood around the hole in the earth, bowed our heads, and said goodbye to Bob, already buried in dust. Then we told him we loved him, walked into the darkness, and didn't look back.

We walked in silence to Three Twelve Road, the paved drive heading up Mount Equinox, flashlights, and the transistor, on. The uglies' cries died away as soon as we hit the mountain, but the lightning storm got worse. The weird thing was, it seemed to be most active directly over Mount Equinox, the heart of the Bennington Triangle.

As we passed the sunken-in gift shop, the memory of my mom's note rushed me like a thousand midnight moths. She didn't die from cancer like Grams and Pops said. She died by suicide. My body swelled with a hurt big enough to drown me.

We shuffled slowly up the twisting road. Red flashlights bounced. The transistor squealed. "Blackbird" played on a loop, carried on howling winds. We didn't talk much, trying to keep our mouths closed. But when we talked, it was about anime and books. What we'd eat if we could have anything in the world. We held our shirts and scarves over our masks for added protection. We took small sips of water. But my eyes stung. And my lips were chapped. And muscles I never knew I had hurt. Raven never complained, but I knew he had it so much worse. Mostly, we just pushed forward, focused on our people and not falling down.

About three-quarters up the mountain, lightning struck a tree close by. The power of it surged through me, like its energy zapped me, too. The transistor screamed in Raven's hand. Akka yipped and pressed to my side. And like a revelation, the dream I hadn't been able to remember from the farmhouse rushed back to me.

Raven blurted, "Whoa. Did you feel that? When the lightning struck. It zapped through me almost, and I remembered something potentially important."

"Seriously, Raven? Me too. What did you remember?"

We said at the same time, "My dream."

"You first." Raven coughed into his mask. Akka paused to do his business in a pile of dust.

Feral energy coursed through me. "At the farmhouse. I dreamed about purple lights and . . . Oh my crow. I mean holy crow." I gaped into his big eyes. "Raven! It all just came back to me. The people. The people were trapped in the Darklights. . . ."

"Oh my God. Yup. Yup. Holy—" He shook his head. "I had the same dream."

I gasped. "Wait, what?"

Raven stared at me like he knew something I didn't. "Uh, yeah. I dreamed about purple lights with people inside. I was in a round red room holding a black orb and whispering, *Open the heart and we're free.* Then I woke up. I can't believe I couldn't remember that until now. Did you dream about the black orb and that weird line, too?"

Open the heart and we're free. That sounded like the Madonna song "Open Your Heart." My scalp tingled. "No. But it's funny. Back at the library, a song got stuck in my head with almost that exact same title. 'Open Your Heart,' by Madonna. My mom loved that song. So, I don't think that could be a coincidence. That black orb and those words sound like clues."

Raven nodded. "Open the heart, open your heart. Any idea what that could mean?"

I shook my head. "No."

Raven side-eyed me through his hair. "Okay. Well, how did your dream end?"

I side-glanced him back. "Like I told you in the farmhouse. I dreamed about going west. But right before I woke up, a flash of gold lit up the world."

Black spots opened behind my eyes. I swayed and steadied against a boulder. The rock was vibrating. "Hey, Raven? Put your hand on this rock. Do you feel that?"

Raven touched the stone. "Weird. It feels like standing beside a speaker booming with base. A rhythm. A pulse."

"Yeah." Dust caked my eyelashes. I had to keep

rubbing it away. "I think it's coming from the mountain. Or maybe . . . from the crashed UFO."

He pointed at me. "A signal."

"A distress signal." I pressed my palms to the earth.
"I can feel it everywhere. Like a heartbeat under my
skin."

Raven tapped his stick, thinking. "A heartbeat.
Like *Open the heart and we're free* from my dream, and
'Open Your Heart,' like the song. Maybe those are con-
nected somehow."

"Wait." I pulled my mom's journal from my pants
to check something; the CD I'd stuffed inside poked
out. Mom. A flood of emotions rushed back. The note.
The truth. The lies. The questions left unanswered
haunting me still. Did she say goodbye to me that day?
Did I even notice something was wrong? Did she try
to tell me about the abductions or how sad and hopeless she felt? And if so, what did I say back? Was I
caring enough? There for her enough? Did I forget to
love her enough to stay?

*Stop, Izzy. Whatever she went through was about
her, not you. She loved you to the stars and back, so get
back to work finding your family. They're the ones who
need you now.*

I sniffed back a sea of unspent tears and snapped
the CD into the Discman, still at my hip, then flipped

to the right page. "Maybe this has to do with the words from your dream and the song in my head." *And*, I thought to myself, *my mom's ghost whispering* Open to me *before she vanished.* I pointed to a line that had been mostly scribbled out near the back of the book: "Inside the light, we are free." I hadn't paid it much mind until now.

"*Open the heart and we're free.* 'Open Your Heart.' 'Inside the light, we are free.' Those are almost the same." Raven stared at the invisible shell of what might be the crashed UFO on Mount Equinox, jacket flapping in the wind. Akka stood at Raven's side and still looked weak. I watched him like a hawk.

"I don't know about you, Raven, but 'Inside the light, we are free' seems to corroborate our theory that the living beings of earth were broken down somehow into light and beamed inside the orbs. And now, everyone's just waiting to be set free."

I flipped back to the sketch of the whole orb with the symbol on its side. The last couple of times I looked at this sketch, I hadn't had a lot of time to really study it. But now, I saw something I hadn't noticed before. "Hey. What does it look like to you?" The golden orb with the geometric symbol hovered three-quarters above the base of the page. Not far underneath, my mom had faintly drawn what looked like a shelf with spaces to cradle two of the same-size orbs.

"Oh yeah. Weird." Raven held his hair out of his eyes and squinted closer. "And there's something in the bottom of the curved indents, too. I can't tell what the one on the right is, but the other one kind of looks like the geometric heart— Oh my God." We gaped at each other. "The symbols are hearts."

"Raven." I shoved my hands in my hair and paced. "We need to crack the orb open to free everyone. That's it. That's what the messages were trying to say. Holy crow." I stopped and tapped the page. "Maybe you have to put the orb into that indented curve in the table/shelf thing to unlock it? Because the only lyrics I remember from that Madonna song are about locks and keys. And it looks like if you put the orb into the cradle, the symbols would match up."

"Gah! Yes!" Raven's eyes went wide. "Maybe the orb is what's putting out that heartbeat signal and . . . Whoa, whoa, whoa. Maybe that other cradle thing is where the black orb from my dream needs to go?"

"Oh, that's good." I stroked my hair and grinned. "Things are coming together."

Raven's excitement suddenly fell flat. "Izzy, I really hope you're right."

We stepped out from under the trees and back onto the road. Raven put his wild mop into a ponytail and kept looking at me like he had something to say. But for a while, we just hiked, saying nothing at all.

Finally, Raven glanced at me and said, "Before we get up there, I need to tell you something." His lungs rattled with dust. His eyes burned like twin flames. "And I'm not sure you're going to like it."

CHAPTER 24

THE CONFESSION

I'D NEVER LIKED SURPRISES. MY BRAIN FROZE when unprepared. So when Raven said he had to tell me something I wasn't going to like, every word I knew slid off the edge of my mind. All I could do was keep hiking up Mount Equinox, worried about what Raven might say. But friends could tell each other anything. That's what friends were for. So when words finally came back to me, I nodded over at him and smiled. "Whatever you want to say, I'll listen like you did for me."

Raven's transistor radio squealed. The radio on my mom's Discman shrieked. Mountain stone crunched under our feet as Raven set guilty eyes on me. "I'm just going to say it, okay? I knew this alien apocalypse thing would happen just like your mom did. I'm sorry I didn't tell you sooner and I feel terrible, especially since your grandparents weren't honest either and I really do not want to make things worse, but—"

"What?" I froze again, confused. "What do you mean you knew? How could you know ahead of time unless . . . ?" I gaped at Raven, trying to process the only idea that made sense. "Were you . . . abducted? Did aliens take you like they did my mom?"

Akka stared up at Raven like he was waiting for answers, too. I wound my nervous fingers into his fur. All the while, the black dust blew.

Raven took a slow breath in and out. "No. But for the last few months I've been having these . . . dreams. About the invasion. About people and animals going missing. About the uglies. And . . ." Tears rimmed his eyes as he fought to get out his next words. "My nightmares came true."

I was too stunned to speak. I just kept shaking my head. Punching my leg. Pushing down the million feelings in me until my mouth figured out how to work. "So, you dreamed all this. You dreamed things and watched them come true months before they happened?"

Raven gave Akka a drink of water. "Yes."

I stared at the mountaintop, gulping back fresh panic. "You knew about the lights." Raven nodded at his boots. "Which means you knew the lights weren't biological weapons. Or our government starting some war, or any other thing we were brainstorming. You knew, without a doubt, the lights were UFOs?" When Raven hunched over and gave a small, sad nod, my pulse shot through the top of my head like a rocket. "Why would you pretend you didn't know? Why would you lie to me, Raven? I don't understand."

A black river of dust snaked the road through the red light. "Blackbird" played on the wind. "I'm sorry. I guess I didn't want to steal your hope of finding your family on the road—"

I held up my palm. "Stop." I tightened my sweater and looked him straight in the eye. "You knew we were the only ones here? All this time while I was leaving notes, you knew nobody would read them. You knew everyone was . . ." I wiped my eyes and nose, suddenly bleeding again. "My grams and pops, my sister. You knew they were gone?"

"Yes." I could barely hear him.

"I can't believe it." I pushed quicker up the mountain, shaking out my hands. Akka trotted after me, and Raven did the same. "So did you know where the UFO crashed ahead of time, too? What about where everyone went—do you know where they are? Do you know things about the aliens?" I turned to face him, walking backward as a shock of dread hit me. "Wait. Did you know about my mom? About her abduction. Her journal and CD and—" I coughed, choking on dust and fury and tears. "Raven. Did you know how she died?"

"No! I didn't know anything about your mom, I promise." He looked so tired but kept hiking on. "And I don't know where everyone is, or about the aliens. But, the other stuff, yeah." He tapped his walking stick on the pavement, hair blowing back in the wind. "That I knew."

"Really?" My heart kind of broke. "So first my grandparents lie to me. Then I find out my mom was lying. Now you, too?" I stormed ahead with Akka, leaving Raven in the dust. I knew Raven felt bad and he was trying to apologize. But I was mad. And sometimes when I got mad, it took a good while for my fire to go out.

Raven caught up. "I am so, so sorry. I never meant to make you feel that way."

"But if you'd have just told me about your dreams, I would've believed you. Maybe if you'd have told me, it would've helped me believe all the stuff my mom went through. And all my own visions and psychic links to her, too. Because since all this, I doubted if what I was seeing was true. I doubted myself. And, for a while, I doubted what my mom went through, too."

"I know." Raven leaned against a tall pine, head hung and catching his breath. I felt his regret three feet away. "I didn't know what to do. I was so scared because . . . I doubted my mind, too."

I was still hurt he lied, but I got it. None of us were perfect, and fear can do a lot of dumb things. Like hiding valuable information in your mom's journal from a friend. I wasn't okay with him lying to me. But these were not normal times. And if I'd been having those dreams, who knows what I'd do. "It's okay. I kept my mom's story from you at first, too. And at least you finally told me the truth. But Raven? Did you see the same things my mom drew? Or did your dreams also have new information?" After another coughing fit, I started back up the mountain. Raven followed. "Blackbird" played on a loop under the whine of our radios.

We were almost to the top.

"The dreams were so evil—but so, so real." Raven rubbed his chipped-nail-polished hands over his dust-streaked face. "Every night for months, the dreams were always the same. UFOs came in a blaze of lights to obliterate life on earth. I saw my family taken into the lights—my mom, dogs, even my dad three towns away, and I saw myself get left behind. I saw clues, I guess? Road signs. Song lyrics. The same sort of things your mom drew. I even saw the farmhouse we stayed in." I gasped. "I know. I even knew the uglies were going to get me. Except . . . the dream never showed me if I'd survive."

"Raven! If you'd have just told me that, I could've helped you."

Raven shook his head. When he tripped over rubble, I caught him before he fell. "Thanks. I guess I just didn't want to put you and Akka in any extra danger." He snuck a peek at me. "I even heard some of the songs on your mom's playlist in my dream. And I saw Akka and you."

I gasped. "You saw me? Is that how you found me the day Bob crashed? Did you know I'd be there?"

"I didn't see that happen exactly, but I was following a song on the wind. And it kind of led me to you."

"'Blackbird.'"

"Yeah. Like my pin. My mom used to sing me that song before bed. She still calls me her 'little blackbird' and named me Raven because she loved that song so much."

I smiled sad. "My mom, then my grams and pops, used to sing that song to me and my sister, too. I still wish you would've told me. My mom, she kept everything she was going through from me." We passed a clearing. I twisted my hands until they hurt.

"I'm sorry." Raven wiped his bloody nose. "Like your mom said, whenever I told anyone about my dream, nobody believed it could actually happen. I don't even think my mom believed me. Some of my friends even called me crazy. And sometimes, I thought they were right."

"That's awful."

"Yeah." He smiled at me through his hair. "But I cut those losers loose after that, so whatever. I'm better off without them."

In a moment of daring, I placed my hand over his. And he let me. For a second, we just stood there, two kids on a mountain covered in alien dust, listening to the Beatles play, holding hands at the end of the world. And it was nice.

Too nice to last.

Akka shot up howling, staring into the trees. An electrical storm churned over Mount Equinox, getting more intense all the time. My amethyst heated so hot and quick, it turned from purple to red and burned my sweater in seconds.

Raven and I looked at each other. "Uglies."

I wrestled the necklace off my body and tied it around the base of my flashlight, letting the burning stone dangle in the air. A gray ugly chittered a call somewhere ahead. Another screamed back like the biggest cicada on earth.

The mountain trembled. Akka growled through his mask, and I couldn't get him to hush.

Then one of our two flashlights died.

"Oh, that's unfortunate." Raven checked the spare in his pocket, but it was dead, too. Only mine worked. And who knew how long it would last.

"Okay, that's okay." I pushed my hair off my face. "One is enough to cover us, and we have the radio."

Raven smiled and nodded but looked scared to his socks. Truth be told, I was, too.

Our earplugs had been sucked into the earth with Bob. I turned the transistor's volume to medium anyway to keep the monsters away. "Blackbird" crackled through the feedback like a beacon of hope. The uglies shrieked in response to the feedback; but somehow, we were getting used to the sound.

The Mount Equinox parking lot only minutes away, Raven and I had just paused to rest when Akka growled at the sky.

"Uh, Raven?" I tightened up on Akka's leash and pointed straight up. "We've got company."

An unlit UFO, three times as big as the others,

hung motionless over Mount Equinox.

"Holy—" Raven mouthed the rest. "Another ship."

I knelt beside Akka and petted him as he snarled. "Did you know this ship would be here, too?"

Raven looked hurt. "No. This wasn't in my dreams. I'd have remembered this thing. Because wow. That UFO is . . ."

"As wide as the entire mountain."

Raven coughed into his elbow. "Do you think it's here to rescue the crashed UFO?"

Akka pressed his body to mine. "I don't know. But we need to get out of sight."

"Yeah." Raven peered up at the ship. "Before it beams us into its lights."

Another flash of lightning hit above the motionless spaceship. The amethyst hanging from my flashlight burned even hotter, too. I wondered if we were being followed by uglies, and why they hadn't made a move. Or maybe it was the ship hovering over the mountain, or the crashed UFO heating my purple crystal. In the back of my mind, I wondered if the aliens knew we were here. And if they did, what was their next move.

We hiked another few minutes, bone-tired and coughing dust. Then, just like that, the mountain road ended and the parking lot of the visitors center appeared.

The three of us stumbled forward, Akka in the lead, me and Raven shaking our heads.

We made it to the top of Mount Equinox alive.

We pushed across the parking lot, our last red flashlight and the crescent moon our only sources of light. The whole vibe up here felt wrong. Wicked. Like we weren't welcome here. "Raven, does the air seem thicker up here to you?"

Raven nodded into the gale of dust. "Right? It's like the atmosphere has weight."

"Yeah. And it smells weird. Like wet firepits and coins and—" I pushed hair off my face; it blew right back. "Static. Our hair is full of static." I ponytailed my mess of curls before my mop drove me wild.

Raven's hair refused to stay down. He eventually pulled up his hood.

"Blackbird" sang louder. The heartbeat signal pounded stronger. And every step we took across the lot, toward the area where we'd glimpsed the crashed UFO, the harder it was to move.

"Why is it so hard to walk?" Raven shielded his eyes. "It's like a force field is pushing us back."

A force field. "You're right. A force field of energy meant to keep us away."

Feedback squealed louder through the transistor toward the end of the lot. Something glinted through the dust cloud ahead where the visitors center should be. I shielded my eyes from dust. "Is that . . . the visitors center?"

Raven squinted into the wind. "If it is, the entire top half of the building has been sliced off. And look." He pointed. "The radio towers behind it are bent sideways."

The tree radio spires that once stood like small, green Eiffel Towers by the mountain's trailhead were curved against the mountain stone at ninety-degree angles.

"The radio towers. Holy crow, Raven. The Mount Equinox radio station is 95.1. 95.1. The number my mom wrote in her journal. And 'Blackbird.' It's been playing louder since we got to the top." Did the radio towers have something to do with how to find everyone missing and bring them home? Could the energy of this force field have something to do with the gold and black orbs? And why were the radio towers and visitors center mowed down?

"Maybe 95.1 has been playing 'Blackbird' on a loop since the UFOs came."

"But how could it play anything after all the power went out?"

We struggled toward the radio station, slow as turtles through sand. When we got there, we found the little green radio station had been sliced in half, too. Stranger still, as soon as we got there, the music stopped.

"Whoa. That's . . . creepy."

Everything went dead still. And then, over the oppressive stench of the mountain and bleached stink of the dust, a wisp of orange perfume blew by.

Mom.

"My mom wrote that 'Blackbird' was playing on her radio the first time she was abducted." I clenched my fists and held Raven's stare. "Maybe 'Blackbird' was my mom's way of leading us here. It brought you to me. Maybe it'll lead us to our families, too."

"How do you think it was playing all this time?" Raven asked, bending to pet my dog.

I thought of my mom. "Because love is the most powerful force of all."

Raven grinned sweet behind his mask. "Cheeseball."

"And proud." A long, dark cloud shifted past the mother ship above us. When it moved, I swore a light flashed on in the ship. "Come on." I grabbed Raven's sleeve. "Let's find the crashed UFO before the Death Star gets us."

"The what now?"

I sighed. "Never mind."

As the three of us huffed and puffed past desks, chairs, and scattered equipment from the buildings sliced in half, it hit me. "Raven. You know what would do a good job of leveling buildings and steel towers?"

Raven thought about it for a second, then covered his mask with his hands. "Oh my God. A crashing UFO."

CHAPTER 25

FOUND

WHEN ME AND MAPLE WERE LITTLE, POPS USED TO read us a fairy tale about a firefly and a bear. "Before the birth of our sun, fireflies lit the earth. But they got so tired lighting the world, eventually, their lights burned out, and they fell into a deep sleep. It took years for fireflies to regrow their fire. And during this dark time, a single bear grew. When the bear saw the sleeping fireflies, it folded them into its fur, carried them to the beach at earth's edge. It said, 'Drink the starlight on the water, then wake and relight the night. And if you're too weary to shine, I will carry you home.' The fireflies drank and shined until their light was spent. Again, the bear carried them to the sea. Until finally, the fireflies shone so bright, they never ran out of flame." I'd heard that story a million times. But I'd never felt as drained as those fireflies until Raven, Akka, and me pushed across the peak of Mount Equinox and the alien force field pushed back.

The three of us trudged past the destroyed radio station to where the forest should be. But like the decapitated buildings, the trees had been flattened and burned. Dust whirled like a hurricane over the dead land and squinted ahead. And there, just like we thought, a runway of flat, fried trees led all the way to the far cliff. Like an arrow pointing to the crashed UFO.

Raven stepped over a snapped pine branch. "So. We just follow this runway, and that whole *heartbeat in the mountain pulse*, which is probably from the UFO like you said earlier. And"—he wiped a trickle of blood from his nose—"drag our poor, broken bodies through this horrendous alien force field, until we hit a UFO. No problem."

"Yup." I checked Akka to make sure he was good. He looked worn out, but from the way he jumped at dead leaves and wagged his tail, I couldn't help smiling with hope.

"Well, what are we waiting for? Let's show these alien turds what we earth kids can do."

"Bark!"

"Sorry, Akka." Raven scratched Akka's chin. "What earth kids and a *dog* can do."

Raven, Akka, and I pushed forward against the wall of energy. We trudged through drifts of dust and charred trees, using all the strength we had, not saying a word. I thought about where Grams, Pops, Maple, and Nora were now. And about how my mom died. How my mom led us here with music and clues. How, if I let my thoughts go quiet, I could feel my family around me. Then all of a sudden, this big wave of love rolled through me like a new feeling all its own. And when I put my hand over my heart, I swear, I heard them say:

We're with you, Izzy, and we won't ever leave your side.

I warmed inside the cold wind and mind-whispered back, *I'm with you all, too. And like the bear did for the fireflies, I swear to bring you home.*

The farther we hiked the broken runway, the more intense the force field and pulse became. Our radios shrieked and sparked the farther we went up the burned-tree trail, even after we'd turned them off. We'd just pushed around a broken pine big as a house when "Purple Rain" by Prince crackled through my mom's Discman—from the radio, not her CD. *Purple means something*, I thought, right before the music abruptly shut off. In the quiet, I could've sworn I heard Grams whisper my name. I covered my face in a rush of hot tears.

That was my grams's favorite song.

All of a sudden, the energy field before us got so thick, we could barely move. Our radios whirred. Thunder rumbled in the distance. Akka stopped and growled, hackles raised, teeth bared directly ahead. "Akka? What's—"

Lightning flashed. When it did, a bubble of space shimmered before us, five feet away. Black dust swirled around the shimmer, but not through it. Like something big and invisible was blocking its way. When the lightning stopped, the shimmer of space in front of us vanished.

I gasped and shone my flashlight at Raven. "You saw that, right?"

"Oh yeah, I did." Raven cocked his head and squinted at the space before us. Without the lightning, you couldn't see anything at all. Raven held out his hand and took one more step. "Izzy. I think we found the crashed UF—"

BOOM.

A force of energy blew us back. Our radios screamed feedback at ten million decibels. We skidded across the ground, speakers blowing sparks. Something hard struck my head. Next thing I knew, Raven was dragging me away from the force field. Akka was trying to lick me through his mask. And a new song started to play, "Song thirteen of Annie's Alt. Mix, 'Everybody Wants to Rule the World,' by Tears for Fears." My mom's voice wailed over the chaos: "Blood p . . m . . . Listen to . . . bridge . . ."

When the music played, the feedback stopped.

Raven knelt over me, holding Akka close. "Are you okay?" I barely heard him over the ringing in my ears and music playing from the Discman. "I think you hit your head." He helped me up. "That's becoming a bad habit of yours." Raven smiled through pain, hair all in his banged-up, dusty face.

"Yeah." I blushed. "Thanks. I'll try not to let it happen again but am not promising anything." I checked Akka over, making sure he wasn't hurt. I sure was lucky to have the strongest dog in the world.

"Hey, check it out." Raven pointed to his pocket. The inside glowed red. "My flashlight works again. And yours is . . . Wow. Look how bright yours is."

"Maybe that blast-back recharged our batteries."

I shone the infrared light at the invisible force field on a hunch. *(Everybody wants to rule the world . . .)* And there it was. The object we weren't even sure existed until a few minutes ago. "Whoa. Whoa. Whoa." Raven got up slow and punched his fists high. "Izzy!"

If I were a cartoon, my pupils would be exclamation points right now. "Raven. I *definitely* think we found the UFO."

A humongous black spaceship emerged through the red mist like a ghost ship at the base of the sea. It was oval, almost round, and jagged at the edges like a meteor. The air surrounding it pulsed with the UFO's heartbeat.

"It's really here." Raven hopped on his walking stick, favoring his right leg, a frenzied look in his eye. "It's just like the ones in my dreams."

We shone our infrared lights inside the force field. I moved closer to the wall of energy separating us from the ship. The closer we got, the brighter our flashlights flared. The louder the music from the Discman played. And the more I worried about the mother ship beaming us up or striking us down. But my mom's amethyst, still dangling from my flashlight's base, had suddenly turned ice cold.

Akka kept a careful distance from the force field as we skirted the dark ship. The UFO was so massive, it hung off the side of the mountain at a thirty-degree angle, tipped up by outcroppings of stone. Nine rings of unlit lights, kind of like the rings on a record, ran between the UFO's rim and center. The outside of the craft was jagged and rough as crystal or stone and carved with markings I didn't recognize. A large, black space in the center of the craft resembled an eye—the place Darklights shone through and snatched people away. Hatchlike doors circled the bottom section of the craft. The way the ship was angled, we could see only two and a half doors. More alien symbols marked the doors, different ones on each. One of the symbols matched the one my mom sketched on the gold orb she'd labeled: They were guarding this.

I mentally crossed my fingers the orb, or orbs, were inside.

This UFO looked identical to my mom's drawings. Was this the one that took her? The one that took Grams, Pops, and Maple and everyone else, too?

Almost to the edge of the eastern cliff, Raven paused, shining his flashlight through the invisible shield. "See that hatch?" He pointed to the large sliding door just behind the barrier shield. His nose trickled blood. I nodded. "Okay. So that side panel beside the hatch? I saw a movie once. I wanna say *Star Trek*? Something about a whale . . . ? I don't know. Maybe it wasn't *Star Trek*. Anyway, they had these hatches that open by touch. Like a key." He looked at me. "We need to find a key to get into this thing."

Wait. "A key. Like the key in the R.E.M. song you had in your head before. And a key like the lyrics in 'Open Your Heart,' by Madonna."

As soon as I said that, a whiff of orange blew past, a full-body chill blew over me, and the Discman's radio and the transistor blasted "I Believe," by R.E.M.

Mom.

Raven rubbed his arms. "I have goose bumps."

Akka grinned and wagged his tail at the space between us.

"Me, too." My nose tickled, bleeding again. I pinched the bridge of my nose to stop it and—oh Han's hair. "Raven! The bridge . . . the song before R.E.M.—'Everybody Wants to Rule the World.' Do you remember the lyrics? About the room where light can't get in?"

He'd gone back to studying the hatch, keeping a careful distance away. "Yeaaah. Does that have to do with finding the key to this door, because I could really use—"

"No. But if I don't get what I just thought of out, I'll forget. Sorry. Anyway, there was interference when my mom introduced 'Everybody Wants to Rule the World,' but I think she said *blood poem*. Not sure what she meant. But then I'm pretty sure she said *Listen to the bridge*. And those lyrics about the room where the light can't get in were in the bridge of the song."

Raven swung his gaze onto me. "Yesss. The bridge. Of the song." He paced the curve of the force field. "Yes. The room where light can't get in and then it's like . . . lalala . . . holding hands as walls fall around us, but when they fall, someone will be right behind you."

My mom's CD suddenly jumped ahead to the middle of the next song, like it was on ghost shuffle. This time it played "Learning to Fly," by Pink Floyd. It reminded me of the mother ship above us, and my mom and her abduction, and—

"Wait." I swung and faced Raven. "Maybe there's a room in the UFO we need to find where the light can't get in. Maybe the answer to finding our families is in the room." I tapped my thigh. "Maybe the orbs are in that room."

Raven leaned on his stick and pointed at me. "That makes sense. And maybe the part about the bridge has a double meaning. Because our noses keep bleeding, too. But before we can find the room, we need to get into the UFO fir—"

"A double meaning!" I pinched my bloody nose. "Like the bridge of the song and bridge of the nose!

That's good, Raven. But what about the blood poem part? What do you think that means?"

Raven acted like I hadn't interrupted him and just smiled. "Actually, I think she said *blood palm*, not *blood poem*. Like in your mom's journal."

I gasped. "Yes!" I pulled out my mom's journal and turned to the red palm print. I never noticed the background before, but teeny-tiny doodles of rectangles and keys circled the red palm. Rectangles that looked like doors. And a palm print red as blood. "Okay, so what would a bloody palm print, a bridge, and a room where light can't get in have in common?"

"The doors, too. Maybe this all has to do with breaking the invisibility shield?" Raven tapped the sketch. "The page's background is the same purple as your amethyst. Do you think that means something?"

The amethyst.

Purple means something.

My mind spun with clues, trying to put things together at warp speed. Then an idea stopped me in my tracks. "When we were at the library reading about amethysts, do you remember what it said? How they have properties that interfere with force fields and magnets?"

"I do, actually. And look." He pointed to my

amethyst. "Your amethyst is glowing. And the air around it is really cold."

My amethyst glowed in cool lilac and was frosty as winter snow. When I touched it, the music shut off, and the feedback wailed at ten billion decibels.

Raven screamed, *"Shut it off!"* I read his lips over the noise and let go of the amethyst. When I did, the feedback died and the music returned. Raven shook his head like it was filled with bees. "What was that?"

Akka cried and hid behind my legs. I scooped him into a hug. "Something about the energy of the UFO, combined with the radio waves from the radio station, the amethyst, and I don't know, the ley lines under the mountain, and maybe even the energy of my mom's ghost, are affecting the force field around the UFO." I wasn't sure yet what the red palm print meant, but the closer the amethyst came to the force field, the brighter it shone and the wilder the electronics went. "Hold up. What if the amethyst can disrupt the energy of the force field?"

Raven stopped pacing and threw out his arms. "Oh my God, yes." Then he started pacing again. "And maybe all those other things, the ley lines and radio waves and UFO vibes from space or whatever, are magnifying the crystal's power. I mean, if it works on

TV and in movies, why can't it work in real life, am I right?" Akka jumped up on me and barked. "See? Akka agrees. Let's try putting your amethyst into the force field. See if your mom's crystal can disrupt the energy and break the barrier down."

"Yes! Okay." I slipped my necklace off the flashlight and folded it into my fist; the crystal was ice cold. "On the count of three, I'll try to push the stone into the energy field and see what happens. If I get blasted backwards, will you—"

"Yup. Me and Akka here won't let you fall." He smiled so sweetly, I almost hugged him. But this wasn't the hugging time. "Let's count you down, Izzy."

"Okay, three, two, one!"

I shoved my hand and the crystal through the invisibility shield. This time, it slipped right through.

A golden shine radiated outward from the crystal. The force field lit up in lilac-gold light. The radios screamed louder than a horde of banshees. The heartbeat hum bump-bumped, bump-bumped, bump-bumped so strong, I swear I felt my molecules ripping apart. And right before my mom's amethyst shattered to dust in my palm, "Blackbird" played through our radios, and the invisibility shield blinked out.

And the UFO appeared, unhidden to the human world.

CHAPTER 26
INSIDE

ONE OF MY FAVORITE AUTHORS ONCE WROTE THAT if you dug to the bottom of hope, it would lead straight back to fear. That fear was the door you needed to open to release all the shiny magic waiting on the other side. And now, as I stood alongside my best boy and new friend, at the base of a UFO that might've beamed up my family and definitely crashed to earth, I knew he was right. No matter how afraid I was, or what we might find. We needed to open the door and get to the other side.

Red flashlight aimed at the crashed UFO, I shook out of my shock and hugged Raven like a force. "We did it!"

"We did it, and . . ." Raven pulled away slowly and

stared at the UFO. "My lungs. Do you feel that? The air. It's almost . . ."

"Clean."

A colorful mist drifted around us and the tilted craft. Some kind of force must've still emanated from the UFO. Because as hard as the wind blew, no black dust came within five feet of its exterior. Inside this cushion of space, the air didn't stink either.

"And our radios are quiet." Raven's voice was loud in the hush. "No more feedback."

"Yeah. It's like there's no sound anywhere at all."

For the first time in a long while, we took off our masks. The air tasted so sweet in my fried throat, I cried with joy. Raven smiled at me, doing the same thing. Akka didn't cry but sniffed the clean earth with wild abandon, because for once, I wasn't telling him no. For a few minutes, the three of us just breathed and shook our heads at the reality of what lay before us.

The crashed UFO.

Side by side, we studied the spaceship. Half the craft jutted off the cliff's edge like it could slip off at any moment. The inside remained dark, no lights in or out. Without the invisibility shield, the heartbeat we felt was gone. But the closer we got to the UFO, the brighter our flashlights grew and the more energy we seemed to have. Like the UFO was a battery and we were charging up. Metallic windows lined the rim, but we couldn't see inside. I kept glancing at the spaceship above us, thinking it might turn on once the shield was down. Certain it had been searching for the crashed UFO, too. But the mother ship stayed dark and silent, which was even creepier.

We returned to the hatch Raven found earlier and inspected the panel alongside. I looked closer as Akka sniffed the base. "There's a symbol on the panel." Raven leaned in close. "I don't remember one like it from my mom's journal, do you?"

"Uh-uh." Raven fixed his ponytail and seemed refreshed. Honestly, I did, too. "I didn't dream it either. I wonder what it means?"

"Hmm." A picture of the red palm print in my mom's journal flashed in my head. Red palms. I glanced at my hands. My nose had stopped bleeding, but my palms were still slicked in blood. A bolt of revelation struck. "Raven? I think I might know how to get into this ship."

Raven had been watching me. He stared at our bloodied hands and gasped. "Are you thinking what I'm thinking?" He nudged his chin at the panel.

"I don't know." Akka panted and wagged like, *Yes, this all sounds very good to me also.* "Let's find out."

Before I let nerves stop me, I pressed my palm to the panel. A surge of power shook through me. My mom's Discman whistled and sparked, and the door hissed open.

"Ahh!" I shouted too loud, and clamped my lips shut. White light poured out from the UFO. Mist rolled down the ramp to our feet.

Raven did a happy dance. "It worked!" He laughed. "I mean, I never doubted you. But this is . . ." His happy vibe suddenly vanished. "I'm nervous." He stared up the ramp, to the bright light inside. "About what we might find—and who we might find or not find inside."

All was quiet in the UFO. Too quiet.

"I know. I'm scared and nervous, too." Akka, on the other hand, clip-clopped up the ramp like he lived here. I gently coaxed him back and stood with Raven. "But I'm with you. And Akka's with you, too." Akka pawed his leg and worfed. "See? We can do this together." I smiled right at him and took his hand. "We are not alone."

When we turned back to the light, I closed my eyes and swore I saw my mom standing beside me. Cheering us on. Then Grams, Pops, Maple, and Nora were there, too. I felt them. Guiding us. Calling to us from inside the ship like they knew we could bring them home.

Behind us, familiar screams echoed from the valley. Raven spun toward their cries. "The uglies are back."

"Bork-bork-bork-bork!" Akka sprang to the end of his leash.

I grabbed Pops's bowie, shone my flashlight over us, and wrestled Akka to me. "You ready to go inside this UFO before we're some ugly's McHuman-McDoggo combo?"

Raven nodded. But his nod was heavy with fear. "Ready as ever. After you."

We'd only just stepped onto the ramp when the mountains erupted with shrieks. Gray uglies flew over the edge of Mount Equinox, heading our way.

Akka lunged away from the ship, back down the ramp. Three baby uglies galloped toward us out of the dust. I pushed past Raven and Akka, swinging my blade at the base of the ramp.

"Feedback incoming. Heads up!" Raven warned behind me before blasting his transistor to high. The pain of sound came like knives in my ears, eyes, and brain. The feedback screamed louder than ever. A giant tentacle flew at my legs a second before the noise blew the uglies away. Raven extended his hand from the top of the ramp and shouted, "Come on!"

I clasped his hand and dragged a borking Akka

back up the ramp. We were almost to the top when a hmm-mmm-MMMMMMM vibration knocked us down. Raven slid to the base of the ramp. Akka skidded toward Raven. I only had time to grab Akka's collar before the massive spaceship hanging over Mount Equinox came alive.

A megawatt spotlight beamed down and drenched the mountain in gold. Wind kicked up and raged. Feedback from the radios increased, shrieking in a vortex of sound. I crouched in the shadows with Akka at the top of the ramp, still gripping Raven's hand. I tried to pull him toward me, boots skidding on the slick metal. But Raven was frozen inside the gold light.

Then the lights lifted Raven off the ground.

"Raven!" I gripped his hand with all my power and tried dragging Raven down, but the beam was too strong. Akka barked and cried. Raven's eyes were on me, his face stuck in a scream from the sound, and I didn't know what to do. But then, clear as day, I heard Pops say, *You know why your watches break, Izzy? Because the power you hold is greater than any device. You are a force all your own.* Chills poured over me, and right then, I knew he was right.

I am a force, we all are. And I won't let anything stop me.

I pulled against the alien beam, dragging Raven down, refusing to let him slip away. Just when I thought I couldn't hold on any longer, the light beam flickered. I yelled a battle cry and yanked my friend free. The mother ship beam shut off. And Raven crashed to the ground.

"Raven!" I shouted over the noise. "Talk to me." I patted his cheek.

"Hey." He gazed at me with all the love in the galaxy, and I smiled back the same.

"Hey, yourself. Welcome back." I pulled him up and grabbed his walking stick, while Akka smooched him up good. "Now let's get the heck outta here before the lights come back."

Gray uglies galloped toward the UFO. None made it past the barrier of sound. Raven, Akka, and I didn't miss a beat. We stumbled up the glowing ramp and through the UFO's door.

The second we got through the hatch, the door whooshed shut. Uglies rushed the door after it closed. A limb severed in the closing hatch as white lights flicked on in the UFO. The limb sparked, twitched, then died. We were safe. But I had a feeling uglies were out there, gathering in the dust, no red light, force field, or feedback to keep them away.

But I couldn't worry about them now.

Every noise from outside cut off when the door closed. Soft white lights lit the floor. Long windows circled half of the giant round room. The way the craft was tilted, our only view was the valley beneath us and spaceship above us, staring down like a big black eye. The room silenced to the shushing of air through vents. And the huffing and puffing of us trying to breathe. The room's air seemed wrong. Dense. We wouldn't last in here long.

Raven raised his head to me, hands on his knees, struggling for breath. "You. Izzy. We just . . ." He leaned on his walking stick. "You pulled me back. From being taken. Can I"—he held out his arms— "hug you?" I grinned and let him crash into me. Akka jumped up for hugs, too. "Thank you." Raven let go, eyes on me.

I lit up like Bob's holiday lights. "Anytime."

We gaped around the vacant room. Akka sniffed the floor and stayed glued to my side. Strange clothing and drawers lined the walls. The ceiling was domed and circled with windows. Triangular segments, each marked with a different symbol, were carved into the metallic black floor. The same types of symbols marking the outside of the ship. The floor's surface shone like hematite, one of the many crystals dotting Maple's room. My pulse sped thinking of her. She should be at home now, tucked up safe in bed. I was so desperate to see her, I could scream.

Everything was in disarray from the crash. Akka's nails tip-tapped the floor as he fought to keep steady. We had a hard time walking due to the sharp angle of the UFO.

I came up beside Raven and focused on one of the vents. "What do you think's coming through here?" he asked, scratching his throat. "My lungs weigh about a thousand pounds."

I extended my neck, breathing deep. "I don't know. But whatever it is, it's not meant for us to breathe."

Raven pushed a button on the wall. A storage hatch opened fast, and a bunch of three-fingered gloves shot out. "Ugh. Alien fashion is . . . just straight-up nonsense." He held one up, twice the size of his hand. "Three fingers. Like lizards. Not like the uglies at all." He cringed and dropped the gloves on the ground. "I wonder where crew *alien Godzilla* is now?"

I coughed. Every second here made me dizzier. "Good question." I eyeballed the tall door at the opposite end of the room. A panel similar to the one outside hung beside it. "I hope that door leads to the rest of the ship because this room is so empty." I picked the dust from my nails and paced. "Maybe the hatch we came in wasn't the main door . . . Maybe we should . . ." Raven started sifting through strewn debris, casting odd, and potentially dangerous, items aside. One device shaped like a trident cracked in half and exploded when it hit the wall. Akka yipped and jumped. He looked like he was fighting for breath, too. "As I was saying. We should make a plan before exploring the whole ship. Make sure we're on the same page. That we're careful." I eyed the cracked trident, now smoking green. "And focused on finding the orbs."

"Right. Sorry about the exploding alien artifact thing." The room stank like rotting meat. "This ship is huge. If we're going to find the orbs, we should check the journal. Make sure we didn't miss anything crucial in the *Ghost Mom, Izzy, Akka, and Raven Save the Earth Plan.*"

I nodded. "Okay." I leaned against the side wall, pulled out the journal, and went straight for the sketch of the orb. "Let's go over what we know about the orbs." I shone my flashlight on the page and tapped the shapes of people and animals my mom had sketched in invisible ink. "The gold orb is what my mom saw in the ship when she was abducted—the one the aliens were guarding. And the black orb is the one from your vision."

Raven's eyes went wide. "Yeah. And we decided the orbs are like arcs or something. The gold one beams people up—like what those alien losers just tried to do to me. And the black one might beam matter back down—like they did the gray uglies."

"Exactly. And here." I pointed at the faint sketch my mom drew of two curved indentations the right size to cradle two orbs. "We need to look for the orbs and their matching cradles, too. Then click the orbs into place and . . ."

"Our families are magically released from the balls and back to earth—oh my God, this all sounds so . . ." Raven rubbed his face. "It sounds so Pokémon. But like . . . if Ash Ketchum can hold all those massive Pokémon in poké balls, chances are good aliens can pull that sort of tech off, right? I mean, look at this spaceship. If we were this smart, we'd all have one, right?"

I sighed. Me and Maple loved Pokémon. And maybe, hopefully, if we could figure out how to save them, I'd get my butt handed to me in a game by Maple again soon. "I can't argue with that. And if our theory's true, aliens would've beamed them into the orbs seconds before the ship crashed." I blinked at Raven, dizzy spots in my eyes. "Then that means the orbs are still here."

I held my knuckles out to Raven for a slow fist bump. He grinned and coughed and bumped back. "And we'll find them. Together."

We climbed the incline of the tilted UFO to the door at the end of the room. Akka scratched the exit and growled like, *Izzy, there is danger in there and we need to eat it, please.*

Raven leaned on the wall beside the panel. "What if there's aliens still alive in there?"

I twisted my hair, thinking of my family. "Then I feel sorry for them because we're not leaving without info about our families, or our families themselves."

There was no more time to waste.

I pressed my palm to the panel to open the door, like last time. But it wouldn't open. The blood on my palm was dried. Maybe it needed fresh blood. So, as nasty as it was, I wiped my slightly bloody nose, slicked my hand, and tried again. But no luck.

"I don't under—"

Out of nowhere, the UFO lurched sideways. Drawers shot out of the wall. I stumbled and fell. Raven grabbed a space where the drawer had been and hung on. I crawled up the ever-tilting floor, holding Akka's collar. All around us, sparks burst from the walls.

Outside, gray uglies pounded the UFO.

The UFO slipped another few degrees. Five uglies stared through the windows circling the ship. But that wasn't all.

"Umm, Izzy. There are a few more spaceships"—Raven coughed—"out there. Small ones. Under the mother ship." Sure enough, smaller crafts had joined the party at the end of the world. Small and round, they glowed with bright, spinning lights overhead.

The room dappled with a disco-ball shine. The gray uglies fought like hyenas over a kill—and we were the kill. They stabbed the domed glass again and again. The UFO slipped even more, and we screamed.

Raven and I tried to grab hands, but he slid too far away. I dragged Akka to me by the leash and scooped him up before the glass dome broke. A flood of baby uglies dropped to the floor like spiders, too fast to stop.

CHAPTER 27

FREE

BABY UGLIES DROPPED INTO THE UFO. THEY CAME at us, red eyes and sharp teeth. One wrapped my wrist and pulled me toward the shattered dome. But I refused to have my life and hopes of finding my family stolen by monsters from space. So, I imagined myself all battle goddess and blood who needed to fight for my life and everyone I loved. Time sped up real quick when I realized I didn't have to imagine myself as a monster-slaying warrior. I already was one.

I slid my knife from my scabbard and struck the ugly's limb until it let go. I dropped to the floor beside where Raven and Akka were under attack. Raven knocked them back with his stick. More fell from the dome. I shouted to Raven, "Radios?"

Raven nodded.

We flipped our radios on high, unprepared for the blast-back of sound. Feedback wailed sharp and violent. My eardrums pulled and stretched and stabbed like they'd burst. I could barely breathe, but the baby uglies had it worse. Their bodies trembled. Their limbs contorted and flailed. Their mouths unhinged and fell open in terrified screams. And as their ugly parents pounded the roof and scrambled down the side of the craft, the baby uglies shook so hard and fast they all exploded at once. Black goo splattered the walls. The floors. Us.

Before we could process what happened, the UFO shifted and lurched forward. We slipped in alien goo, dropped to our butts, and skidded across the floor. I landed in a pile of alien gloves at the ship's edge.

Stumbling to my feet, I glimpsed the panel by the exit hatch. A symbol in its center flashed gold—the same symbol I'd just seen on the three-fingered gloves. The gloves were a key, too. "Raven, I have an idea!" I grabbed Raven and Akka, and we hurried toward the exit door.

When I put the glove on and pressed it to the panel, the symbols locked into place. The door hissed open. Red light poured out. And the rotten-meat stench we smelled earlier was so strong, it almost knocked us down. We pushed inside—Raven holding his nose and me holding a glove—and the hatch hissed shut behind us.

This ceiling was flat, but circular like the last. Infrared lights snaked the roof in a grid. A band of windows wrapped three-quarters of the room. Benches rimmed the curved walls. We turned our radios to low and scanned the red-lit room. No chairs. No bridge. Just hatches on walls with vials inside. The empty vials gave me the creeps. Vents hissed in this room, too, but the air in here was fresh. Like the air pushing through was oxygen.

Out the windows, a fleet of UFOs and the mother ship cluttered the sky. To my surprise, the skies were dusted mauve. It was almost dawn.

Akka had a hard time walking but scrabbled up the tilted floor. After we'd checked for danger, Raven sidled next to me. "Izzy, this is it. The round red room from my dream."

"The vision where you were holding a black orb?"

"Yeah." He nodded, wiping blood from a cut on his neck.

"Weird how the air seems made for humans, too."

Raven nodded. "Yup. And look what I found on the floor." He held up a Nike jacket. "At some point, there were people on this UFO. This room was probably built to hold humans."

I coughed and almost choked. My mom might've been in this very room.

A panel with a glowing symbol like the last edged the doors. Raven approached it, holding his nose. "Good thing you brought that ugly glove."

I nodded, cringing at the stink. "Maybe. Let's see if it works." I took a deep breath through my mouth and clicked the symbols together. The doors hissed open without drama, which was nice for once. Except right away, the stink grew worse.

A small room, a third as big as the last, spread out in pale blue light. A shimmering gold circle rimmed the center of the room, like maybe it was a hatch, too. Two enormous captain's chairs faced equally huge windows and a thick panel of dashboard-like screens. The screens lit in every color of the rainbow, showing what looked like star maps and constellations. We could just see the spaceships haunting the lilac dawn sky. The mother ship remained dark. Like they were waiting for something, but I didn't know what.

I clamped my nose. "Raven. I think this is the cockpit."

Raven approached the captain's chairs and gagged.

"Oh. Wow. Umm, you might want to look at this." Akka burst out of my grip, galloped toward Raven, and sniffed whatever sat in the chairs. "I guess those two explain the smell."

Raven swiveled one of the chairs toward me and I jumped back, hand over my mouth, scared near to death. Two giant beings slumped motionless in the seats, still strapped in. "Dead aliens." They were horrible. Almost human, but not. Skin the color of arctic ice. Dark liquid crusted their ears and noses, three long fingers on each hand. Retching at the stench, I checked to see if they were breathing. They weren't. Akka sniffed the ugly giants so hard, I had to pull him across the room.

"Hey." Raven waved me toward the bridge. I swallowed past the stink. "Look at this." A hatch with two curved indentations sat between the captain's seats. Indentations the perfect size to fit two baseball-like orbs. "Maybe the orbs really are here."

"Raven!" I shook him a little. "Yes!" We sifted through debris for anything resembling orbs. Akka growled his way back to the aliens, sniffing them good. I pulled him away, wondering why they didn't make Akka afraid.

"Ohh, wait. This is the bridge. Right?" Raven scanned the screens of constellations I'd never seen before in my life. "That's what they call it in *Star Wars*?"

"Yeah." I bit my nails and dropped my hand when it hit me. "Wait. The *bridge*."

"Mm-hmm." Raven rubbed his hands together. "Like in the song."

"'Everybody Wants to Rule the World.'"

"Right. The bridge in the song about a room where the light can't get in." Raven tapped his walking stick on the floor. "But every room we've checked has lights in it."

I paced. "I know. But maybe that's not what she was trying to say."

I stopped to pull Akka away from the dead aliens—again—and caught a glimpse of the sky. More spaceships circled the dusty purple clouds.

Raven tapped to me on his walking stick. "They're here to take it back, Izzy. The ship. They've come to take it back."

Akka poked his nose out from under one of the chairs. "Worf."

"Akka, hang on." I coughed and wiped my face with my sleeve. "I don't care about the aliens. They can't have this hunk of junk until we get what we came here for." I thought of Grams cooking break-fast with me. Pops teaching me to drive. Maple and

FartMaster19, how if I got her back, I'd never complain about her again.

"*Bark!*" Akka whined and scratched the far corner of the floor. This time, I followed.

"Raven!" I scooped up Akka's find and held it high. "Akka found the gold orb."

Akka panted up at me, smiling like, *I AM GOOD BOY.* I kissed and hugged him up.

"Whoa." Raven turned the orb over in his hands. "It's got the symbol on it. And look. Your mom's sketch was missing a part of the symbol. You know what this looks like?"

I grinned. "A geometrical heart." I took the orb in my hands. It felt powerful. Like it had a pulse. "Like *Open the heart and we're free*, from my mom's journal and your dream."

"Yup. And the Madonna song." Raven frowned around the room. "I wonder if the black orb is here, too? There are two spots for them on the bridge. The black one has to be here."

The longer I held the orb, the stronger I felt it beating. A pulse that matched the beat of my heart. Then suddenly I remembered my mom's ghost from the library saying, *Open, open*, to me. *Open* . . . I looked closer. A thin, indented ring circled the golden orb. "Hey, look. I think it's made to break."

Raven, still searching for the other orb, looked up from a pile of weird alien junk. "Like the half orb from your mom's sketch. Maybe it's supposed to be cracked like an egg."

I held the pulsing orb, going over songs from Playlist at the End of the World, when I thought of something. "Raven. Other songs on my mom's CD talk about lights and hearts, too. Just think of them all. . . ."

Raven pushed hair out of his face. "I've been going over the lyrics, too. And your mom's messages on the CD. Like the one about the bridge, and the other one . . . *Find the light and don't give up* . . . or something like that. And the first song on her playlist. 'Don't You (Forget about Me).' There's a line about someone taking someone apart, and someone else putting them back together—at the heart."

I gasped. "You're right. Taking someone apart . . . like how the UFO lights have to pull human matter apart to beam people into their ships and into the orbs. And in order to beam people out of the orbs and back down to earth we need to put the hearts together. That's it!"

Raven threw some weird alien garbage over his head. "Oh, that's good."

Eating my nail beds to shreds, I returned to the cradles on the bridge. Each had raised symbols on the base. Symbols, like the others around the UFO. But the other symbols were flat, like they were sketched on the surface. These were raised. Like they were made to click into place. "These markings. Maybe they lock together with the carvings on the orb. Like a puzzle."

Akka scratched at one of the dead aliens, stirring up the stink. "Akka, no. Please." Akka reluctantly returned. But as soon as I looked away, he was back to licking their hideous hands.

"Wait. What have you got—" Raven shrieked. "Akka! Good boy!" Hidden in the dead alien's fingers was the black orb. Raven wrenched it free from the gruesome thing's clutches. At his touch, the black orb glowed. It bore the same geometric heart as its twin, as well as the same ring of light circling the outside. But this one's heart and ring lit purple. Like the Darklights. "Izzy. This is the orb from my dream." His eyes shone in the orb's light. "I didn't imagine it."

Meanwhile, Akka panted up at us like, *I tried to tell you I found a clue, but anyway you're welcome. Akka gets num-nums now.*

I gave Akka the best scratches in the world and told Raven, "This is probably the realest thing we'll ever do. And right now, we need to open these orbs and set whoever and whatever's inside them free."

Akka pawed my leg like, *Hullo. I am waiting for*

treats because I am a good boy. I kissed my boy's head. "Sorry to make you wait. You are the best good boy ever." Raven gave him the last bit of squished granola bar in his pocket, which Akka gulped in ecstasy.

Before Akka was done chewing, Vermont shook with a low hum from the mother ship. Raven stood, his face as worried as mine. "Whatever freaks are driving the mother ship are getting ready to shine the Darkli—"

Hmm—mmmm-MMMMMMMMMMMMMM-MMMMMMMMMM.

The hum from the spaceships grew. The screens on the bridge flashed. Electronics sparked. Our radios screamed. The three of us ducked under the rim of screens as the spotlights of gold beamed onto our UFO. The world shone in the brightest light.

Then the crashed UFO lifted off the ground.

"Ahh!" Raven and I screamed. The crashed UFO shifted and straightened out. Debris rolled across the floor. The hum from the lights echoed through my blood. Through the machinery. Maybe even through time.

"Raven. We have to put the orbs in the cradle things. Break the circles. Open the hearts and set everyone free before the ships take us." The UFO trembled so hard my teeth shook.

The smaller ships turned on a new sequence of colored lights. The crashed UFO shuddered, then rose inside the beam. We must've been about twenty feet off the mountain. My vision blurred. I felt upside down, like my face would hit ground.

Raven nodded. "Okay, let's do it."

Raven and I clasped hands, like the song said, and Akka squeezed in between us. "On the count of three, set your black orb in the cradle. And I'll do the same with mine."

"Got it."

Interference screamed through every speaker, including those of the severed radio station. Another song burst through the Discman speakers, "'I Am by Your Side,' by Corey Hart." *Static* "I am here." I grinned as the song played, and held Akka tight. Energy poured through me from the orb. Raven shook with the force; tiny bolts of static lit the ends of his hair.

"One. Two."

"Bork-bork-bork!"

"Three!"

Raven and I locked the orbs in the indentations, symbol to symbol, heart to heart. I thought of everyone I loved (*Waiting for you . . .*) as they clinked into place. The orbs lowered into the bridge and the hatch closed.

Behind us, the hatch in the center of the floor slid open and revealed a see-through floor. Spotlights beneath the crashed UFO revved on in beams of violet and gold. We were high enough off the mountain for our lights to shine far and wide.

The flashes of light were the last things we saw before a sonic boom blew out around us in a wave like a supernova encapsulating the world.

I fell to the floor.

The UFO crashed back down to the mountain's peak.

Akka barked as if far away.

(Waiting for you . . .)

And sunlight flooded Vermont once more.

CHAPTER 28
A NEW DAY

AFTER MY MOM DIED, A HOLLOW SPACE FILLED ME up. A space so dark, all I wanted to do was hide. Everyone told me, "Time heals all wounds." But time kept ticking by. And I was still trapped in the dark and couldn't find my way out. Then one day, Grams and Pops bought me a journal with butterflies on the cover. "She's still around," Grams said. "Always with you," Pops told me. "Writing to your mom will help you heal," my therapist insisted. I didn't know if I believed it. But as sad as I was, my mom was still my best friend. And I missed her more than I hurt. So, I started writing my mom little notes I called *Letters to the Milky Way*. I told her everyday things. What I'd tell her if she were here. Who I thought was cute.

Funny things Maple said. Why I was sad. Or just I love you. I miss you. And I wish you were here, hoping she'd hear me.

Back then, I didn't think she had. Now, though, I think she was there all along; I just hadn't noticed the signs. Hearing her music in the grocery store. Finding heart-shaped rocks. Coins from the year of her birth. Getting chills when thinking of her. I used to think those were just coincidences. But now I know they were my mom, showing me how much she loves me. Trying to get me to fill that empty space in myself with a new, brighter-than-ever-before light.

And inside the blast of otherworld gold light, I think I saw her. Standing over me and smiling, whispering, *Isadora, I get every message you send me. Now wake up, and know, I am always with you.*

———————

"Izzy . . . Izzy, are you okay?"

"Bark-bark-bark!"

Somebody was shaking me. Calling my name.

I gasped awake to my best boy licking my face. Raven grinned excitedly, happy as a kid staring at a pile of gifts. Tears streamed down his scraped, dirty face. "Izzy. Wake up." He wiped his eyes. "I think we did it."

We were in a field by Route 30, not far from the Townshend Dam. The sun was just rising over the hills. The skies were pink and gold. It was the most beautiful dawn I'd ever seen. Vermont was as green as ever—except for the trees that found autumn early and shone in bright shades of crimson and gold. A cool rush of wind pushed crisp leaves across the pavement. There were no crashed vehicles in the street. No black dust. And there were no gray uglies in sight.

"It wasn't all a dream or anything, right?" Raven smiled down at me. Long hair rushed past his face. The purple granny blouse was shredded and splotched with old blood. Akka sniffed me like a meat bone, nudging me with his cold, wet nose. "Izzy? Can you hear me?"

"I hear you all right." I scooped Akka up in the biggest hug of his life. Akka looked great. Clear eyes, wagging tail, no blood or black tongue. No sign of anything wrong. I ran a finger over my chest where the amethyst burned me and felt a crusty scar. "No. It was all real."

The clues, the journal, the lyrics, the UFOs, the monsters, the orbs. The invasion. The abductions, the aliens, the truth about my mom, the life-and-death journey Raven, Akka, and I had just been on. How we fought. How we survived. How we believed. And how we were alive.

I sprang like a wild wind into Raven's open arms. "We're okay." I let him go, grabbed Akka's leash, and stood. "We survived. But I can't tell if what we did worked."

And that's when I felt my mom. Goose bumps popped out all over me. A warmth settled and bloomed in my heart. And from someplace close by, a song played. "Here Comes the Sun," by the Beatles. And even though I couldn't hear her voice, I knew she'd brought it to me.

"Raven, do you hear that song?"

We stared up the road toward home, just listening to "Here Comes the Sun" get louder and louder until a truck came into view. Raven and I blinked in awe at the truck with the actual human person waving at us from the driver's seat like we'd never seen an actual human person in our lives. We waved back slow and stiff as zombies. Akka worfed and wagged a friendly hello. And when the truck passed there was no denying it.

The truck whizzing past was Bob.

"Uhh, Izzy? Are you seeing what I'm seeing right now or—"

"You're not dreaming. That is definitely our hero Bob. And Bob's person to boot." It made me so happy that Bob found his way home. "Hey, Raven?"

"Yes, Izzy?"

"I think the whole orb thing worked."

We stood there in the field, listening to that song until Bob and his person were gone. Letting the lyrics and music sink in. *(Here comes the sun . . .)* And everything I'd been through, the horrors, heartache, and pain, shuddered out of me until only hope was left. If that car and person were alive, then chances were good our families were, too.

Maybe we changed the world after all.

"It's a bit of a walk. And I don't know about you, but if the lights from the orbs beamed my mom, Louis, and Harry back to earth, then I can't wait to get home. What say you, Isadora Wilder?" Raven picked his walking stick out of the grass and straightened his blouse. "Should we get back on the road?"

"What do I say?" I dared myself into a hopeful smile big as the sun. "I say—"

"Bark!" Akka did that whole-body wag of joy the second he heard the word "home."

I laughed. "Akka took the word right outta my mouth."

And we started up Route 30 the way we came.

The woods were restored to health. No trees cracked in half. No houses or fields destroyed by uglies. Along the way, more cars passed. Sounds we knew and loved had returned to the world. I almost cried at the sweet singing of birds. Akka's ears perked and swiveled toward each note—twin satellites tracking their songs. He smiled at me like he'd never heard anything so fine. The crows joined the chorus next— CAW, CAW, CAW—and the chipmunks calling from the woods were quick to follow.

"It's beautiful, isn't it?" Raven glanced at me, shy.

"The most beautiful ever."

A clean breeze blew. No sign of bleach. No ozone smell. The air was that morning-dew smell of cool green. I breathed in deep, letting that sweet Vermont green fill me all the way up. I couldn't put together exactly how we got here. How the alien technology worked. Or how the earth was back to green. But here, in this moment, Akka happy and healthy, Raven and I chatting like old friends about all we'd been through, and all we hoped was to come, it felt like anything was possible. Like standing in the sunlight and birdsong with the best dog in the world and a new friend beside me was the most precious and glorious thing, and I had no need to ask why.

For the first time through all this, I fully believed

we'd see our people again. I let it in this time. I let the thought of hugging Grams in. Of Pops arm-wrapping me as I cried. Of running at Maple full speed and pressing her close as two sheets of paper to me. And laughing hysterically with Nora anywhere at all. I let it flood in. And when I did, I think I might've glowed.

"For you." Raven picked me a purple wildflower, all blush and smile. "It's not much. But I thought you might like it."

"I love it." I couldn't stop my tears. I didn't want to. "Thanks, Raven." I took the pretty flower (purple means something), then tip-tapped my thigh with one finger and beamed at the sunshiny road. "These were my mom's favorite wildflower." I took a deep breath, looked at Raven, and smiled. "And now you're one of my favorites, too."

Raven grinned big and stared at his feet. "Good. And same."

Akka nudged Raven's hand, dancing tongue out for pets. Spoiler alert: it worked.

As we came into the center of Townshend, other sounds drifted toward us. Voices, cars—people. Akka barked, tail wagging with ecstatic cheer as another dog came into view.

"Akka. You're not alone, bud." I thought of his best friend, Moss, and hoped he'd be home, too. I smiled, all warm and happy inside. There's no love on earth as pure as the love of a dog.

Raven, Akka, and I walked to Townshend to the sounds of our earth waking up, big hopes inside us of seeing our families and friends alive. And finally, we made it to Raven's home. A cute little saltbox in the center of town. "Well, this is me. The moment of truth." When we got to the sidewalk, dogs barked inside. Raven and I shrieked louder than anyone in history. Akka almost lost his mind wanting to play with Harry and Louis, but now wasn't the time. And before his cute, 1D-loving mom stepped outside, I hugged him first.

"Thank you, Raven. For everything. Me and Akka couldn't have done this without you. And . . . we couldn't have asked for a better friend at the end of the world."

Raven laughed, Akka jumped in for love, too. "The feeling is mutual. Especially because I literally would not have survived without you."

Then I did something I'd been wanting to do for a while.

"Raven?"

"Yes, Izzy?" He told his mom to hang on and she ducked back inside.

"Um, would it be okay if I kissed you?"

Raven snapped up in shock. Then nodded quick and nervous and shy.

When our lips met, for a moment, we shone. Everything we shared—every memory, thought, worry, and joy beamed from us like a bit of awkward magic.

But there was no fear.

"That was . . ." Raven ran a hand through his hair.

"Yeah."

"Sooo. Are you sure you don't want my mom to drive you home? I know she wouldn't mind."

"No, actually. It's not far. And I'd kinda like to walk with Akka. Let everything sink in alone, you know?"

"Yes. I absolutely do. Well, okay then. Come find me when you're ready, and we can do something normal for once?"

"I'd like that."

"Oh, and here." He handed me a paper he'd ripped from his journal and stuffed into his jeans. "I wrote this poem for you."

Before I could reply, Raven petted Akka goodbye and left, sneaking glances at us until he ran inside to the wild music of excited dogs. Then he was gone.

And as Akka and I started home, I felt connected to everything. To this moment, to moments past and every person, and this great big, beautiful earth. I knew then no matter what happened in my past, present, and future, I would be okay. I felt my place in all things and was right where I belonged.

"You ready to see our family, Akka?" My best boy pawed my thigh and nuzzled me close. Then stared at me with all the love in the cosmos.

And it was just me and Akka. And for a while, the world was ours.

CHAPTER 29

HOME

AS ME AND MY BEST BOY PASSED THE RIVER BEND Farm Market, cars were revving to life. Horses ate fresh green grass in the field across the parking lot. Dogs walked their humans down streets, shining in early dawn light. Bees and squirrels, every other woodland beast and bug, too, emerged from bushes and air as they always had before. But I smiled. And Akka did, too, watching them buzz and shuffle on their way. Because we knew how it could've been. How it was only minutes before. We knew. And we'd carry that knowing with us as long as we walked this earth.

I passed Nora's house, grinning so hard my cheeks hurt. Nora and her family were up. They shuffled around the kitchen making breakfast and doing normal, morning-time things. I wondered if they knew what happened to them. If deep down they felt how close our world was to being destroyed, and if it made them feel the way it did me: so much more alive. Akka pulled toward their house, wondering why we weren't stopping for snacks and hellos. "We're gonna let them have their time, Akka. They're safe now. And don't worry. Nora will give you way too many cookies real soon." Satisfied, Akka put nose to breeze, leading us home.

At the circle by our mailbox at the end of my road, my mom was fresh as new daisies on my mind. I remembered her story. I remembered her. All she endured. All she did to help us get to right here, right now. All the thought and energy and tears she put into the clues and journal and music, and how excruciatingly painful that must have been. I remembered all the love she gave us while she was alive, and the light she gave me still.

I missed her. So much. I traced the outline of her journal, still tucked up safe in my jeans. My mom wasn't all-the-way gone. She never would be.

I walked faster. Mom's Discman, still hanging from my jeans, suddenly turned on by itself. "Blackbird" came through the headphones, and I broke a little with joy, hope, and tears as I started up the driveway we shared with our neighbors, Fee and Ben. A familiar "*Rarf-rarf-rarf!*" had me screaming for happiness and Akka shaking with excitement.

Moss!

"*Bark-bark-bark-bark-bark—!*"

I stopped at the end of their driveway, unhooked Akka's leash, and before I set him free, I cupped his fuzzy muzzle with tears and a big old smile. "Okay, good boy, it's okay, you can go."

Familiar faces emerged from their house. The Vanescos waved me forward. I met them with love, then raced the whole way home.

For the first time maybe ever, I knew exactly who I was, where I was going, and where I'd come from. I may not have had all the answers, but my old boots were crunching gravel on my driveway, pebbles pinging to grass at 4821 Derry Lane. My hair rolled out behind me in a curly mess of waves. My skin was battered and bruised. My *Moonlight Society* T-shirt and jeans were ripped and covered in dust and blood. The sweater I'd double knotted around my waist was dirty and frayed (*Strong, you are*). But that big, beautiful mess?

It was all me.

Akka and Moss racing loops around my heels, I caught the first glimpses of my family. Grams, Pops, and Maple were out front, decorating early for Hallow-een. They must've heard Akka and Moss barking and playing, because they stood together by the driveway, facing me.

And I tell you, there was nothing—nothing—like this feeling on earth. When I found them right where they should be, there was no worry about what would happen next. Now that we were together, nothing else mattered. Nothing. When we locked eyes, we lit up like a sky filled with stars, and it was like heaven on earth.

"Izzy!" Maple crashed into my arms like a stick of dynamite, and I hugged her like she'd explode if I let go. "Where were you? Why didn't you tell anyone you were going out? We were worried when we saw you were gone." Grams said Maple could talk a bird out of its wings, and goodness, was she right. Maple finally peeled away, Grams and Pops waiting patiently behind. "And why are you bloody and dirty?" Maple frowned, leaned in, and whispered, "If you snuck out, why didn't you take me with you?"

"Hey, Maple bud." I held back tears as long as I could. "Sorry I worried you. I was just walking Akka and got in a mess. But next time, I swear, you're gonna be right by my side. Because, you know what? I missed you more than OMG-I-Love-Corn and that's no lie."

Maple laughed through big-love tears and punched my arm. "Well, I'm happy you're back. Because I missed you, too." She twined her hand into mine. "More than FartMaster19 and that's really saying something, so be proud."

"Oh, I am, Maple bud. I will always be proud of you."

Maple stepped aside when Grams burst into tears.

"Isadora Bellamy Wilder, you get right on over here!" Grams came at me hard, warm eyes beaming love. "I'm so thankful you and Akka are all right. You had me scared half to death!"

"Grams!" I melted into her arms and never wanted to let go. Pops stood behind Grams, smiling and sweet as ever, letting the love of his life have her time. "I'm sorry! Sorry I left without saying goodbye. Sorry I didn't take the sweater. Sorry it took me so long to—" I choked up in the driveway. Moss barking. Maple dancing with Akka on his hind legs in the sun. So full of sorry and happy, I couldn't get any more words free.

Grams pulled away and stared me hard in the eyes—her eyes, my eyes, Maple's eyes, Mom's eyes. "Now, now, there is no need to be sorry. Not for one thing." Grams gifted me a big sunny smile. "You're here. You and Akka are safe." She looked me over, lingering for a beat on Mom's Discman before nodding, like somehow she knew everything we'd just been through without really knowing at all. "But goodness, Izzy. Look at you." She grabbed my chin and turned my face. "What in the world is this black dust on you? It looks like you've been cleaning chimneys. And . . . Is that blood?" She shook her head and wiped my cheek. "You look like that Princess Manatoe, or whatever her name is, I forget."

"Mononoke, Grams." I laughed, wiping the happiness from my cheeks. "Princess Mononoke."

"Mononoke, then." Grams pulled me back into her warm, cozy arms, which felt like home. "You can tell me your story inside, with a nice cup of blackberry tea. For now, I'm just glad you and that furry menace are finally home."

"Bark!" Grams knelt in the driveway and gave her best boy all the love in the world.

Pops wiped his hands on his jeans as Grams followed Maple, Akka, and Moss to the neighbors'. For a second, we just smiled at each other, eyes twinkling, like we were trading secrets. Until I started up laughing and jumped into his arms.

"Hey there, Izzy," Pops said with his deep, gentle voice. He folded me into the warmest bear hug ever. In his arms, there was no more pain, only love.

"Pops. I missed you. So much." Somehow, he still smelled like burned popcorn. He pulled away, motioned to the journal poking out the top of my jeans.

"I see you've been doing some closet digging. I gave your mom that journal, right before you were born." Years of sadness and happiness and memories of yesterdays flickered like tiny movies into my sweet pops's eyes. He swallowed hard and quietly smudged away tears. "We believed her, you know. We just couldn't stop her pain."

"I know, Pops." He wrapped his arm around my shoulder. And as we started for the house, I was sniffing my own tears away. "But it's all good now, okay? She doesn't hurt anymore, and she knows just how you feel."

A waft of wind circled us, infused with a distinct orange scent. Pops glanced around like he was looking for her. Like deep down in his heart, he knew it was true.

"I had a funny dream last night, you know it? Grams, Maple, and me, we were trapped inside a dark room and couldn't find our way out. But you and Akka, and a blackbird of all things, found us and set us free." Pops's eyes twinkled. "Isn't that strange?"

My heart fluttered wild. "Yeah. That is definitely strange."

Pops nodded and motioned to his bowie knife on my hip. "You were wearing that in my dream." He motioned to the Discman. "And that old relic of Annie's, too. And you survived, Izzy. You did whatever it took like I taught you."

We stepped onto the deck and faced a near clear blue sky. "Yeah, Pops. I survived. And now, I'm gonna live."

I stood on the back deck in the same place I first saw the lights. The place our nightmare began. My lungs still hurt, but they didn't burn. Grams wrapped me up on one side, Pops on the other, and we stared out over Vermont, not needing to say any words. Maple raced after Akka and Moss in the yard.

Everything was so peaceful. Grams and Pops drifted back inside. The beauty of life echoed around me. I closed my eyes. And in the darkness came a golden vision of my mom. She rose from her nest of Milky Way stars and stared straight into me. *A new day has dawned. No matter where you go, I go with you.* Then she faded back into the sky.

I slipped the Discman's headphones on and played the last song on Annie's Alt. Mix. This time, when my mom spoke, she was laughing. "Song sixteen of Annie's Alt. Mix always makes me feel so happy, 'The Ghost in You,' by the Psychedelic Furs." *Static* Then,

"I hope when you hear this, the sun is shining on a new day, and it makes you smile, too."

When the song came on, I grinned big and turned up the volume. I danced on the deck and listened until the end.

Maple shouted up from the yard, "Izzy, come play with me, loser!"

I burst out laughing, set the Discman down, and ran.

ACKNOWLEDGMENTS

HELLO, DEAR READER, I AM SO GLAD YOU'RE HERE. Before I thank the many incredible friends who supported me on Izzy's journey, I'd like to share a bit of this book's journey with you. After all, we survivors have to stick together. And it sure is nice having a friend at the end of the world.

10-28-2017. I was in edits on *The Land of Yesterday* when Izzy first whispered her story to me. I was already contracted to write *The Spinner of Dreams* next, but this girl's voice was so strong and unique, I couldn't get her out of my head. So, I did what any good writer would do. I swept my first-pass pages dramatically off my desk and drafted the first chapter of a book I wasn't supposed to be writing. (Just kidding.

I'd never do my first-pass pages so wrong!). Still, I did take a day to set Izzy's voice in stone.

3-23-2018. I sent my agent the premise and first chapter of this alien invasion dystopian apocalypse upper middle grade story, which was completely different from my first two books, thinking she'd be like, NOPE. But my amazing agent replied the same day, saying she loved it! So, the second I finished *TSOD*, I started *Izzy at the End of the World*.

*Fun fact: this book was inspired by real events that occurred in the same town, on the same mountain, in the same house as I gave Izzy—the home I shared with Bob and our kids. And just like Izzy, everything I'm about to tell you is true.

10:00 p.m. Bob was playing guitar on the couch when he spotted an odd light in the sky. He watched it for a bit. The light didn't move. He thought maybe it was a planet until it started moving slowly toward our house. It kept getting bigger and closer, and finally stopped halfway between the horizon and us. Then Bob knew exactly what it was. He ran upstairs, burst through the bedroom door, and whisper-yelled, "Hun! There's a UFO!" We thundered downstairs a million miles a second. When we got onto the deck, the UFO sprang. The deck trembled. The trees swayed. The huge craft soared directly over our house, lights spinning and everything, and then it was gone. We'd never felt such primal fear in our lives. I gave that same fear to Izzy. Then I gave her more of me, too.

Like me, Izzy was abandoned by her father before birth. Her mom died under mysterious circumstances. Her grandparents raised her, loved her, and told Izzy her mom died of a brain tumor (as my gran did about my mom). Izzy discovered the same truth I did as a teen—my mom died by suicide. Finding out the truth had me grieving her all over again. I wanted answers. But there were none to be had. I was so desperate to feel my mom's presence, but she never even came to me in dreams. Not until I started writing *Izzy at the End of the World*.

Suddenly, my mom was everywhere, sending me clues. In dreams of her, The Cure would be playing in the background. Out in the world, The Cure found me in stores, on the radio, even on TV. I became so re-obsessed with The Cure they were all I'd listen to while drafting *Izzy*. And get this: their first album debuted on the exact day and year my mom died. I was blown away. But the musical synchronicities didn't stop there.

Then, "You are My Sunshine," the song my mom always sang to me before bed, would play wherever I went. And "Sunshine on My Shoulders," by John

Denver, came next, which was hard, because it has the most beautifully sad lyrics ever. And because my mom loved John Denver so much, she almost named me Sunny. In these moments, I felt her with me. Like she was showing me that even if I couldn't see her with my eyes, I could feel her with my heart.

Then I started seeing the number 312 everywhere, too. On signs, clocks, mailboxes, license plates, time-stamps, TV. More otherworld messages from my mom. The address of our first family home was 312. A home my mother thought of as family and missed dearly when it was gone. Seeing that number felt like her cheering me on and saying, "I know this book hurts to write, but Izzy Wilder's story is bringing me closer to you."

Speaking of Wilder. Izzy's name came to me randomly, so imagine my surprise when I got my DNA results back and discovered my missing father's side of the family had a ton of Wilders! I mean, what? The ties between my life and Izzy's kept piling up. It was comforting to feel I wasn't in this alone, especially considering what happened next.

7-3-2020. My husband Bob, the superhero after which Izzy's truck was named, suffered a massive stroke from a brain tumor we didn't know he had. He went in for emergency brain surgery and was diagnosed with Stage 4 Esophageal Cancer.

We couldn't believe it. This was a guy who survived third-degree burns over nine percent of his body. Chainsaw wounds. A brain bleed/cracked skull from falling head-first off a ladder. Getting shot between the eyes with an arrow, and so much more. So, when he got his diagnosis, he said with absolute nonchalance, "Cancer, Shmancer. Don't worry, honey. I'll be fine." But, uh, I couldn't not worry. So I set Izzy's story aside to care for Bob.

But somehow, things only got worse.

We were evicted from our home. Thanks to Covid-19, the only available place to go was Bob's mother's house in our old state of Vermont. So, just three weeks after Bob's brain surgery, my herculean husband, five kids, and myself, moved states. It was all too much. There was so much going on with our family—not to mention the pandemic raging on in our background— working on my *Izzy* revision was impossible. Even if I had time, which I didn't, I had zero spoons to give creatively. Every ounce of energy happily went into caring for Bob and the kids. I finally asked my editor if I could extend my deadline to focus on my family, and of course, she said yes. During that time, Bob started feeling okay enough that I could get back to work.

A dear friend (you know who you are!) sent me $600 for a hotel to finish Izzy's story in peace, knowing that writing in my house with eight pandemic-isolated people wasn't going to work. Still, as kind as the gift was, I debated going. When your partner is dying, every moment is precious. But I had a contract and career too, and I finally decided to go.

And when I arrived, my mom was there waiting for me.

March 12th (3-12-21). Inside the room was a vintage record player with a stack of records my mother loved, and others by artists on the Playlist at the End of the World. I put on old records and wrote in a flurry of words, distraction free. I had two days left to finish my extremely overdue book when Bob's oncologist called. His newest scan results said he now had Leptomeningeal Disease, cancer of the spinal and brain fluid.

Once again, everything stopped. My heart. Our hope.

The world.

I called Bob sobbing. We talked about the news. Despite the grim prognosis, still, Bob told me not to worry. He'd made it this far. He'd do radiation and burn the dumb cancer away. I said I wanted to leave the hotel and come home. But he said no, finish the book, he'd see me soon. So, I pulled myself off the floor and finished the book. For me. For Bob. For every child and adult who's ever stared down their deepest darkest fear. I got up. But I wasn't up long.

4-8-21. Just three weeks later, my husband, and biggest fan for twenty-seven years, died.

But like my mom, I know he's still with me. When I step outside at three a.m., into the Vermont air and mountain fog, crying out there by his truck (right where he left it), I feel him all around me. It's beautiful and hideous and intense, and this is grief. The full awareness of love in everything. The same wellspring of love that allowed me the grace to write this book and tell the story of a fourteen-year-old girl who lost almost everything and fought with all she had to love. To hope. To survive. And to get on the road and live.

Bob's dying wish was to do a Route 66 road trip, but he passed before we got a chance. When I mentioned this on Twitter, a kind friend set up a GoFundMe page, and before we knew it, thousands of dollars were donated to our grieving family. There are no words to express my deep gratitude for giving Bob his dying wish.

On that note, let the festival of thanks begin.

Endless thanks to those who helped make Bob's Memorial Trip happen. It truly, definitely, fully saved us. Never doubt my love for you.

Thank you to Black Beauty, my 2011 Toyota Sienna (183,000 miles and counting), which carried us grievers over twenty-five states and 10,000 miles in five weeks. We went (almost) everywhere Bob wanted to go and scattered his ashes along the way. Like Bob the truck from *IATEOTW*, you got us through certain peril with grace and style, and I am so proud of you!

Eternal thanks to my always brilliant agent, Thao Le, who loved Izzy from the beginning and helped her story come to life.

Many thanks to my unbelievably insightful and patient editor, Emilia Rhodes, for championing Isadora's story and giving me the time I needed to grieve. Huge thanks to the Clarion and HarperCollins team for giving Izzy the platform to speak her truth.

Thank you, thank you to Bex Ollerton, the perfect cover artist for *Izzy at the End of the World*! (As soon as I saw your *Steven Universe* fan art, I was like YES, THIS IS THE ONE. Ha.)

To my indispensable critique partners and first readers, fierce hugs for your input, time, and love! To Hayley Chewins, who always knows just what to say to help make my book shine. Beth Revis for your invaluable *Star Wars* input and advice. Ally Malinenko for reading, teaching me about the circle, and understanding. To Mike Lasagna for shouting about *Izzy* and checking in with me daily while Bob was dying, and for months after. Your care meant so much to me. To Sarah Cannon, Cindy Baldwin, Samantha Clark, and Jacqueline West, for reading and loving Izzy's story enough to blurb. I love you all.

A special thanks to my kiddo, Autumn Reynolds, for doing a sensitivity read on *Izzy*. I love, love, love you!

Thank you to Keri Roberts, my previous boss from the Windham County Humane Society, for the info on Akka's seizures and meds.

A million thanks to Saadia Faruqi for so many reasons. I hope you know how grateful I am to call you a friend. Thank you to Danielle Mages Amato for getting it. For knowing all too well what this feels like, for sitting quietly with me, and for telling me about the people in cars (I can almost feel the wind on my face again).

To anyone who read an early version of this story I might've forgotten in the chaos, please forgive me. Everyone who gave me feedback helped forge this book into what it is now, and I thank you unconditionally.

To everyone who messaged me to check in since Bob's diagnosis. Those who gave us words of solace and care during the darkest time in our lives, thank you. It meant so much to know I wasn't alone.

An infinite helping of love and thanks to my kids, Michael, Jonah, Autumn, Ava, and Indy. You are my hands to hold, and hearts to mold, and five of the greatest stories ever told. Thank you for letting me snot and cry and sing Dad's favorite songs badly and at the top of my lungs *Step into the freezer!* and for trying to take pictures despite the garbage in the way. For Von Maur. The hotels. The lifestyle. Starbucks. For checking in on me during those dark days after Dad died. *A special thanks to Ava for cooking dinner for us each night, and for making sure I ate. There are no words to express the enormity of my love for each of you. You're the greatest thing Bob and I ever did, and I am so, so happy you are here.

And thank you, Bob. We never had an easy time, did we? Not even once. But we raised each other alongside our kids. We taught each other to be and not to be (that is the question, yo!). And for all the messes we made and hurt we gave, in the end all we had was love. The last nine months with you meant everything to me. I love you, Honey. I'll see you in the stars.

Last but certainly not least, thank you, dear reader. For listening. For reading. For going out into the world each day and just being you. Wherever and whoever you are, know that I am cheering you on. That I see that light in you. And no matter what happens, you've got a friend in me, and I believe in you.